BREATHLESS:
TALES OF CELEBRATION

edited by

RADCLYfFE and
STACIA SEAMAN

2010

BREATHLESS: TALES OF CELEBRATION

ISBN 10: 1-60282-207-7
ISBN 13: 978-1-60282-207-8

This Trade Paperback Original Is Published By
Bold Strokes Books, Inc.
P.O. Box 249
Valley Falls, NY 12185

First Edition: December 2010

Credits
Editors: Radclyffe and Stacia Seaman
Production Design: Stacia Seaman
Cover Design by Bold Strokes Graphics

Contents

Introduction

When we close the book on happily ever after, we do so with a feeling of satisfaction. The lovers have met challenges, overcome obstacles, and ultimately have found their way to a future together. And yet, we wonder: What does the future hold for these characters? Once the dizzying rush of new love fades, what takes its place? After a lifetime together, will their bond remain strong?

In *Breathless: Tales of Celebration*, twenty-one authors revisit some of their favorite characters to show us the entire spectrum of love: from giddy infatuation to lifetime commitment, from buying a home to starting a family, from asking "Do I?" to saying, "I do."

Radcly*ffe* and Stacia Seaman 2010

WINTER PENNINGTON is the author of *Witch Wolf* and *Raven Mask*, the Kassandra Lyall Preternatural Investigator series. She is currently working on *Darkness Embraced: A Rosso Lussuria Vampire Novel*, which will be published in 2011. She is an avid practitioner of nature-based spirituality and enjoys spending her spare time studying mythology from around the world. The Celtic path is very close to her heart. She has an uncanny fascination with swords and daggers, and a fondness for feeding loud and obnoxious corvids. She can be contacted at Winterpennington@gmail.com, or visit her blog at www.winterpennington.blogspot.com.

"Harvest Sins" takes place in the time between *Raven Mask* and *Bloody Claws*, the planned third book in the Kassandral Lyall series.

Harvest Sins

Winter Pennington

Detective Arthur Kingfisher smiled at me as I entered the double doors of the Oklahoma City Police Department. I did not return the smile. It was ten o'clock in the morning. I do not make a habit of smiling at the person responsible for waking me up. In my experience, it only encourages them.

Lady knew, it wasn't the first time and it wouldn't be the last time I lost precious sleep just to help the police.

Holding a recycled paper coffee cup in my hands like a lifeline, I skirted around an officer in a dark blue uniform. I'd managed to convince myself that swinging by Starbucks and spending five dollars on a cup of white mocha goodness was not frivolous, it was necessary. Thank the corporate gods they were open on Thanksgiving.

"Heya, Kass." A lock of sandy brown hair fell over Arthur's eyes and he pushed it back. Arthur approached me wearing a light blue men's dress shirt and navy slacks. White penguins romped on his black tie.

Arthur had been promoted to detective not long ago. I was still trying to get used to seeing him in a tie. He wasn't a tie kind of guy. A tie with penguins, however, was another story.

"Morning," I grumbled.

"Aren't you just bright-eyed and bushy-tailed?" His very blue eyes sparkled with cheer.

I had a moment to think *if only you knew* before taking a long swig of coffee. Arthur didn't know, so I was safe. "Where's the surveillance footage you wanted me to take a look at?"

"What, were you up all night banging Vampira?" He gave a cheesy smile.

I didn't answer his question, since it wasn't any of his business.

"Her name is Lenorre, not Vampira. She's a Countess, Arthur. Show some respect."

Lenorre was one of the head countess vampires of Oklahoma. Every state has a handful of counts and countesses that oversee the vampire community. Lenorre's sovereign trickled through Oklahoma City and the surrounding area. I'm not exactly sure how many counts and countesses are in Oklahoma, as I'd never really thought to ask Lenorre, but I do know for sure that there is another countess in Tulsa. Okay, so sometimes the media can be informative.

Lenorre and I had been dating for a while. We'd only taken our relationship to the level of sleeping together a few weeks ago. She'd surprised me on my birthday by buying a new shoulder holster to replace the one she'd broken. She'd worked something out with my friend, Rupert, who owns a gun shop in the city. Rupert, like me, is a licensed paranormal hunter. Both Rupert and I legally hunt down bad paranormals that the local cops usually can't catch due to, well, a number of reasons.

Though, unlike me, Rupert had never been a cop. Also, unlike me, Rupert wasn't a lycanthrope working with the police and hiding what he was from them.

After having been infected with lycanthropy three years ago, I quit the force and became a preternatural private investigator. I get to make my own hours and no one looks at me funny for never working the night of the full moon.

Arthur eyed me speculatively as he led the way back to the interrogation room. "Damn, you're kind of grumpy."

"Kind of?"

"You're no fun this early." He practically pouted. I had thought friend and beta werewolf of the Blackthorne pack, Rosalin Walker, was one of the cheeriest morning persons I knew. Apparently, I had sorely underestimated Arthur's morning abilities.

I frowned as he held the pale brown paint-chipped door open. Two folding chairs had been pulled out into the middle of the room. The table that was normally in the center was hugging the far wall to make room for a television set on a rolling cart.

I dropped into a chair next to Arthur. He grabbed the remote, and the reflective blank screen blinked to life. I knew the surveillance footage was from a gas station, but beyond that I had no idea what would be on the tape. I didn't know whether to steel myself or not. I took a deep calming breath, trying to ignore the harsh bite of Arthur's cologne.

The camera showed the back of an employee's blond head. The camera angle was wide enough to reveal most of the store with only a few blind spots. The store wasn't large, four aisles, a row of glass doors lining the far right wall, a single glass door set into white brick at the end of a candy aisle.

If someone had ducked down behind the counter in front of the employee, I wouldn't have seen them.

The door opened and two figures in matching black jeans, sweaters, and black ski masks entered. It was then that I knew Arthur was making me watch a robbery, but why I wasn't so certain. Unless a crime had to do with the preternatural, the cops didn't call me in.

I leaned forward. "Pause."

Arthur hit a button on the remote, pausing the video. I compared the height marker in the doorway to both of the robber's masked heads. If you've ever wondered why most gas stations have these, now you know. It gives the police a better idea of a suspect's height.

"The first person is about five-six," I said. "Could be male or female." The second robber was close behind. Arthur pressed Play and the second robber entered, then the door closed. The tape froze again.

"The second one, I'm pretty sure is female. She's close to my height. There aren't many men that are around five-one."

Of course, Arthur had probably watched the video several times by now, but even so, he was quiet and allowed me to check off my own markers. It would help us avoid missing anything.

The two approached the counter. The woman wasn't wearing lipstick, which was a smart move, but even if her breasts weren't obvious under the sweater, her build and height still told me she was female. If she'd been wearing makeup, it'd have been a dead giveaway.

One of the first things you learn when examining a crime scene is this: always expect your perpetrator to do something stupid. Crime is not perfect. People are not perfect. At some point or another, everyone fucks up. My job was to find their fuck-ups.

"It wasn't a spur-of-the-moment," I said. "They're both wearing gloves. Whatever they're about to do was premeditated."

Arthur nodded his agreement. "Keep watching. You'll see."

I kept watching. The woman in the video fell behind and kept an eye on the door. The other robber stepped up to the counter, lips moving. The employee opened the cash register and started handing money to the robber.

The masked robber took enough time to count the bills that I noticed the large hands inside the black gloves. I would've put money down that the robber was male. How he'd so easily persuaded the employee without a weapon, I didn't know.

The masked woman paced in the background, her body language jerky and quick, like she was uncomfortable and scared. Her dark eyes kept flicking to the door, as if she was considering running out at any moment.

The masked robber raised his face and gave the camera the full weight of his blue-green eyes. He smiled, showing the dainty tips of elongated canines.

"Well, crap," I said, watching the two black figures exit the building. "That explains how he persuaded the employee without a weapon."

Arthur turned the television off.

"We know he's a vampire. What do you think about her?" Arthur asked.

"If she is, she's new to it," I said. "Vampires control their body language very well. She didn't. She was scared and jumpy. Have you questioned the employee?"

"Yes."

"What did he say?"

"He doesn't remember anything."

"If he didn't remember anything, how could he have remembered to call the police? If the vampire had wiped his mind, he wouldn't have even bothered calling you, Arthur. You said earlier this happened around five thirty this morning? That's cutting it awfully close to sunrise. Vampires are quick, but if his lair is halfway across town…" I shook my head, thinking furiously. If the vampire would cut it that close to sunrise, his daylight resting place had to be close by.

"It doesn't make sense, does it?"

"No, it doesn't. Your vampire didn't even call his power."

Arthur looked at me as if I'd started speaking another language he was trying very hard to understand. "Call his power? How can you tell when they do that?"

I shrugged. "I don't know if it shows on camera, but their eyes and skin change. They don't glow, not exactly. You remember seeing someone's eyes under bright lights when they're highly emotional? How the color seems to get richer and more vivid?" Arthur nodded. "That's how it is. Their skin is naturally kind of luminous, but it becomes even more so when they call their power. It looks like your vamp didn't say anything to the employee other than asking for the money. Usually, when they go all vampiric and start playing head games, they give a verbal command of forgetting. He didn't say anything after taking the money."

"Do they always have to say something?"

A memory of Lenorre going all vampiric on Arthur swam to the surface. When we'd first met, Lenorre had been helping me locate a really nasty werewolf. We'd taken Claire Delaine, a woman who had been attacked by the werewolf, away from the police and under our wing. Lenorre had given Arthur the verbal command to forget everything, and I knew from personal experience that her eyes had changed with her power. Her very gray eyes turned to liquid silver, surreal, stunning, and a little unnerving.

Of course, I didn't tell Arthur that my girlfriend had wiped his mind. That would have defeated the purpose. The last he knew he'd taken Claire somewhere safe and she was off living a happy and preternatural-free life. The truth was, she had been infected with lycanthropy, and with Rosalin and the rest of the Blackthorne pack's help was learning how to adjust to life on the wild side.

"From what I know, yeah," I said. "Is the employee still here?"

"We sent him home," he said, standing. "But we can go talk to him and ask him why he doesn't remember anything. I'll drive."

On the way out I checked the clock on my cell phone and cursed under my breath.

Fortunately, I didn't have to drive out to my parents' tonight. Even though I'm pagan, I do take part in Thanksgiving with my folks. This year, both of my parents had gone to visit my mother's brother in Missouri. So my sister and brother and I had agreed to an early Thanksgiving. That being done with and out of the way, Rosalin was supposed to make dinner at Lenorre's.

I fished the black sunglasses out of my coat pocket and exhaled a deep breath before getting into Arthur's dark blue Crown Victoria.

❖

By the time we made it to Jordan Jacobson's apartment, I was out of coffee and a very unhappy camper.

Jacobson was twenty-one and living with roommates. The roommates weren't home and when Jacobson answered the door, it looked like he'd been sleeping.

Arthur sat on a futon that was pressed against the wall in front of a small entertainment center. Jacobson offered me a green recliner and I shook my head, preferring to stand and observe.

"Mr. Jacobson, this is Preternatural Investigator Lyall."

Jacobson tensed and shot me an uneasy look.

"We have a few questions for you," Arthur continued. "You said earlier that you thought the vampire had erased your mind?"

"Yeah."

I felt more than saw Jordan's blue eyes following me as I moved around his living room, pretending to eye the movies stacked on the entertainment center. The brown carpet was old and worn. I inhaled, sorting through a myriad of smells. I caught the distinct whiff of old french fries and ketchup. I turned to glance in the kitchen, spotting the open-lid trash can. How long had it been since the trash had been changed? There were dirty dishes in the sink that smelled like rancid milk. I shuddered. If I ever wanted to throw my mother into conniptions, I'd show her Jacobson's house. I started heading for the hallway.

A lot of the time, odors mingle and form one big smell. It takes a conscious effort for me to sort through the various ingredients. When I focus, it's like my body starts separating the scents.

Jacobson was in the middle of explaining to Arthur that he didn't know to call the police until he realized the cash register was empty when he stopped in mid-sentence. "What's she doing?"

"I don't know," Arthur said. "Investigator Lyall?"

It was the *Investigator* part that made me turn from the hallway. Apparently, we were throwing titles around to make Jacobson nervous. Fine with me, I could do that.

"I'm going to take a look around while you question Mr. Jacobson." I stared at Jacobson. "Is that all right with you?"

"I don't think my roommates would appreciate having an investigator sorting through their stuff."

"Don't worry." I smiled, hoping it wasn't as predatory as I felt. "I'll leave everything in its place."

I heard the sound of chair legs scraping the carpet as I continued down the hall.

"Mr. Jacobson," Arthur warned.

There were three doors at the end of the hall. I opened the first door on the left. It smelled of Jacobson, salty with an undercurrent of dirty socks and crisp cologne. A twin-sized mattress sat on the floor under a window. Someone had nailed up a dark blanket in place of a curtain. A stereo with an alarm was within arm's reach of the bed. I stepped into the room.

Dirty clothes littered every surface. I opened the sliding closet door to find more clothes and a mess of shoes that would've made a gay man proud. I highly doubted the mess and tacky blanket would make one squeal with pride, though.

I kept exploring, ignoring the smell of unclean bathroom. I discovered the master bedroom at the very end of the hall. The room was much cleaner with a neatly made four-poster bed in the center of the room. Ah, a woman's touch. No, I wasn't gathering that from the bed alone. The scent of floral perfume and scented candles hung in the air.

I checked the closet, relying on my vision as well as sense of smell. The closet was lined neatly with clothes, one side his and one side hers.

Something about Jacobson wasn't right. His story wasn't right. He was too tense and nervous, obviously hiding something.

Crossing to the nightstand by the bed, I picked up a small picture with a metal frame. A woman with dark eyes and bleached blond hair stood next to a male with shoulder-length brown hair. He was smiling widely, and if it hadn't been for the unkempt eyebrows, he might've been one of those guys other guys call pretty. The white and dark green building of Jacobson's apartment formed the backdrop. I tapped my hip with the corner of the photograph, scanning the room.

"You're fucking kidding me," I whispered, as a thought bubbled to the surface of my mind. I raised the photograph again.

The guy had the girl tucked into the crook of his arm. The look on her face was softer and more reserved than his bold, broad stare. His eyes were blue-green.

I couldn't help it, I laughed. I raised my eyes to the ceiling. "Seriously?"

If the Gods heard me, they didn't answer.

I returned to the living room and tossed the small frame to Arthur. He caught it without fumbling.

"Where are your roommates, Jordan?"

Jacobson's eyes went wide and he rocked back in his seat. "Shit."

"Um, yeah. Shit about covers it. So, where are your friends?"

When Jacobson didn't answer, Arthur put the picture down on the wooden coffee table.

"We can do this the hard way, if you want to," I said. "Detective Kingfisher can arrest you and I can go search your apartment more thoroughly. I'm sure I'll find old bills or something else that will identify them." I crossed my arms over my chest, careful of the Mark III in its holster beneath my peacoat. If it had been any day other than Thanksgiving, I would've threatened to have the police check his bank records. Of course, even for searching the apartment the cops would've needed a warrant, but I didn't mention that. When threatening, some things are better left unsaid, and besides, I'm not a cop. "Your choice, Jacobson."

Jacobson decided to do it the easy way and gave us the names of his roommates. Christina Simmons and Joshua Roberts. Joshua was a vampire wannabe, which explained the lack of fangs in the photograph and the fangs on the surveillance footage. Then again, the photo could've been taken before he'd been turned, but he hadn't been turned, and that was the point.

Jacobson went to the bathroom and emerged carrying a case with two dainty fangs in it. When Arthur took the case, he started laughing.

"Damn kids these days," he said. "What in the world would make you think a preternatural expert wouldn't see through these?"

Jacobson shrugged. "We didn't know there would be a," he seemed to have forgotten the word, "paranormal investigator."

And that was the truth. They thought they could fool the cops by pretending a vampire had wiped Jacobson's mind. The kids didn't know enough about vampires and the aftereffects of being charmed by one to make their story convincing. At first, it might have worked on the cops, but I suspected once Jacobson's manager realized he'd failed to do the nightly drop, he'd have gotten caught.

Arthur called for backup. Once two cops I didn't recognize showed up in their squad cars, Arthur told them to park down the street and wait inside until Christina and Joshua got home. I was thankful Arthur wasn't going to force me to stand around twiddling my thumbs, but I hadn't expected him to drop it in someone else's lap just to take me back to my car.

On our way out of Jacobson's apartment, I asked him, "Are you sure you don't want to stay?"

"No, they can sit around and wait to arrest them," he said. "I'm taking you back and going to get lunch."

I opened the door and slid into the seat. "Sounds like a plan to me."

It's true what they say, sometimes the universe does smile. It might not have been smiling on Jordan Jacobson and his roommates, but hey, that was their own damn fault.

❖

"Kassandra."

Lenorre's voice was smooth and velvety, her British accent only slightly noticeable. I blinked my eyes open. The bedside lamp was on, casting a soft glow from its frothy globe.

I stretched, shoving my arms under the pillow.

"You're awake," I mumbled, trying to push away the last clinging strands of sleep.

Lenorre touched my cheek with cool tapered fingers. "So are you."

The blouse she wore was the color of hematite, bluer than the pure gray glory of her eyes. It showed the slim and curvaceous perfection of her waist, the gentle swell of her breasts. The color brought out the preternatural luminosity of her white skin.

"You're dressed," I noted, letting the appreciation of her attire fill my eyes. "What time is it? Have you fed?"

"'Tis eight and yes, I have fed."

I sat up, pushed my tangled black hair out of my face, and guided the hair to fall down my back. "Gods, it's already eight?"

"Rosalin informed me your little detective friend sought your aid. So I thought to allow you to rest. What happened?"

I told her. When I was done, Lenorre's eyes shone with soft amusement.

"That was rather foolish," she said. I nodded my agreement, reclining against the mound of pillows. Lenorre lay next to me, tracing the line of my jaw with the tips of her fingers. I turned my face into her palm, brushing my lips across her skin.

One touch, one simple touch and a heated look was all it took to make the breath catch in my throat. She bent at the waist and I knew she was about to kiss me.

"You should *really* let me brush my teeth first."

Lenorre got to her hands and knees. "I have a better solution," she said, stretching her body across the bed and reaching for the nightstand. I wanted to go to her, to slide my hands across the tight swell of her ass and to her waist. I wanted to tuck my hands under the silken material of her blouse, to feel her cool skin beneath my fingers.

I hadn't realized I'd made a noise until Lenorre turned her head to look at me.

"That look," she said in a breathy voice, eyes dark. The top drawer of the nightstand slid closed with a quiet click. Amusement rose in her expression to mingle with that seductive darkness. "Why are you holding yourself?" she asked wryly.

"I don't know, exactly," I said, lowering my arms.

She stayed where she was, glorious body stretched out like an offering, gaze meeting mine invitingly over her shoulder.

The wolf inside me pricked her ears in curiosity.

"Kassandra, what are you thinking?"

I closed my eyes and licked my lips.

"That's a very distracting position."

Lenorre gave her honeyed laugh. "Oh?"

I opened my eyes. The shirt fell away from her stomach, giving me a peek-a-boo view of her pale skin underneath.

Good Gods.

"Come here," she whispered. There was no power or pull in her voice.

Stubbornly, I shook my head. "If you plan on wearing that to dinner, that's not a good idea."

"Ah," she said, understanding. She sat back on her heels and held out her hand. It took me a moment to realize she was holding a small box of mints. I laughed.

"The better solution is keeping a box of mints stashed next to the bed?" I asked, taking one.

She tossed the small box aside, hands rising to unbutton her shirt. "I know how much you appreciate good hygiene."

"Are you trying to make me choke on my mint?" I asked, tucking it behind my teeth. I pushed the blankets aside and stopped her by putting a hand over hers. My T-shirt was long enough to cover the crimson lace shielding my intimate bits. Lenorre liked the sight of red against my skin.

"No," she said, "I am only trying to spare my clothes."

I touched the silken collar of her shirt, stroking it between my thumb and index finger. On her knees, she was still taller than me and I had to look up to meet her gaze. "What if I don't want to spare them?"

"You are the one that gave me a choice." She touched my thighs, hands sliding up to cradle my hips.

I grabbed two fistfuls of my shirt and tugged it over my head, before tossing it to the floor.

Her hands slid over my stomach, threatening to go higher.

"Take your clothes off without making a show of it," I whispered against her lips, "or I'll rip them off."

Her generous eyelashes fluttered. She did what I asked, but even with quick and adept hands, there was some show to it. With Lenorre, how could it be otherwise? She was a vampire; watching her undress was like watching some dark and seductive goddess unveil her beauty.

I reached behind her back, unhooking her bra and dragging it down her arms.

The sight of her made me ache between the legs. I ignored that aching need and bowed my head, taking the soft skin of her breast into my mouth.

Lenorre moaned my name and buried her hand in my hair.

I drew back, whispering, "Harder."

Her hand twined in my hair, twined in such a way that I cried out.

I bowed my head again, kissing the top of her breasts.

Tension strung her body. She used the grip she had to turn me, pulling me back against her. Her hand slid down my stomach, fingers sliding effortlessly beneath the red lace. She played those fingers at my cleft, threatening to sink lower into the honeyed sweetness she had summoned.

"Yes."

Lenorre tugged my hair, forcing my head back and exposing the line of my neck. I thought she would touch me, thought she would finish that last downward slide, but she didn't.

Instead, she whispered my name and I shivered. Her mouth traced my shoulder, leaving a trail of kisses behind. She stroked the damp lips between my legs, placing a kiss over the pulse pounding in my neck.

I tensed, afraid that she was going to bite me.

Lenorre noticed it. "You are afraid I will bite you?" Her fingers stopped their steady teasing.

"Yes."

"Would that truly be such a bad thing?"

I licked my lips. I was afraid to answer. She had only bitten me twice and neither of those times had really been as a means to feed.

When I didn't answer, I felt her lips moving. "I am a patient woman," she said. "I will wait, but for now…" I flinched when she drew my skin into her mouth, sucking on it oh so carefully to avoid breaking it. The dents of her fangs dragged across my throat, drawing an invisible thread of desire to my groin. The pleasure of it startled me, made things low in my body swan dive. My stomach muscles spasmed with anticipation.

"Do you trust me, Kassandra?"

"What are you going to do to me?"

She answered me with actions, not words. Her mouth worked at my throat, teasing me with lips and teeth. I rocked back against her, swooning, shivering as the edge of her fangs caressed my skin.

"The neck is a very sensitive area. Particularly yours." She kissed me and licked me, trailing her fangs tauntingly across my skin as if she knew where every sweet spot was located in my neck and shoulders.

I shivered helplessly. When her lips found a spot on the curve of my left shoulder, she caught it lightly between her teeth and I moaned. Her mouth sealed over it, tongue playing against it, sending a small orchestra of shudders down the front of my body.

I moved my hips, praying she understood I wanted the hand she so idly held against me to start doing something.

"Yes."

"Yes?" she whispered, pressing a kiss behind my left ear, breath warm and tickling.

"Gods, yes! I trust you. Please," I breathed the words, "Lenorre, touch me."

She obliged. I made a sound of frustration when her fingers brushed past my clit. She pushed herself inside me and I fought to hold myself upright. Her grip in my hair did most of the holding.

"Lenorre," I said, eyelashes fluttering as she slid her fingers in and out of me. "Lenorre, I want you to stroke me."

She laughed and the laugh vibrated against my neck, forced another shudder from me. Her hand moved up my body to stroke me and I sank into her, closing my eyes.

I felt her breath against my neck before she again asked, "Are you certain you trust me?"

"Yes."

"Good."

Two things happened at once: her stroking rhythm quickened, and I felt her open her mouth to bite me. My entire body went rigid with fear and pleasure. When the bite came, the orgasm overrode it, slamming into me and forcing my spine to bow against her body. My hips bucked forward and in one final stroke and cry, reality tumbled away.

Lenorre loosened her grip in my hair and I swayed forward. She laughed softly, helping to guide me onto the pillows.

I lay on my stomach and stared at her, body spent and mind cloudy. I reached up with an arm that still felt unreal and touched my neck, checking for blood. There was none. Her mouth was clean and perfect.

"You didn't bite me?"

"I did not bite you hard enough to bleed you, no. You have said you are not ready."

I had, but it didn't erase the fact that even that little bite had thoroughly rocked my world. Lenorre had thrown her power at me once. She had projected Zaphara's feelings onto me, so that instead of her fangs buried in Zaphara's skin, I had felt her fangs in mine. It occurred to me that was probably one of the reasons I was still hesitant about feeding her. In truth, I wasn't ready. She knew it and I knew it. Lenorre also knew that if she pushed it, I'd resist even more.

She traced the raven tattooed on my back, her nails tickling the swirling knot work decorating its body. I closed my eyes, relaxing. Her fingers brushed the tail feathers toward the base of my spine.

"Have I told you how truly beautiful you are?" she asked and I opened my eyes to look at her.

"Once," I said, remembering. "At least, that I recall."

The corner of her mouth twitched. Her fingers brushed my ass as she smiled tenderly, head resting on her bent arm. "Have I told you that you are a thousand times more beautiful nude and in my bed?"

I sat back on my heels and reached for her waistband. She rolled onto her back, allowing me to unhook her slacks. I pulled them down, revealing the black material stretched over the delicious mound of her. The slacks landed in a fall of cloth with the rest of our discarded clothes.

I moved to kneel between her legs, kissing above the line of her undergarments.

There was a knock on the door.

I gave a low growl, lips trembling against Lenorre's skin. I felt her body react to it.

"Is it locked?" I asked.

"Yes," she said.

"Should I stop so you can get it?" I inhaled deeply, trying to get a sense of who was knocking. Who did I get to be mad at?

Regretfully, Lenorre nodded and I sat up. She grabbed two robes from the back of the closet door, shrugged into the black one, and handed me the dark green one that I often wore. I put it on, belting the waist.

A moment before she opened the door, the smell of earth and forest, of another wolf, filled my senses. I could suddenly taste cool ginger on my tongue. Rosalin.

Lenorre stepped back to admit her. Rosalin, being a lycanthrope, didn't need to see the clothes on the floor or the messy covers and my hair to know what Lenorre and I had been doing. I expected her to comment or to at least smirk, but she didn't. Her honey brown eyes looked serious.

"Rupert is here," she said. "He said he needs to speak to you. It's urgent."

I blinked. "Urgent?"

She nodded, auburn hair bobbing in its ponytail, and said to Lenorre, "He wants to speak to you as well."

"We will be up shortly."

Rosalin looked my way, an expression in her eyes I didn't understand.

"I'm sorry for interrupting," she said. "Dinner is almost ready. I wouldn't have disturbed you if Rupert hadn't insisted."

"It's okay, Ros." I climbed off the bed. "What's wrong?"

She wouldn't meet my gaze.

I tried again. "Rosalin."

Lenorre gave her a quizzical look.

Rosalin's chest rose and fell unsteadily behind her pink T-shirt. Her eyes glistened with tears. I approached and touched her arm. A few months ago I'd accidentally claimed her as my wolf. It hurt to see her so sad and to not understand why. I didn't think it was because of what Lenorre and I had been doing.

"I hate holidays," she said, words choked.

I put my hands on her shoulders and pulled her into me. Rosalin's arms slipped around my waist and I felt the sob go through her. She was a few inches taller than me, especially when I wasn't wearing shoes, but I reached up anyway to stroke her hair.

That one touch did it. Rosalin collapsed against me, holding on to me like she was drowning. We went to our knees on Lenorre's carpeted floor. I held her body close. She clung to me.

I looked at Lenorre, trying to ask her with my eyes if she had any idea what was wrong.

Lenorre knelt beside us and caressed Ros's hair. "The loss of your parents?"

Rosalin buried her face in my shoulder. She fought the silent sobs long enough to say, "Yes."

Neither Lenorre nor I asked any more questions. We didn't need to.

I sat on the floor and held her. She'd lost both of her parents in a car accident when she was twenty-one. Some years had passed, but still, the loss was enormous. Her brother Henry was the only family she had aside from pack.

Rosalin drew away from me, wiping her face with her shirt. "I'm sorry," she mumbled. "I'm keeping you from Rupert. I interrupted you. I'm sorry. I didn't mean to, but once I saw you—" She choked on a sob and buried her face in her hands. "Fuck! Why can't I stop crying?"

I kept a hand on her back, keeping her from drawing away completely. I felt the wolf inside me, saw her in my mind, eyes sad, ears lowered. I felt her sadness, her desire to comfort one of our own.

Sighing, I held Ros close, brushing my cheek across hers in a gesture that was more wolf than human. Her tears were cool against my skin. I licked her face, taking in the salty sweetness of those tears. A great loneliness gripped my heart. I felt Rosalin's need for comfort, a need so true and intense that it was like starving. Her pain hit me like a crashing wave.

Lenorre touched my shoulder and I turned to look at her. She brushed her finger across my cheek and came away with a trembling teardrop. I hadn't realized I was crying.

I reached for her, my lover, and she came to me, pressing as much of her robed body as she could against mine while I held Rosalin. She encircled my waist with one arm and I wrapped an arm around her as well as Rosalin.

"You don't need to stop crying, Rosalin," I whispered. "We're here. You can fall apart. It's okay. We'll hold you."

The great sobs that had shook her body picked up again. Rosalin screamed, one long and angry scream, her face contorted with the pain. She threw her head back and howled. Even if I wasn't a lycanthrope, I would've caught the mourning and sorrowful tune of her song.

The wolf's need rushed through me and I tilted my head back, echoing the lonesome call in a long, clean note.

Rosalin nestled into me tighter and offered her voice to mine.

Distantly, I felt Lenorre shifting her arm, sensed the ripples of other energies entering the room. The air was heavy with the scent of rich soil and patchouli.

Another call came, echoing Rosalin's. I raised my face to find Trevor, one of the more submissive wolves of the Blackthorne pack, standing in the doorway with tears in his brown eyes. He dropped to his knees and we, my wolf and I, knew that he was waiting for permission.

I held my hand out and he crawled to us, keeping his head low to the ground so that all I could see was the bleached blond of his surfer hair. In his jeans and blue shirt, he knelt by Rosalin, reaching for her uncertainly, as if he was afraid of how she would react.

A high and concerned whimper emitted from his throat.

Rosalin brushed his hand and Trevor plastered his body against hers, bumping us roughly enough that if it wasn't for Lenorre's support, we would have fallen over.

The smell of forest fell over us like a comforting blanket. Someone nudged my hand and I opened my eyes.

Claire's full lips brushed across my knuckles. Her wide hazel eyes searched mine. I knew by the confused look that Claire probably had no idea why she felt the urge to join us. Though she was gaining better control over her wolf, the wolf's urges were still strong within her, strong enough that she probably came to us without realizing it.

I knew she had a room upstairs, but until that moment I hadn't known she was having Thanksgiving with us. I touched her cheek, pushing the brown tresses away from her face. She accepted the invitation, and Trevor moved so that she had room to join our little snuggle party.

I smelled air and rain, like sky and slick streets. Zaphara stood above us. She was fey, not a lycanthrope, and I didn't always get along with her, but the energy spilling from her skin caressed mine, calling to the blood in my veins, like two droplets of water colliding. She did not wait for my permission, but knelt and rested a hand on Rosalin. Her aubergine hair was pulled back in its usual tight braid. Her model features were striking, but it was her eyes that made me hold her gaze. Her eyes, shining like amethysts, were filled with such soft compassion I was reluctant to turn her away.

Rosalin's tears slowed, but even after the tears stopped fallng, we held her. We comforted her. Lenorre's energy was a cool balm against my back, like a slight breath of winter wind. I cradled the arm she had wrapped around my waist.

"Thank you," Rosalin whispered, to me, to all of us.

Trevor responded, "We're your family."

Rosalin looked at me, eyes still damp and red from crying. She smiled sadly.

"It's true," I said, brushing aside a strand that had broken free of her ponytail.

"I know," she said, "but uh, you guys are kind of smooshing me."

I laughed, leaning back against Lenorre.

"It seems your wolf is feeling better," Lenorre said.

"Yes," I said, not bothering to argue whether she was my wolf or not. In that moment, I agreed with Trevor. We were family.

Claire peeked at me from around Trevor's shoulder. "That was amazing," she said, tears still damp on her cheeks. "I've never felt so whole…so at peace with myself."

Rosalin actually giggled. "Welcome to the pack."

"But you're not a part of the pack," Claire said to me.

"No, but she has the mark of an alpha and you answered her call," Zaphara said rather cryptically.

I met her gaze and the look in her eyes was more Zaphara, less compassionate and more tricksy and mysterious.

"What made you want to join?"

"I'm fey," she said, as if that explained everything. I let it go.

"We should speak with Rupert," Lenorre said.

I clutched the robe, holding it carefully in place as I tried to get to my feet. I didn't get very far, considering Rosalin was practically sitting in my lap and Trevor and Claire were still pressed against her.

"Yeah," I said, "we should before he starts wondering what the hell is going on."

Lenorre helped me to my feet and drew my back against her chest, hugging my waist.

"Shit," Rosalin said as she got to hers. "Fucking shit!"

"What?"

She ran for the door, calling over her shoulder, "The bird!"

Trevor and Claire hurried out after Rosalin. Zaphara crossed her arms over her chest, considering me.

"What?" I asked.

"Nothing. I believe Rosalin will be relieved when she finds that I rescued her bird before it was beyond edible."

"What did you do, pull the stove out of the wall?"

She scoffed. "No, why would I do that?"

I played my nails across Lenorre's arms.

Lenorre's laugh thrummed against my back. "Kassandra is implying that she does not believe you know how to find your way around a kitchen, Zaphara."

"I don't," she admitted. I hadn't actually thought it was true, but had thought the joke would irritate her. "However, opening the door and taking the turkey out when the timer went off wasn't exactly difficult."

"Who knew you cared," I said.

"I wouldn't have," she said in a bland voice, if Zaphara's sultry voice could ever be bland, "if I wasn't going to be partaking in eating it."

Such was Zaphara.

❖

We met in the upstairs parlor. Rupert sat in one of the white armchairs, wearing a dark sweater and black jeans. The brown spikes of his hair were gelled into place. When I entered, he stood and offered a black case that he'd been holding in his lap.

"What is this?" I asked.

"A belated birthday present."

"From you?" I asked, taking the heavy case.

"No." His blue-gray eyes went to Lenorre.

I gave her a suspicious look. "What did you do?"

She smiled, silvery eyes sparkling in the brightly lit room.

"Open it and see."

I sat on the edge of the couch and opened the case. I recognized the beveled slide serrations and shiny steel. The breath caught in my throat. I ran the tip of my finger over the word *Kimber* engraved on the side of the gun.

I'd been wanting that gun for a while. I'd actually mentioned it once to Rupert. The last I knew, he didn't have any in stock, and even if he'd given me a discount, it was still a little too expensive for my tastes.

"Kass, you can close your mouth," Rupert said.

I couldn't help it. I stared at Lenorre. "You didn't have to do this."

She traced the white streak in my hair. "I wanted to."

Something hit the couch and I jumped. I turned to find a shoulder rig that Rupert had practically launched at me.

"That one your girlfriend shouldn't be able to rip apart so easily," he said.

I looked at Lenorre. "You told him about that?"

She lifted her shoulders. "It came up briefly when I was replacing the other."

I grabbed a handful of her curls and tugged her head down to mine, kissing her softly.

"Thank you," I whispered, this time against her lips.

"You are more than welcome." She touched my throat and something about the way she did it made my cheeks flush with heat, reminded me of what we'd been doing earlier and what we had left to finish.

"I will meet you in the dining room. No doubt Rosalin is setting the table." She looked at Rupert. "You are welcome to join us, if you wish."

Rupert nodded. "Thanks."

"I'll be there in a moment," I said.

I watched the way the high heels made her hips sway, the way the slacks hugged her very delicious form and spilled down her legs, the way her onyx curls fell, dancing at her waist.

"You're really in love with her," Rupert said, almost casually.

"Yes." I sighed. "I am hopelessly, completely, madly, and sinfully in love with that woman."

"Huh." He looked uncharacteristically thoughtful. "You know, I haven't exactly been nice to her, but I'm starting to think maybe the Countess is good for you, Kass. She seems good to you."

I narrowed my eyes at him. "You're not giving her enough credit, Rupert."

He grinned, blue eyes hardening coldly. "I'm not giving her more than that, Kass."

"You don't have to," I said. "I will. Are you going to stay?"

"Do you want me to stay?"

"You're a brother to me," I said. "Of course I want you to stay."

The smile he gave me made his eyes warmer. Well, as warm as they got. "I'll stay."

"Good." I led the way to the dining room. The table had already been set, and Lenorre sat at the far end. I took the empty chair next to her.

Lenorre's lips brushed my ear. "After you are well fed we have other matters to attend to."

I met the seductive look in her gray eyes. "Trust me, I'm all yours."

Lee Lynch <leelynch6.tripod.com> has published fifteen books, including the classics *Toothpick House* and *The Swashbuckler*. Her most recent novel is *Beggar of Love*. Her monthly column "The Amazon Trail" appears in gay publications across the country. Lynch is the recipient of the The James Duggins Mid-Career Author Award, the Lesbian Fiction Readers' Choice, Golden Crown Literary Society Trailblazer, and Alice B. Reader's awards, and has been inducted into the Saints and Sinners Hall of Fame.

The characters in "The Top" first appeared in *Sweet Creek* and *Toothpick House* (www.boldstrokesbooks.com).

The Top

Lee Lynch

Annie Heaphy had been to Oregon several times to visit Vicky, usually when her life was flipping ass over teakettle. They would always drive to the coast for a day, but this time they headed inland, where Vicky had promised to spend Christmas Day with a couple who ran a natural food store. Vicky's wife, Jade, was stuck in Mumbai, where her company had sent her for three months.

"Good career move," Vicky had explained.

"Bad for the heart," Annie had muttered as the old wave of love for Vicky washed through her. Lately she'd started beating herself up again: should she have agreed to move cross country with Vicky all those years ago? Would they have stayed together? It was sad, but Vicky and Jade made a better match. Although Vicky was still her best friend, the friendship was laced with regrets.

Vicky's small law firm had clients who were sometimes a three-hour drive away, dug into little valleys and hidden in the hills. Going south, Vicky had told her, she always stopped for lunch at Natural Woman Foods, did a little shopping to support them, and brought home one of Donny's excellent cinnamon pull-aparts. Every year Vicky sent one for Annie's birthday. It always made Annie's girlfriend, Chantal, kind of pissy, because Chantal wanted the star attraction to be the cake her gay son, a baker, made. That Annie wouldn't share her ex's gift with anyone but Chantal, while she shared Ralph's cakes with everyone Chantal invited over, was a sore point. Annie's sore point was the party itself. She was vastly uncomfortable, her face glowing hot and red, as she opened birthday presents and gave out the expected thank-you hugs along with wisecracks.

They could smell the roasting turkey even before Chick, who Vicky said was the other half of the Natural Foods couple, opened the door for them at the top of a steep narrow staircase that ran up an outside wall. Chick's hug and exclamation of delight welcomed them to a real home, perched though it was above the store. Outside she'd been chilly from the icy fog; in here, a living room woodstove pumped out the most genuine heat she'd ever felt. She wanted to melt into the couch, hang like a drape, stretch out like the braided rug, and hoped Donny and Chick never redecorated.

She'd left Chantal back in Morton River Valley with her daughter, son, and their families. Chantal Zak was an adorable pudgy fifty, and Annie didn't know if she could stand another minute with her. Could she breathe better in Oregon because the air really was better, or was it because Chantal was on the other side of the country? Maybe she just wanted a little break; she so wanted them to stay together. She didn't have to make a decision today, not Christmas Day. Or did she? She was waiting for Chantal to call at 5:00, after a long day with her kids' grandparents.

Chick led Vicky and Annie through the kitchen, where a woman in overalls said, "Come on in! I'm Donny." Donny slid the turkey out of the oven with the help of a radically short-haired younger woman who called, "Yo, dude, dude-ess, Jeep here."

As the last arrivals, Vicky and Annie were introduced to a host of women, each of whom was engaged in some task: setting the table, playing with a little round-faced boy, braiding evergreen branches into a wreath, peeling foil off steaming bowls of potluck offerings, playing holiday songs on guitar, adding ornaments to the Christmas tree, lighting all the candles on a menorah. She immediately forgot most of the names, but let herself be seated, with some ceremony, at the long table, across from Vicky. She removed her tweed cap and shook out her shaggy fair hair.

The witchy-looking woman who'd been making the wreath stood by what looked like a round pig trough, the kind Annie had seen at county fairs. It was big enough for a prize hog to bathe in, but filled with gifts. The woman raised her hand, and as if by her power, all the lights went off, including those on the Christmas tree. Annie spied two assistants—or were they acolytes?—at the lights. The witchy woman, who seemed familiar somehow, spoke of coming home to celebrate solstice. She went on about the plant-themed gifts brought by all the guests (Vicky had provided handcrafted vanilla-scented sachets), and about Yuletide, Yule, and the heathen feast Jul. She placed the wreath in the center of the table, explaining its history over the centuries.

"The darkness gives us rest," she pronounced, "and the light gives us life." The woman lifted a long butane lighter, the kind used for barbecues, flame shooting to a candle set in the middle of the wreath. Annie glanced around for another exit and made note of the front door. Wasn't anyone else worried about fire?

Immediately, that door opened and a tall figure loomed in it for a moment, then stepped inside and closed the door, silently, behind her.

"Jesus, R," the newcomer said, with a quiet authority. "Are you trying to burn the place down?"

The woman called R raised her hands and the lights came on. The room looked dazzling now.

Donny said, "Come on in, Joan."

Joan pulled off her cap, its Sheriff's Department emblem matching the one on her jacket. She did not remove her gun belt or radio. "Sorry I'm late." She took the empty seat next to Cat—not a name Annie would forget.

"We're just eating," Donny said and stuck platters of turkey on the table. "If R is done searing the wreath."

The woman called R bowed her head and, with a smile that broadcast long-suffering tolerance and a humble superiority, sat.

All hell broke loose then, with bowls passing, serving spoons scraping, a splat of jellied cranberry sauce on the little boy's lap, and everyone talking at once. This reminded Annie of Christmases when she was a kid, with the aunts and uncles, the off-color guffaws, the goosing, the spilling, the pouring of cider from a thick glass gallon jug—which Chick was doing for her right now.

Chick's presence felt like the sun emerging on a gloomy day. Chick pressed her hand on Annie's shoulder as she went by. Had Chick said "Hot butch" to her?

There was wine on the table, but she didn't want the scratchy-eyed feeling that came later, when it wore off. She stuck to cider and to figuring out who this R woman looked like. The woman next to her, Sarah, was saying she was an architect. How she and Jeep were from Reno, Nevada, originally and were going to Idaho to get married and would have a baby as soon as she could manage it, but they'd had no luck with that so far. Sarah sat with the smiling little boy between her and Cat. "Luke's mom," she explained, "is visiting her other kids in Mexico." When Annie raised her eyebrows at this, Sarah stroked Luke's head and added, "It's complicated."

Annie was reminded of Chantal and her kids. Why couldn't she have gotten together with a childless dyke? She was with kids all day at work: driving them, teaching life skills to those who could use them, feeding and cleaning up those who couldn't. Then to spend a weekend with Chantal fussing over her visiting grandkids, endlessly cleaning up after them—and corralling Annie to help keep the house spotless—it got a little much.

Chantal had always been persnickety. Now, though, Annie worried she'd become obsessive. She was still a terrific lover, but was more and more particular even about sex. Had Annie washed, you know, down there? Brushed her teeth? Locked the doors? Turned off the lights? There was little spontaneity, though the lovemaking was frequent and enthusiastic. At least their periods were over. That had entailed a whole other set of rules.

The woman, R, had stopped saying her weird kind of grace. Annie whispered to Sarah, "What's R's real name?"

"Oh," said Sarah. "It's Rattlesnake. I mean, maybe not her birth name; I hope not her birth name. Rattlesnake's the only name I hear her called."

"Does she use a last name?" She'd seen R before. She would have asked Vicky, but Jeep was speaking expansively to her about the secondhand shop she owned and her fiddle.

"Are you going to play today?" Vicky asked. Jeep flushed red, squirmed, said she doubted this was the time or place, but she let her violin case peek over the table so Vicky could see it. Annie wondered if she came across to others like Jeep did: the blushing butch.

R got up and moved behind Vicky, hands on her shoulders. "How are you, Victoria?"

Vicky craned her head around to look at the woman and gasped. Annie started to rise. Had the witch done something to her old lover?

"Rosemary!" cried Vicky. "Is that you?"

Rosemary? That was Rosemary from Yale who came out with

Claudia? If so, she'd aged. Aged terribly. The extreme short hair—she'd always been gawky, but—had she had a mastectomy?

Rosemary was talking to Vicky, but looking at Annie. "Oh, Claudia hasn't exchanged a word with me since I married."

Annie had been disgusted at the news from San Francisco, via Vicky, of Rosemary's marriage to a man. When Rosemary came out, it had been the political decision of a radical feminist and she'd proceeded to tell all the lesbians she met how to be lesbians. Annie's old friends from the bars still laughed about her.

Yet she'd learned from Rosemary to be enough of a feminist that she'd brushed marriage aside like she would a spiderweb across a doorway. While the commitment marriage demanded had its appeal, she was uneasy about the whole concept of having, and being, a wife. She didn't want to own Chantal and that's exactly what Rosemary had preached back then, that marriage was about making women chattel in the power of men.

"And she's got twin sons, don't you, R?" Clara called from the far end of the table. Clara had been flitting in and out of the kitchen nonstop and finally sat. As far as Annie could tell, this spare woman in her seventies, and her big-bellied husband Hector, were the only straights there. "All grown up, but they came to get you with their father when you had the cancer, didn't they, R? They got her the best treatment."

Hector added, "Doesn't have a pot to pee in herself."

"My hair still hasn't grown back."

She exchanged a look with Vicky. R's sharp and universal discontent hadn't changed with her name. "R"? "Rattlesnake?" Marrying? Bringing up sons? Commuting between that world and this micro-lesbianville in the mountains? Where was the rabid man-hater? Who was Rosemary now?

Then she laughed at herself; life did lead to strange decisions. Chantal might well be getting ready to dump her, for all she knew, and be uninterested in working on what they had together. At the end of the day, what had she to offer? Happy in a dead-end low-paying job she happened to love, her birth family all gone, and her longevity pretty genetically iffy. To get healthier, she'd taken up bicycling and took a spin every day after she got off work at 3:00 p.m. The first downhill whirl, that was a daily thrill. Breathing came easy as she explored her valley's nooks and crannies before Chantal got home from the office just after 5:00. She loved the new solidity of her thighs. So did Chantal.

Rosemary hadn't gotten any less weird, and she wasn't exactly Hollywood hit material herself, she thought. Watching *The Closer* reruns with Chantal was the other highlight of her day. She genuinely enjoyed Chantal and looked forward to a week in Provincetown every summer and a visit to Rockefeller Center every Christmas where they would take in a show at Radio City Music Hall and spend the night at Dr. Turkey's place.

They had a history together, she thought with some warmth. Dr. Turkey was Chantal's name for Annie's oldest friend, Turkey, who was now a professor of sociology. Someone chose that moment to pass the platter to her. She smiled at the memory of Chantal's running family joke. Every Thanksgiving she would tell the littlest grandkid about Annie's famous friend in New York City who invented turkeys.

She gave the platter to Sarah and accepted gravy from—what was the name? Jeep.

"So," Jeep said, "you're an East Coaster?"

She grinned. "I've always been a fan of wizard-style towns, like where Harry Potter shops."

With a rush of enthusiasm, Jeep said, "That's exactly how I imagine New York City, or Boston, or places like Hoboken, New Jersey, and, let's see," Jeep scratched at her dark, brushy hair. "New Orleans, though that's not exactly the East Coast, is it?"

"A different kind of magic," she said.

"It's dark back there, right? I mean, compared to the Left Coast?" Jeep was spooning green beans with sliced almonds onto her plate, trying valiantly to keep the gravy from soiling them. Annie slipped her knife from her pocket to help with the dam.

"A silver Swish Army knife? Now that's slick."

Annie quickly opened all the tools. "This is the best," she said, jabbing a finger at the saw.

Jeep reached in her pocket and displayed a well-worn green Girl Scout knife. "A Kutmaster, from the 1960s. Old."

"Oh, man. That thing has definite street cred," Annie said, thinking that the 1960s weren't all that long ago. They exchanged knives and inspected them.

Jeep ran her thumb along Annie's blade. "You keep that sharp."

Sarah laughed and said, "Chick! Look at the bois with their dueling pocketknives."

In a flash, everyone seemed to zero in on them, all smiling and curious. Quickly, they handed back their knives and concentrated on the food. "Great grub, Donny—everybody!" Jeep said.

"They're shy!" Sarah teased, but the talk went back to food.

She recognized herself in Jeep, though she was into hats, not strange haircuts.

After she turned fifty, her enthusiasms had become selective. She was older than that Girl Scout knife. Jeep was obviously still giving megawatt energy to everything equally. She was young and adventurous—and ready to accept settling down forever. She watched Jeep wave knife and fork in the air to illustrate a point. Sarah reached across her to capture Jeep's hand.

"Oh. Right. Chill," Jeep said and laid down the knife. Jeep's adventures were with Sarah now.

So maybe it wasn't Chantal, thought Annie. Maybe it was herself, slowing down. Chantal might be sensing that and scared that Annie had lost interest.

"So, really, where are you from?" Jeep asked.

Annie was glad to be taken away from her simmering brain.

"I grew up in Beantown, but I live in Connecticut." She'd learned that people out west had only a vague idea of the original thirteen colonies' geography and that it did no good to offer details.

But Jeep perked up, if it was possible for her to be any perkier. "Katie's filming in Connecticut right now. In some little town—Waterbury? Do you know where that is?"

"You bet. It's just northwest of where I live in Morton River. Who's Katie?"

Jeep glanced across her at Sarah. "A mistake I made once," she told Annie.

Sarah's tone was gentle. "Don't say that, Jeep. You had some oats to sow. And you found us this wonderful community."

Jeep nodded, looking at her plate, lips tight. "I'm just glad it's done," she said, then, eyes alight, told Annie, "We live over our store, too. Do you know we have a store?" Jeep smiled at Sarah. "Chick and Donny helped out. So did Clara and Hector."

"Garage Sale Dandy, she calls it," said Sarah.

"Oh, super name," Annie told them.

"You need to come by tomorrow," said Jeep.

"You're open?"

"Yes! You'd be surprised. The day after Christmas people sell us loot they don't want and can't return, then get something twice as good or twice as many. Like if you wanted to bring in your 'cauldron' present. Kids with Christmas money buy used video games. It's not a great day for musical instruments, which I mostly sell and buy on eBay anyway, but why drive all the way to a mall when Garage Sale Dandy has it all? That's our motto."

"She's so busy I help out the days before and after Christmas," offered Sarah.

"Sarah's on school break. I gave up my job wrassling preschoolers with disabilities to run the store full-time, and they hired Sarah to replace me. How cool is that? She's taking classes in special ed."

"I'm working on the certification. They always need special ed teachers. See, Jeep? You found me my calling, too."

"I thought you were an architect?" Annie asked. "The buildings in Waterfall Falls are right out of an old Hollywood Western."

Sarah sighed. Jeep explained, "Sarah can design any kind of building: retro Western, modern, you name it. But finding a job? Hard enough in the big cities."

"And I refuse to sit in front of a computer doing CAD work for some guy. That's incredibly boring."

Jeep leapt up then to take care of something in the kitchen with Donny. Sarah and Cat fussed over Luke's cranberry stain. Annie looked at her watch. Too soon for Chantal's call, but she felt unbalanced here. How did you tell if you should be living your life differently? If moving, or splitting up, or enjoying the heck out of what you had was right? She'd caught herself looking at the houses on the way from Vicky's. Imagining herself in a rental in Eugene or out in a very small town, like Waterfall Falls. Everyone here seemed happy. She felt happy.

When a few women rose to leave the table and her offer to help in clearing or cleaning had been refused, she asked if she could see the store.

"Of course," said Chick, showing her the indoor stairs and

flicking a light on for her. "I'll come down and give you a tour in a few minutes."

She bounded down the stairs like a top spun hard and set free. As she wandered the place, she noted that it was no hole in the wall. Food, personal care, supplements, even organic wines. There were two booths and a couple of tables that probably came from Garage Sale Dandy. She sat by a window. The corner sign read *Stage Street*. Was there a theater? Then it hit her. Waterfall Falls must have been a stagecoach stop. Wow, she thought. Despite growing up a T ride from Boston's Freedom Trail, history had never seemed so close. Otherworldly ornamental cabbages—light green, purple, ethereal white—grew in a long wood and tin planter out front. That's where the horses once were hitched. Wow, wow, wow. She wished she could show it to Chantal.

The truth was, she missed her Chantal. Maybe she should quit waffling and, now that it was legal for them to marry in Connecticut, go ahead and do it. Vicky had gone along with Jade's wish to marry. She'd go home, get down on her knees, and ask Chantal to marry her. Would that get them back on track? It might fix her own wavering affections. They'd have a sweet wedding and a honeymoon that would jump-start them. She imagined Chantal saying, "Com'ere, sugar," in her throaty voice, leading her, that swing of her hips promising everything a woman can promise. Annie, as usual, wanting to fill her hands with those hips, insisting that she undress Chantal herself. That golden moment when Chantal's breasts would come free of her bra and fill Annie's waiting hands. What a rush that was, every time.

"Congratulations, Mrs. Heaphy," she'd say. Chantal's light blue eyes would go dreamy. She would kiss Chantal's near-constant wedding-day smile. This was what they'd needed to do, she'd say with her hand between Chantal's legs, her own excitement another "I do." Chantal on her back, beyond ready for Annie to demand entry and reach far inside so Chantal could close around her fingers, and open, and close, and come with all her being. Then, whispering that she was still feeling it, turn to touch Annie with her delicate fingers.

It was more like half an hour before Chick arrived downstairs. Annie was whistling as she aligned items on the shelves.

Chick said. "Let me give you a big old hug. I didn't have enough of a chance earlier."

Annie found herself enveloped for a second time by a woman taller and softer than Chantal. Chick's scent took her back to the seventies, when essences, rather than perfumes, were used. She put her arms around Chick's back and gave her a quick tight squeeze. When she stepped away, it was with reluctance.

"You feel good," Chick told her.

"If I had my druthers, I'd stay like that all day."

"Don't you have a girl back home?"

She tried to cover her shock. It wasn't, she understood in a flash, it wasn't the sex, the fussiness, the kids or the sameness of her daily life. It was this: the plain human affection Chantal had once given out like the sun gives light was gone. Touch was rote: a peck hello or good-bye, some moments in bed after the big event. Then it was back to business, whether it be sleeping or working, making a phone call or doing chores. Annie felt untouched. Did time do that to every couple? Was she expecting too much?

"Are you all right, Annie?" asked Chick.

"Yes. Yes, I am. You just made me think of something I've been trying to figure out."

"Stop working on the shelves. We pay people to do that. Come sit down." Chick led her by the hand to a booth. She was all too aware that it was evening and the earth was spinning away from the light of the sun. It seemed so sad. Every day had to end. Did every love have to also?

Tears came to her eyes when Chick looked at her and asked, "What's going on?"

She carried a rainbow bandana for special occasions and hated to mess it up as it was the only one she owned, but she pulled it from her back pocket now and dabbed at her eyes and nose. "Maybe it's the time of day or the time of year."

"Or being so far from home?"

"I don't feel far from home. This could be home as easily as Morton River is home. It's confusing. I could pick up stakes and resettle out here, like Jeep and Sarah did, and I'd hardly notice."

"Oh," said Chick, her hands on Annie's free hand, "I think you would. Notice, that is. Do you want to leave her?"

"Not really." She hesitated to make her thoughts real by saying them aloud. "Lately, I've been feeling like a top coming out of orbit, all wobbly."

"Do you love her?"

"Yes, mostly. She really, really wanted me. That was a good feeling."

"And now?"

"Do I destroy something, and maybe someone, for not being perfect?"

"Don't expect perfect, Annie Heaphy."

Chick was a big woman. Next to skinny Donny, they could illustrate the old nursery rhyme, "Jack Sprat could eat no fat. / His wife could eat no lean. / And so between them both, you see, / They licked the platter clean."

She had put on weight, too; it wasn't just Chantal. Their imperfections were perfect together.

Upstairs, chairs were scraping and feet were stepping, muffled by rugs. There was a silence, the sound of a keyboard and of a violin tuning.

"Sarah's a talented pianist, but wait till you hear Jeep," said Chick.

They sat there, holding hands across the table, smiling at each other while listening to Christmas songs on the fiddle. What would it take to get Chantal looking as warmly at her again?

Where was Chantal, anyway? She could see the wall clock. It was 5:25. She always called on the dot, like she planned her whole day around it. What was she thinking? This was Chantal. Of course she would plan her whole day around it. So why hadn't she called?

She told Chick.

"Are you worried?"

"Well, yes. Chantal always has to do the calling and control the timing."

"And that bothers you?"

"Not really," Annie answered. "I'm kind of lazy about making decisions." She grinned. "Isn't that what femmes are for?"

Chick said, "You've found our secret. Come on, let's go back upstairs. It's time to exchange gifts."

Rosemary lay on the couch, attended by the same women who had controlled the lights earlier. The sheriff and Cat were putting on their jackets, looking sort of separate and sort of together.

Chick whispered, "Don't tell a soul in this county that you saw the sheriff here tonight."

"Oh," she said. That was another blessing with Chantal. Neither of them would want to be grand marshall at a gay pride parade, but they refused to be closeted. So, she thought, she's a super lover, we have history, we're not into closets. Was that enough? Maybe they could change something, anything, like where they went on vacation, or she could break the butch barrier and hug Chantal big, a Chick hug, regularly. And Chantal's fussiness, was it a reaction to—what? Something she was doing? Something Chantal was afraid of? Was Chantal desperately trying to keep a lid on their life?

While the others exclaimed over the gifts, she thought again about marriage. Chantal had mentioned it more than once; she'd never suggested doing it. But then, that was one of her charms: Chantal was an old-fashioned, small-town lady who would wait to be asked. All of a sudden her life was spinning again, and she was filled with an edgy excitement. After years together she'd considered that they were as good as married, but maybe that was a way of taking Chantal, and what they had, for granted.

It was her turn to pull a gift from Rosemary's cauldron and be embarrassed by everyone watching. She reached in and grabbed something small, fully intending, as she turned, to pass it on to one of the others. Chick was right behind her.

"I don't need any gift except being in your home and with your friends today," she said, her voice loud in the hush of expectancy. "I want you to have mine."

"No, Annie Heaphy," Chick said. "You're not giving this gift away, too."

She furrowed her brow, taking in what Chick had said as she removed the wrapping.

Chick slapped her knee and laughed.

It was an old wooden top, painted all around with flowers. She loved the feel of it between her fingers, smooth and tiny and still.

Her phone rang.

This short story from Nell Stark and Trinity Tam features Valentine and Alexa from *everafter*, before they were turned. Book two in the series, *nevermore*, was released in 2010. Nell Stark is also the author of the romances *Running With the Wind* and *Homecoming*. Spread the infection at www.everafterseries.com.

The Twelve Days of Courtship

Nell Stark and Trinity Tam

1 Alexa

I first met Valentine Darrow on the Monday after Thanksgiving.

If it had been up to me, I wouldn't have gone out at all that night—the semester was officially in its death throes, and I was overwhelmed by case studies and exam preparations. But it was Nicole's "quarter of a century" birthday, and there was simply no way to plead out of the festivities. And so it was that I found myself in the Niagara at just past one in the morning, having been charged to order a round of lemon drops.

At first, I thought the bartender was the most attractive man I had ever seen. But when I realized my mistake, my purely aesthetic appreciation became something far more primal. After almost ten years of being out, I knew what attraction felt like. That was not this. This—the electric shock that coursed down my spine, the dry mouth, the moist palms—was desire. I wanted the woman behind the bar with a blazing intensity that was as unexpected as it was sudden. I wanted to grip the biceps that leapt into sharp relief as she shook a cocktail, and I wanted her slender fingers to dip between the buttons of my shirt and trace the skin beneath. I wanted her at my mercy, and I wanted her above me.

I wanted her. I didn't even know her name.

And I certainly couldn't order drinks from her, feeling like this. I leaned one shoulder against the wall and took a few deep breaths. What was going on with me? I'd stopped drinking over an hour ago and felt completely sober. Was this my body's way of telling me that my current dry spell had gone on too long? My last relationship had ended before the semester began, and I'd been too concerned about my classes to date casually. Clearly, I needed to carve out some time for a social life that didn't revolve around my straight friends.

After a few more breaths, I dared to return my gaze to the bartender, feeling reasonably sure I could hold a conversation with her without making a fool out of myself. As I watched, she raised her head and surveyed the crowd for thirsty patrons. When her eyes met mine, she froze.

With her appreciative stare, my confidence returned and the paralysis that had anchored me to the wall dissolved. I moved forward until I could prop my forearms on the bar and glanced at the nametag pinned to her tank top, just above her left breast. *Valentine.* The name suited her—feminine, yet striking.

And then I realized I was blatantly cruising her. A flush rose to my cheeks, chasing away the chill of the wintry night.

"Valentine." Her eyes were as blue as a robin's egg. I fished my credit card out of my leather pants. "Seven lemon drops, please. And one Coke."

Her fingertips slid over mine as she took the plastic—a deliberate move, I knew, but my breath hitched nonetheless. Had she noticed?

"Would you like me to keep it open?" she asked over her shoulder, granting me a vision of taut muscles and a slim waist as she gathered her ingredients.

"Yes, please."

She poured the Coke first, and I sipped at it gratefully. As she lined up the shot glasses, a grin rose to her full lips. "I don't trust a woman who doesn't drink."

I arched one eyebrow, determined to keep my composure in the face of her cockiness. "Why is that?"

"Not indulging in a simple vice implies that you're saving yourself for something much more extravagant."

I laughed at her presumption. "It's obvious you don't know me."

She paused, vodka bottle poised above the row of shots. "I'd like that to change. Let me take you out to dinner. Tomorrow."

For a moment, I was in danger of saying yes. Valentine the Bartender was beautiful and confident and I enjoyed the way she looked at me. But what could we possibly have in common? Besides, I wasn't about to indulge myself when the specter of final exams loomed on the horizon.

"You're very smooth. But no, thank you."

"All right." Her shrug was nonchalant, her smile pleasant. The warm feeling in my stomach soured. Whatever chemistry I'd felt between us was nothing special to her. Valentine was obviously a player.

I couldn't help but watch the grace of her slender fingers as she arranged the glasses on a small tray, but petulance at her easy dismissal overruled my attraction. I deserved someone who would cherish me—someone who could both excite me and match my intellect. Valentine mixed drinks in a neighborhood bar on the Lower East Side. She probably took home a different woman every day. I'd been crazy to even contemplate her offer.

"Thank you," I said coolly.

"Enjoy your night." She turned back to the register, leaving me relieved. And aroused. And frustrated.

But at least I had escaped unscathed.

2 Valentine

I found the right classroom in Vanderbilt Hall with ten minutes to spare. After poking my head inside the door to make sure she hadn't yet arrived, I leaned back against the corridor wall to wait.

Alexa Newland. If she hadn't paid with a credit card, tracking her down would have been much more difficult. As it was, all I'd had to do was make enough idle chat with one of her friends to discover that she was a law student, and then make a late-night call to a friend of mine who was working part-time at the registrar's office. And just like that, I had a copy of Alexa Newland's class schedule.

Shifting the hot cup of coffee from my left hand to my right, I surveyed the passersby. I wanted to see her before she noticed me. Technically, this probably qualified as stalking, but I wasn't trying to be creepy. I just needed to talk to her again. She had written me off last night, and I was going to prove to her that she shouldn't have been so hasty.

As the minutes passed, my pulse actually started to race. I might have been back in high school all over again, nursing my first crush on another girl. In the intervening years, I'd never had to pursue women; they had sought me out, and I'd been happy to be found. Alexa was different. We hadn't spoken for more than two minutes, but something about her called me to the quest.

I looked right again, then left. And there she was, approaching the classroom briskly, glancing down at her watch as she walked. She wore charcoal slacks and a dark green blazer over a cream-colored silk shirt. I glanced down at my worn jeans and scruffy leather jacket and wished I'd gone for upscale instead of rugged.

"Good morning." I pushed off the wall when she was just a few feet away. Her eyes widened, black eclipsing the emerald irises that had captivated me last night, and a blush bloomed over her cheeks.

"Valentine? But what are you…" Her surprise became suspicion. "How did you find me?"

"Ah, that." I flashed her as charming a smile as I could muster on three hours of sleep. "I looked up your class schedule."

"How?"

"I can't reveal my sources," I said, holding up one hand when she looked like she wanted to steamroll right over me. "But my purpose isn't nefarious, I promise. I just wanted to offer you some caffeine, since you were up late last night and this class is early."

She moved forward until she was close enough to touch, and my fingertips itched with the urge to tuck a stray lock of crimson hair behind her left ear. She looked from the cup to me, then shook her head.

"I gave up coffee in college. Excuse me."

Without another word, she breezed past me and into the classroom.

3 Alexa

The next morning, I returned to Vanderbilt Hall with a mix of trepidation and anticipation swirling in my stomach. Would Valentine be there again? Or had I succeeded in blowing her off?

In all honesty, I hoped I hadn't. Late to class, caught by surprise, and blindsided by the same visceral desire that had beset me on Monday night, I'd been less than polite. Cold, even. Now I wanted another chance.

Thankfully, when I rounded the corner she was leaning against the wall next to the amphitheater door and holding a Starbucks drink tray. Yesterday, sporting a worn leather jacket that clung to her broad shoulders and framed her slim torso, she had looked every inch the hot bartender. Today, dressed in khakis and an orange wool sweater, she looked insouciantly preppy. She smiled when she saw me, a slow and easy smile that made me want to twine my fingers in the front of her shirt and—

Fantastic. Now I was blushing again.

"Hi," I said, clutching my bag as though it would help me regain my inner balance.

"Good morning." She proffered the tray. "How do you feel about chai lattes? I brought one made with soy, one with skim, and one with two-percent. Just in case."

"You went to a lot of effort." I moved closer. "Tell me, what does my taking one of these drinks entail?"

"It's pretty easy," she said, a teasing lilt to her voice. "All you have to do is grab whichever one you like best, and then I'll know what to bring you tomorrow."

"And that's it?" Where, I wondered, was the second request for a date? How long would she be content to ply me with caffeine before asking for something in return?

"That's it."

I reached for the soy latte. "Will the leftovers be used in other attempted seductions?"

A flash of hurt crossed her face so quickly that I wasn't sure I'd even seen it. In another moment, she was leaning in close to put her mouth level with my ear. "This is not a seduction," she murmured. "Not yet, anyway."

And then she brushed past me to toss the tray into a nearby garbage can. The wordless rebuke stung.

"I'm sorry," I said. "That was an ungrateful thing to say."

"You don't have to apologize." Valentine's gaze slid up my body slowly—a deliberate once-over that she wanted me to notice. "You're a beautiful woman, Alexa. I'm sure you get plenty of unwanted attention."

I foundered, not knowing how to reply. Despite myself, I wanted *her* attention. And I was pretty sure she knew it.

"Well…thanks for the chai," I said lamely.

She tapped the side of her head. "Soy. I'll remember. See you tomorrow."

In three long strides, she was around the corner, leaving me anticipating tomorrow before today had even really started.

4 Valentine

On Thursday, Alexa was waiting for me, despite the fact that I'd arrived twenty minutes before her class began. She was dressed as impeccably as ever, in black slacks and a silver turtleneck sweater that hugged her breasts and the subtle curves of her waist.

"What took you so long?" She extended her hand expectantly, a grin playing around the corners of her mouth at my obvious consternation. Before this moment, I'd been in charge of our little encounters. Now I felt ambushed.

I kind of liked it.

"Um, hi," I said, handing over her drink.

"So, here's how this is going to work from now on," she announced. "Whenever I ask you a question, you are obliged to answer. For every question I ask, you can ask one in return. But I reserve the right not to say anything."

"That hardly seems fair. Is that your best offer, Counselor?"

She crossed her arms over her breasts and fixed me with a steely stare. "Take it or leave it."

"Okay, okay. Deal."

"First question. What is your last name?"

"Darrow." I said it as matter-of-factly as I could, hoping that she wouldn't make the connection to my father. That was a conversation for later in our courtship.

She held out her right hand. "It's nice to meet you, Valentine Darrow."

I indulged myself by brushing my thumb over her knuckles as I slid my palm against hers. "Likewise, Alexa Newland."

All too soon, she pulled away. "Now that we've been properly introduced, your turn."

There was so much I wanted to know, but I felt certain she wouldn't answer most of my burning questions. So I started with something innocuous. "Where are you from?"

"Eau Claire, Wisconsin." The words sounded like a challenge, and I wondered why she was defensive about her hometown. But when I opened my mouth to ask, she shook her head. "Obey the rules. Second question. What do you want to be when you grow up?"

"What makes you think I'm not grown up already?"

Her eyes narrowed to green slits. "That was a question, Valentine. You don't get to ask one until you answer mine, remember?"

I liked the way she said my name, and the assertive edge to her words was making my throat dry. "Psychiatrist," I said, wondering if she could detect the rasp in my voice. "I have a master's in counseling psych already, and I'm going to take the MCAT in a few weeks."

Her eyes widened in surprise, and I leapt at the opportunity. "My turn. Tell me what you thought I was going to say."

Instead, she looked down at her watch. The blush had returned to dust her cheekbones. "I need to get to class."

I wanted to protest, but she had made the rules and I'd agreed to them. Whatever it took to hold her interest. Besides, her obvious chagrin partially answered my question; she'd underestimated me and was feeling more than a little ashamed of putting me in a box. That could only work to my advantage.

"All right." I took a step backward so I wouldn't reach out and touch her. It was too soon for that. "Until tomorrow, then."

5 Alexa

I flat-out ran from the bus stop to the entrance of Vanderbilt. The bus had been late, and now I only had five minutes to get to class. When Valentine saw me approaching, her frown gave way to a smile of relief.

"What happened?"

I let my fingertips brush hers as I took the cup of chai. "I get to ask the questions first, remember?"

She rolled her eyes. "Fine."

I'd thought long and hard about what to ask next, but the nervousness of her movements prompted a different query. "Were you worried about me?"

"Yes, of course! I have an overactive imagination, and I kept—" She cut herself off, suddenly abashed. "Worried. Yes."

I had to smile at her quick, uncalculated response. "Everything is fine. Just a late bus."

"Okay. Good." She rocked back and forth on her heels. "So. My turn. Just in case something like this happens again, can I have your phone number?"

My first inclination was to give in. My second was to keep playing hard to get. Fortunately, there was a way to compromise.

"No. But give me yours."

She was rattling off the final digits when Nicole, who always breezed into class precisely on time, approached. I could sense the rabid curiosity in her from across the hall.

"I have to go. Thanks for this." I raised the cup in one hand and grasped Nicole's arm with the other to tug her into the lecture hall before she could say a word.

"Lexie," she singsonged as soon as we were inside. "Who was *that*?"

There was no use in trying to evade her interrogation. Besides, I was in need of a confidante; this kind of persistent seduction was far beyond my experience. Nic would be able to advise me on how I should approach the next step. Valentine wasn't going to keep bringing me free lattes indefinitely, after all.

"Her name is Valentine Darrow," I said as we slid into our seats. "She was tending bar at the Niagara on Monday."

Nicole grabbed my arm in a grip Superman would have envied. "That was Valentine Darrow?"

"Yes. Do you know her?"

Nic dramatically thrust both hands into her perfect hair. "You can be so dense sometimes!" she hissed. "Think about it—how do you know that last name?"

I racked my brains, feeling like an idiot. It wasn't easy to keep up with the Who's Who of New York, especially when Nicole's guilty pleasure was socialite gossip, but I did my best to know just enough that I wouldn't be labeled an ignorant Wisconsin farm girl.

"The only other Darrow I can think of is the Secretary of the Treasury," I finally said, exasperated. "Edward Darrow."

"Who got his start in the city, of course, and just so happens to have a daughter named Valentine." Nicole sat back in her seat, looking pleased with herself as I grappled with my surprise. Valentine's father was a Cabinet member?

"I had no idea. What do you know about her?"

"She's a lesbian," said Nicole.

I swallowed a laugh. "Yes, I gathered that."

"She's into you."

"Nic." I gave her my best serious look. "You did not hear that through the rumor mill."

"Oh, sweetie." She squeezed my shoulder lightly as the professor stepped up to the podium. "All I had to do was watch her watching you for five hot seconds."

6, 7 Valentine

The weekend was taunting me. I'd wanted to sleep in after a long night's work at the bar, but my internal alarm clock had woken me at seven o'clock in the morning. Just in time to make it to Alexa's class, chai in hand...if it hadn't been Saturday. Tired but restless, I'd been unable to fall back to sleep.

Now I stood at a festive street corner across from Central Park South, waiting to meet a friend for brunch. A cacophony of Christmas music blared from nearby storefronts, but I found that for once, I didn't mind. The holidays hadn't felt festive to me for a long time, ever since my coming out had provoked the ire of my entire extended family. For the past several years, Christmas had meant protracted meals with aunts and uncles who ignored me and cousins who never stopped taking verbal potshots. But now, the music and lights and window displays made me think of Alexa. I found myself wondering whether she would go back to Wisconsin for winter break, and what kinds of oddball traditions her family had, and what little thing I could give to her that might make her laugh.

Later that evening, by the time my shift at the Niagara was halfway over, I still hadn't come up with an idea. I had, however, been propositioned twice—once by an attractive Mrs. Robinson type who claimed I made the best dirty vodka martini she'd ever tasted, and once by a punk kid with purple hair who asked me out as I was in the process of handing her over to the bouncer for trying to use a fake ID.

When I turned back to the bar, Alexa was standing at my end. She cradled a half-empty glass of wine in her right hand, and I paused to appreciate how the deep red of her hair was mirrored by the shade of the liquid.

"You've been here for a while," I accused, gesturing to her drink.

"I've been lurking in the shadows." Her gaze was warm on my skin, like a caress. "Watching you work. Watching other women desire you."

"Have you, now." The possessive note in her voice thrilled me, but I kept my tone light. "Did you notice me turning them down, too?"

"Yes. Why did you?"

I decided to lay it all out on the line. "Because I don't want them. I want you."

She set her glass down, but not before I saw it tremble. My words had affected her. Good.

"What makes you so persistent?"

I leaned on the bar, putting mere inches between my lips and hers. "I'm just keeping my eye on the prize."

Her gaze dropped to my mouth, then back to my eyes, and I gripped the marble to keep myself from leaning in and stealing a kiss. "When you're done with your wine," I said, "let me make you a cocktail. On the house."

But she shook her head. "I need to go home. Lots of studying to do tomorrow, and I should get started early."

"You don't slow down, do you?" Her intensity struck a chord in me. Could she feel it, too—the beginnings of a connection that went far beyond mere attraction? Or was it all in my head?

"I imagine I take it easy just as often as you do," she challenged.

We shared a conspiratorial smile then. And I knew I was right about this. About us.

8 Alexa

Valentine's entire demeanor brightened when she saw me. Her enthusiasm was addictive, and I felt myself smile. It seemed impossible that I had written her off just one week ago for some kind of cad.

"Good morning." She presented the paper cup to me with a flourish. "How did your studying go yesterday?"

"Not so fast. My question first, remember?"

"New week, new rules?" She sounded so hopeful.

"Not a chance." I sipped from my chai as I decided how to phrase the question that had been killing my concentration all weekend. "Nicole recognized your name when I told her on Friday. Why haven't you ever mentioned your father? Or the rest of your family?"

The light went out of her, then, as if I'd flicked a switch. "I don't get along with them," she said stiffly. "We have extreme differences of opinion when it comes to politics, as you can imagine."

"Okay." I kept my voice soft, regretting my impulse to prod. "I'm sorry if I reopened an old wound."

She waved away my apology. "It's nothing." Her gaze turned speculative. "Do you mind if I ask about your family?"

"Oh, there's not much to tell." I struggled not to feel self-conscious as I revealed my humble upbringing. "I'm the middle child of five, we grew up on a farm in western Wisconsin, and they have no idea why I escaped to New York at the first opportunity. But they love me, and they don't have any bias against my sexuality."

Valentine nodded, and I was happy to see the hint of a smile return to her face. "I'd like to know more about them."

"Tomorrow." On impulse, I took her hand and squeezed it briefly. Her fingers were so warm. "See you then."

9 Valentine

The next morning, Alexa caught me daydreaming. One minute, I was visualizing a cheery Christmas scene chez Newland—featuring a large fireplace, comfortable couches, and a brightly decorated tree—and the next, she was plucking the cup from my grasp.

"What were you just thinking of?" she said as she pulled off her gloves and blew on the tips of her fingers.

I couldn't resist; I gently gripped her wrist and let my own warm breath cascade over her skin. A shiver ran through her, but I pretended not to notice. "I was just picturing what your childhood Christmases must have been like. Will you go back for winter break?"

"No." She stuttered on the monosyllable. "I'll stay here to work on summer internship applications."

I began to massage her palm, very lightly, and was rewarded with a tiny gasp. "I bet you're applying to all kinds of prestigious opportunities, aren't you?"

A single nod. "You're breaking the rules," she said when she found her voice.

I leaned in close and brushed my lips against her cheek. "That," I murmured, "is because I'm officially beginning my seduction of you today."

She trembled. I could have kissed her properly; she would have let me. But it would have been too soon. And I had to get this right.

10 Alexa

How had a simple kiss on the cheek succeeding in distracting me for twenty-four consecutive hours? Resolved not to let Valentine get the upper hand so easily today, I turned the corner briskly…only to find an unfamiliar, dark-suited man in her place. He held a small envelope in one hand and a cup in the other.

"Alexa Newland?"

"Yes?"

"Ms. Darrow regrets that she is unable to meet you this morning," the man said. "She asked that I pass these along." After handing over the chai and the missive, he bade me a "good day" and left.

I opened the envelope slowly, both excited and apprehensive about its contents. What obligation had called Valentine away so suddenly that she hadn't been able to let me know about it beforehand? Or was she deliberately keeping her distance for some reason?

The card inside had my first name printed on the front. I opened it to find *Come to dinner with me* written on the inner left page. The other side read *Friday night.* Out of habit, I flipped the card all the way over. *Say yes* was printed on the back.

"Yes," I whispered.

But since she wasn't there to hear me, I was going to make her wait.

11 Valentine

"I'm so sorry about yesterday." I hurried forward as soon as Alexa rounded the corner. Anxiety about her state of mind had kept me up half the night. At first glance, she seemed more curious and concerned than angry, but I couldn't yet read her expressions with confidence. "My father ambushed me into making an appearance for him. I don't care what he's the secretary of, he shouldn't be able to rope me into service at the spur of the moment whenever he fucking feels like it!"

Realizing that I was ranting, I took a deep breath and handed over the chai. "Sorry. Did you get the card?"

"Yes." She closed the distance between us and reached up to adjust the collar of my shirt. Even that brief touch made my heart pound.

"And?"

"And yes."

I blinked down at her. There was a tenderness to her smile, as though she recognized my emotional fragility. "Yes? To tomorrow?"

"Yes. That's my answer." She turned toward the door to her class. "I want to hear all about how your father dragged you away from me, but over dinner. Pick me up at eight o'clock?"

I took her free hand in mine and twirled her like a ballroom dancer, right there in the hallway. She blushed, of course, but her laugh was genuine.

12 Alexa

The phone rang just as I finished zipping up my dress, and I looked down to see Nicole's photograph. "I'm putting you on speaker," I said by way of greeting, "while I do my makeup." I had only ten minutes until Valentine arrived.

"Lexie! You *must* tell me what you're wearing."

I picked up my eyeliner. "The strapless one."

"Oh my God, I knew you would. She's not going to be able to keep her hands off you!"

Leaning in toward the mirror, I inspected my work. I always received compliments on my green eyes, but the liner made them stand out even more. Good. "I'm not going to sleep with her on the first date, Nic." No matter how much I wanted to.

"So you say. But this is Valentine Darrow we're talking about. She's used to getting what she wants. And I *know* you've thought about it."

The memory of Valentine as I'd seen her that morning popped into my head—slouching in jeans and a gray hoodie against the wall, cupping my drink in both hands as if to absorb its caffeine through the paper. Her hair was still tousled and her eyelids were at half-mast, and I had been nearly overwhelmed by the desire to drag her right back into the bed she had clearly just rolled out of.

I felt my cheeks grow warm and raised the mascara brush, gripping it like a weapon. I had to keep my wits about me tonight. "I'm not interested in becoming a notch on someone's bedpost."

"The woman has pursued you for *weeks*," Nicole protested.

"She's just fascinated because I'm not swooning all over her like the usual suspects." I didn't really believe that, but I needed to say the words out loud. I was at serious risk of falling for Valentine after only two weeks, and I couldn't afford to drop my guard *before* our first date.

Nicole ignored my rationalization. "I'm dying to know where you'll be eating. Text me when you get to the restaurant. My God, she could be taking you anywhere: Per Se, maybe, or even Jean Georges!"

I took a step back from the mirror and smoothed the dress over my hips, feeling butterflies stir in my stomach. Nic was right. Valentine probably had the keys to this entire city. I paused, lipstick poised half an inch from my mouth, suddenly wondering whether she thought my change of heart might have to do with her father's money.

And then the doorbell rang.

"Good-bye, Nicole." Heart pounding, I forced myself to focus. Lipstick. Shoes. The bell rang again. I grabbed my purse from the dresser and locked the door behind me with unsteady hands, then descended the stairs as quickly as I could manage.

I opened the door. She stood before me in a pinstripe suit, her golden hair a spiked halo. I caught the faint scent of cologne as she offered me a single, dusky pink orchid. Behind her, the holiday lights of a nearby storefront twinkled merrily.

And deep inside I knew that for this Christmas and all the ones after, she would be mine, and I hers.

Rebecca S. Buck is from Nottingham, England. Her first novel, *Truths*, in which Jen and Aly appeared, was published by Bold Strokes Books in April 2010. Her second novel, *Ghosts of Winter,* will be an April 2011 release. Right now she's trying to work out which of her many and varied ideas would make the best next novel, and is deciding on her options for postgraduate study. To find out more visit her website: www.rebeccasbuck.com.

Miss December
Rebecca S. Buck

I heard Aly's feet on the steps leading from the studio and darkroom downstairs to our cosy flat above. She'd been in the studio for several hours. I'd missed her, forcing myself to stay upstairs and let her get on with her work.

I was slouched on our comfortable sofa with the laptop, entering details from a pile of invoices into our computerised accounts. Driven by Aly's outstanding talents as a photographer, our business was thriving. Any doubt we'd had about being able to keep up payments on the photographic studio and flat had disappeared. Taking care of the running of the business had become a full-time responsibility for me and, to my surprise, it was the most rewarding work I'd ever done. The best part was I got to spend hours at a time in Aly's company. Months into our relationship we still weren't bored with each other. That was something I'd never experienced in a relationship before.

So much had changed. This time last year, the weeks before Christmas, I'd been lonely and confused, frightened of the world, living a lie. But summer had brought me Aly, my precious truth, and now I met the approach of this Christmas with difficult-to-contain excitement. I had Aly's gift all taken care of, and from her recent suspicious behaviour, I sensed she already had mine. Hidden in the bottom of her closet where she thought I wouldn't look. I hadn't looked. Yet.

I heard her footsteps approach. I smiled to myself and tried to look as though I was still working hard on the accounts. The pressure of her hands on my shoulders was warm through my T-shirt as she bent to kiss the back of my neck, just below my left ear. I couldn't help the shiver of pleasure that swept through me. She knew exactly how to get the reactions she desired from my body.

"Jen, babe?" she said. I knew there was something she wanted.

"Yes, Aly?" I replied, without turning to look at her. Her fingers massaged my shoulders slightly.

"Are you busy?"

"It depends."

"On what?"

"On what you want." I turned and grinned at her.

"How do you know I want anything?" She pouted playfully.

"I know you too well."

"Sometimes I miss the Jen who had no idea what she wanted, you know?" she said. "It was far easier to have my wicked way with you then."

"You want your wicked way with me? Well, you only have to ask…" I closed the laptop and placed it on the coffee table. I turned completely so I could look into her eyes as she leaned over the back of the sofa. I melted into her dark gaze, as I always did. Aly had a habit of running her hand through her short, jet black hair as she worked, and as a result, she was decidedly dishevelled. In a loose white shirt over black jeans tight to her slender figure, she was devastatingly attractive. I felt a familiar heavy heat developing low in my belly. Fuck, could I ever get enough of this woman?

She reached out her hand, with a rattle of the silver bangles she always wore, to stroke my face. She was looking at me contemplatively. "I always want my wicked way with you. But I have work on my mind right now."

"Work?" The anticipation that had been building in my body subsided abruptly.

"Yes. You know the calendar?"

"Of course I do." We'd decided Christmas was the perfect time to put together a calendar of new photographs and market it through our website. The pictures would be artistic and unusual shots of normal women made glamorous through Aly's skill with the camera and the staging of her photographs.

"My Miss December didn't show up today."

"Oh bloody hell," I said. "I'm sure I told her the right date. It was Emma, wasn't it? I'll phone her right—"

Aly's rapidly widening grin stopped me mid-sentence. It was hard to think about anything else with those pink lips so close, smiling with so much intent. "What?"

"You're so very efficient," she said, eyes dancing. "I'm glad I employed you."

"Well, being as you don't pay me, I think you're very lucky."

"I am very lucky." Her expression was serious for a moment and my heart swelled with pleasure. Even after all these months I found it hard to believe this remarkable woman felt lucky to be with me. I looked on Aly as the key to my freedom, the woman who had helped me find myself. That I meant as much to her was incredible and wonderful. "But I don't want you to call Emma."

"Oh? Are you going to ask someone else?"

"Yes."

I narrowed my eyes at her. I couldn't decipher her inscrutable smile. "Who?"

"Well…" She paused and a mischievous look came into her eyes. "What I was planning for the December shot was a sort of Victorian Christmas gothic scene."

"Christmas gothic? Sounds great," I replied, mildly sarcastic, dying to know why her eyes were sparkling in that way.

"It will be. And you know it reminded me that there's a woman I know who once made her living dressing as a very fetching Victorian." She winked at me suggestively.

"You are joking, aren't you?" I couldn't help a slight smile. "I was a museum tour guide in a rubbish fake costume. It certainly doesn't qualify me for modelling."

"Actually I don't care about your prior experience. And I'm not joking." There was a slight challenge in her eyes. And rather a lot of arousal. Fuck, it was impossible to say no to Aly when she looked like this. "I want to photograph you."

"I've told you before I don't like having my photo taken."

"Oh c'mon, Jen, I'm a photographer, and you've never let me take a picture of you. Besides, it will be artistic."

"Artistic?"

"Don't you trust me?"

"Your calendar is risqué as well as artistic."

"I wouldn't want you to expose yourself or anything." She pressed her warm lips to mine, her hand caressing the back of my neck, pulling me closer. "That's for my eyes only. But I really want to do this. Please give it a go, just for me. I'll make it worth your while." Her words were full of seductive promise.

"And how will you do that?" I'd already given in to her and she knew it.

"You'll find out later." She kissed me again, her tongue pushing between my lips, a suggestion of what would come later.

"If I don't like it, we don't use it."

"Of course. Come downstairs to my lair."

She grabbed my hand and we made our way down to the studio. It was very bright in the high-ceilinged room with its white walls and screens. Aly led me to where she'd already established the scene for her December photograph. Her idea was to stage all of her photographs in front of a plain white backdrop, with the focus on the model and the few props around her to suggest the theme. I'd seen several of the earlier months of the year so far and my favourite was July, featuring a girl with an unexpectedly severe bleached blond haircut and several earrings in each ear. She was apparently enjoying a summer picnic but posed with her back to the camera, in a gingham dress evocative of the fifties, with the back fastening provocatively undone. The focus was intentionally slightly off. The photos were unusual, sexy, and artistic. I was so proud of Aly's talent.

I took in the scene in front of me now. Aly had positioned an ornate chaise longue, all mahogany carving and crimson upholstery, in the middle of her bright white backdrop. Next to it was a real Christmas tree, with glass baubles and authentic wax candles, their wicks black and already burned down, melted wax dripping onto the branches. She'd placed several ornately wrapped gifts, decorated with silk ribbons, around the tree. A pile of traditional paper-chain garlands and unused ribbons sat on the end of the chaise longue. Everything was in tones of green, crimson, and gold. The scene was stunning and I was sure my intrusion would not be an improvement.

"Aly, you need a real model for this."

"I think you're missing the point of the whole project, babe."

"No. I know it's about using women who aren't the usual model-type. But I've got nothing distinctive about me at all." I watched as Aly ran appraising eyes over my wavy, long, light brown hair and lower to my very ordinary and slightly too curvy figure. Contentment with Aly had induced me to put several pounds on my hips. She maintained it was an improvement, while I begged to differ. Now, under her gaze, I felt sexy.

"You're perfect, Jen," she said softly. And I believed her.

"So what am I supposed to wear, then?"

Aly grinned delightedly and picked up a nearby bag to show me the contents. A flowing skirt of black velvet was very convincingly Victorian. My eyes widened as she showed me a boned corset in black satin, laced with a crimson ribbon. She caught my expression.

"Don't look so shocked. We're going for Victorian after all."

"Aly, I—"

"Just try it, for me."

I sighed and took the clothes. "Okay. But you can go away while I change. That way you'll get the full effect."

"I'm going to see how my latest prints are progressing." Aly smiled with obvious pleasure. Oh, she was definitely enjoying this.

As soon as she was gone, I stripped out of my jeans and T-shirt and donned the costume. The heavy folds of velvet caressed my legs and draped to the floor. The corset was tight at my waist and had a complimentary effect on my breasts. I had to admit, I felt attractive. I smiled as Aly came back into the studio, eyes all over me.

"Will I do?" I asked.

"I don't think you know how stunning you are."

I looked at her suspiciously as she came closer. "We're not enacting another one of your fantasies are we, my love?"

"You've taken over all of my fantasies, Jen." She clasped my corseted waist and drew me to her. She kissed my bare shoulders, running her mouth over my collarbones and the hollow at the base of my throat. I couldn't help but moan under the caress of her mouth, her breath. She pulled back to inspect my appearance. "Just one more thing."

She reached into the pocket of her jeans, drew out a small velvet bag, and handed it to me."Open it."

Her words were heavy with tenderness and a trace of uncertainty. So different from my usually confident and assured Aly. My heart beat harder in response to the emotion in her voice. Curious, I quickly released the drawstring and drew out a length of black ribbon, upon which hung an oval cameo. A white relief of a striking woman on a pale green background.

"It's beautiful, Aly," I said breathlessly.

"It's authentically Victorian. Do you know who it is?" She looked very pleased with herself.

"No, should I?"

"It's the Roman goddess of truth, Veritas."

"Oh…"

"But the Greeks called her Alethea."

"She's your namesake?"

Aly shrugged as though she was vaguely embarrassed. "Yes. It's an early Christmas present."

"Thank you so much, my love! It's perfect." I hoped she knew how much it really meant. I kissed her. "Will you fasten it for me?"

Aly took the ribbon and moved behind me. Her warm fingers brushed against my neck as she fastened the catch. The back of the cameo was cold against my throat, the ribbon soft and silky. When she was done, I turned to face her.

"Perfect," she told me, satisfaction in her voice.

"Now, reluctant though I am to ask, where do you want me?"

"There's a leading question. On the chaise longue, please."

I sat tentatively in the middle of her carefully arranged scene.

"Lie back a little more. Against the cushion."

I giggled and did as she said. She reached for her camera, with its long lens, and peered through the viewfinder at me.

"Like this?" I asked.

"Perfect." She put the camera down again and picked up the paper chain of garlands and ribbons.

"So, what are you going to do with those?" I asked.

"These are what make this more than just a picture of a reclining woman. These are what make it sexy," she said. "And different."

"How do you mean?"

Aly's dark eyes locked to mine as she leaned over me and pressed her lips to mine, a harder and more sensual kiss this time. Her strong fingers ran over my exposed shoulder and down the length of my arm, to my wrist, which she grasped and raised above my head.

"What are you doing?" I mumbled against her mouth.

"Give me your other hand."

My heart throbbed and my blood raged through my veins, full of heat and desire, as I did as she asked. With one hand she held my wrists together as, with the other, she wrapped the paper chain garland around them. She straightened and looked down at me. I moved my wrists slightly and the paper rustled.

"Not very effective," I said, hearing my own arousal in my voice.

"But that's the point. You don't want to escape."

"You mean the woman in your photo doesn't want to escape."

Aly grinned. "No, babe, you don't want to escape."

I drew a deep breath and tried to regain my composure, a hard task with her looking at me as though she was ready to consume me. I gestured with my chin to the length of crimson ribbon she still held. "And that?"

"Christmas ribbon." She shrugged as though it was perfectly innocent.

"And what are you going to do with it?"

"Ah. Let me show you. Close your eyes."

"What?"

She kissed along my jawline and to my mouth. I inhaled her breath and my desire intensified. I closed my eyes. Aly wound the thick, silky ribbon over my eyes and tied it loosely at the back of my head. Not a particularly effective blindfold—if I opened my eyes I could see plenty. But that wasn't the point. The suggestion was what mattered. I kept my eyes closed and my breathing deepened. Aly ran her hands over my chest, to the tops of my breasts where they swelled above the corset. I gasped and pressed my thighs together, hoping to relieve some of the almost painful need building between them. She reached up to my hair and I felt her spreading it out over the cushion beneath me.

"Oh God, Aly…"

"I love you, Jen. You're beautiful. Now, don't move…" I felt her pull away from me, heard her footsteps as she went to pick up her camera. Every movement of the air, every sound was heightened. I could smell the earthy, fresh scent of the Christmas tree, the bitter aroma of the burned-out candles. I heard a click as Aly took her first photograph, and my stomach contracted. The notion of being captured in this moment, which had become so intense between us, both alarmed and aroused me. The idea of Aly looking at me through her camera was, I discovered, more erotic than I would have suspected. I loved to feel her gaze on me, and somehow the camera intensified it. That was unexpected. Maybe even a little kinky. I'd long stopped worrying about such things. Aly and I set our own boundaries and delighted in pushing them.

The camera clicked again and again. Aly said, "Just turn your head a little bit towards me. And bend your left knee."

She took more pictures. Then the room fell silent. I heard only my own breathing, felt only the throb of my pulse and the heavy velvet against my bare legs.

"Aly?"

"I'm right here," she said, very close to me. Her mouth found mine and I met her bruising kiss with equal enthusiasm. She pulled roughly at the ribbon lacing of the corset, opening it and running her hands over the skin she exposed. I wanted to touch her and lifted my hands. She grabbed my wrists, still loosely joined by the paper chain, and pressed them back into the cushion. I moaned, understanding the mood she was in and responding to it, as I always did. As her mouth moved lower to draw my nipple between her lips, grazing my hardening flesh with her teeth, I kept my hands where they were and arched my back, giving myself to her.

"Aly…oh…I want…" I groaned, unable to articulate my desires but safe in the knowledge she knew them. One of her hands came up to squeeze my breast, pinching my nipple firmly between her thumb and forefinger, as her other slid lower, pulling at the rich velvet of the skirt until it was around my waist. She pushed her hand between my thighs, beneath my underwear, and into my wetness with an aroused moan of her own.

"Tell me you want me, Jen," she said breathlessly.

"Can't you feel it?" I gasped.

"Yes, but tell me."

"I want you more than I've ever wanted anything, Aly. You're my everything…ah…" She entered me as I finished my sentence, taking me with the force of her desire. I met her thrust with a return movement of my hips. She paused, her fingers buried deep inside me. I relished the intimacy as she covered me with her body and kissed me, her hot tongue twining with mine.

"I want to see you," I told her.

She tore the ribbon away from my eyes. My gaze met hers. I saw her arousal in her dilated pupils and knowing I was the cause sent a whole new wave of desire pulsing through me. I was intoxicated by my power to affect her so profoundly.

She moved her fingers inside me slightly. I breathed deeper and had to touch her. I wrenched my hands free of the paper garlands in one quick movement and began to loosen the buttons of her shirt. Her eyes flashed at my sudden reassertion of my needs. Between us we removed her shirt and I ran my fingers over her small, perfect breasts, loving the sensation of her nipples hardening beneath my touch.

"Watch me now," she whispered. Slowly, she slid lower. Easing her fingers out of me, she pulled my underwear down my legs quickly. Teasing, I kept my knees close together. She put her hands on the tender insides of my thighs and pushed, compelling me to open for her. I let her have her way, my eyes fixed on her face, seeing her desire as her gaze fell upon me. Slowly, she moved closer and closer.

"Oh, fuck, Aly…" I whimpered as her breath teased my hot, wet flesh. I pushed towards her and she gripped my hips, holding me down. I groaned, keeping my eyes on her as she pressed her mouth to me at last. The first sweep of her hot, strong tongue sent an electric shock through my whole body. It was almost too powerful and I tried to pull back. She moved with me and relentlessly massaged me with her lips and tongue. I moaned again. When the movements of her tongue became lighter, teasing, I tried to raise myself to her again but she pressed down, stopping me. I had no choice but to give in to her control of my pleasure, to her merciless desires. I looked down over my body and watched her intimate kisses until I could bear it no longer, then tipped my head back and gave myself up to it.

She was consuming me, possessing me—giving everything to me. She sucked my hardened flesh between her lips, teasing with her teeth, as she pushed three fingers into me. I knew she could feel how close to the edge I was, the way my body welcomed her inside as my spread thighs trembled. She curled her fingers around expertly and I gave way suddenly to a shuddering climax, helpless to repress my throaty cry of release.

I was still sweating and panting as she moved up to lie on top of me, her mouth finding mine. I tasted my own arousal in her kiss. I wrapped limp arms around her, enjoying the crush of her breasts against mine.

When I could trust my voice again, I smiled and said, "I hope that isn't the way you thank all your models."

"Only the very sexy ones," she replied.

"Should I feel taken advantage of?"

"Absolutely."

I laughed. Aly was so perfect. Nothing was ever so intense there wasn't an element of fun involved. I loved her relaxed humour.

"How were the photos?"

"Exactly what I wanted."

"You're biased, of course."

"Not so biased I don't know a good photo. You're the perfect Miss December. And I love the idea of all the women who buy the calendar looking at your photo and wondering who you are. Maybe wanting you. But you're all mine."

"Is your possessive streak coming out again, my love?" I teased.

"I can't help it. You mean so much to me, Jen." Her eyes were intense briefly. These moments of sudden deep emotion were common with Aly, but moved me every time.

"You know you're every bit as important to me. This is going to be the best Christmas of my life. The first honest Christmas of my life. It's because of you, Aly."

"It's not all about me, Jen. I just helped."

"More than you know. If you'd told me last Christmas I'd have been celebrating this year like this, I'd never have believed you." I smiled happily.

"I guess life's full of good surprises," Aly replied, stroking my hair. "And we're going to have a brilliant new year."

"Yes, we are. You know you've made me believe in fate?"

"I think things turn out the way they're meant to, and we were meant to find each other." She laughed, lightening the mood once more. "So, you like your present?"

"I adore it." I pressed my lips to hers. Aly writhed against me and I could feel her temperature start to soar. I knew she wanted more. So did I. "In fact, I think I need to show you how much I love it. How much I love you."

I slid out from underneath her and rose to my feet. I unfastened the skirt and let it slide into a velvet puddle at my feet so I wore nothing but Aly's cameo. She sat upright and I watched her eyes roaming over my naked body as I reached for her waist and unfastened her jeans, tight against her toned stomach. I pulled them lower, running my fingers over the tattoo on her hip, and lower still, until she was alluringly naked in front of me.

I dropped to my knees, catching the scent of her arousal. She parted her thighs and ran her fingers through my hair. “I love you, Jen,” she murmured as I took her in my mouth, determined to demonstrate how powerfully I felt the same way. She was my love, my life, my truth. And she tasted so fucking good, I could never have enough.

Erin Dutton lives near Nashville, Tennessee, with her amazing partner. She enjoys writing stories that reflect the strength of love, both within a relationship and within family. She has written six previous romances, the most recent of which is *A Perfect Match*. The characters from "Homemade" first appeared in *A Place to Rest*. For more information about Erin and her work, visit www.erindutton.com.

Homemade

Erin Dutton

"I thought we weren't working today," Sawyer Drake called as she strode through the swinging door that divided the dining room of Drake's restaurant from the kitchen.

"You're here, too." Jori didn't miss a stroke in the dough she mixed in a silver bowl on the counter in front of her.

"I'm looking for you."

"Sure. But I've been in the kitchen—I'm always in the kitchen. You've been here for over an hour and this is the first time you've come in here looking for me."

"You just can't stay away. I only stopped in on my way to pick you up."

"You weren't supposed to pick me up for another two hours, anyway." Jori purposely kept her tone light. They were both here for the same reason, their dedication to Drake's. And given that Sawyer had finally found a career that inspired such devotion, Jori would never make her feel guilty for it.

Sawyer moved behind Jori and wrapped her arms around her waist. "You're supposed to be all mine today."

The familiar feel of Sawyer's mouth against the side of Jori's neck raised goose bumps on her arms. After six months, she still felt a thrill every time Sawyer touched her, and she still would after six years or sixty. Conscious of the other chefs working nearby, Jori nudged Sawyer gently in the ribs with her elbow and Sawyer released her.

"I came in to check on tonight's desserts—"

"Babe, that's why you have an assistant."

As the head pastry chef, Jori not only planned the dessert menu but also made most of them herself. She'd only started handing more responsibility over to her assistant since she and Sawyer started dating. They made it a point to spend one night a week away from the restaurant, and one whole day at least every other weekend. Today was supposed to be that day.

"Anyway, Erica caught me. Now I've got to make two dozen Christmas sugar cookies."

"What? Where is she?" Sawyer's tone made it clear that her sister and co-manager had overstepped by commandeering Jori.

"*She* is right here," Erica said as she entered from the hallway that led to her office. "Do you have something to say?"

Sawyer stepped closer to Erica as if squaring off. "You've got Jori baking cookies on her day off. This couldn't wait until tomorrow?"

"No. It couldn't. And I need her to deliver them when she's done."

"We don't even do delivery. What the hell is going on?"

"Sawyer, it's no big deal." Jori turned the dough onto the counter in front of her and picked up a rolling pin.

After the birth of Erica's daughter, she and Sawyer had put aside their sibling tension and agreed to run the family restaurant together. But they still had the occasional power struggle, and Jori hated being in the middle of them. She wanted to side with Sawyer, stand by her woman and all. But she knew how stubborn Sawyer could be and she often thought the solution to Sawyer and Erica's problems was somewhere in the middle. If they could both just give a little ground, they might find it, too.

"Yes. It is." Sawyer planted her hands on her hips. "This is the kind of stuff I should know about, Erica. You're always going to think of yourself as sole manager."

"Get over yourself, Sawyer. This was a last-minute order from a very important customer. I've already discussed it with Jori and she agreed to make the delivery." Erica walked out without waiting for a response.

"I hate it when she does that," Sawyer grumbled. "You agreed to this?"

"I thought I could be done with them and home in time to meet you. This is the last batch. If you give me a hand we'll be done in no time." Jori tossed a cookie cutter at Sawyer.

Sawyer glanced at it. "Reindeer?"

Jori shrugged. "The customer requested festive and kid-appropriate." Jori nodded toward the cookies she'd already finished, lined up on sheets of waxed paper on the counter. "You can either box those up or cut more out of this dough."

"I got the dough." Sawyer twirled the cookie cutter around her index finger and moved close to Jori. She bumped her hip lightly against Jori's. "You take the boring job."

Jori smiled and moved aside. She unfolded a white cardboard box and carefully filled it with the brightly decorated assortment of snowmen and Christmas trees. As she worked she watched Sawyer press out the reindeer shapes. Sawyer had once told her that she liked to watch Jori work—specifically her hands. Jori had never thought there was anything special about her hands, but every now and again she caught herself watching Sawyer's hands and she totally got it. Sawyer's hands weren't as quick as Jori's in the kitchen, but then again Jori had hours more practice.

Besides, she didn't think about cooking while watching Sawyer's hands; instead she was enveloped in memories of Sawyer's touch. Whether Sawyer held her tenderly or stroked her fervently, the undercurrent of her love was always present.

"Hey, I thought you were supposed to be boxing cookies?"

Jori jerked her eyes away from Sawyer's hands and fumbled to resume packing up the cookies.

"While you were over there daydreaming, I finished." Sawyer held up a baking sheet. "Are these ready for the oven?"

"I wasn't daydreaming." Jori sprinkled a pinch of fine sugar on top of each cookie.

Sawyer leaned close enough to whisper in Jori's ear. "You were. And I know exactly what you were thinking about. You want me to touch you."

Jori trembled.

"You want me to take you someplace private and—" Sawyer laughed softly and her breath tickled Jori's skin. "But first, we apparently have to deliver these cookies."

When Sawyer moved away to put the tray in the oven, Jori pulled in a deep breath and took a second to enjoy the arousal singing through her body.

❖

"I really didn't think this would take very long," Jori said as Sawyer put the bakery boxes in the trunk of her Solara. "I'm sorry. I've spent most of our day on this." Jori slid into the passenger seat of the convertible and checked the clock on the console. It was after two o'clock.

She studied Sawyer, trying to figure out her mood. Sawyer had gotten quiet as they'd packed up the cookies and headed out to the car, but she seemed more nervous than aggravated. "Do you have the address Erica gave us?"

"Yes." With a small smile, Sawyer reached across the console and covered Jori's hand. "It's only a few minutes away."

Jori relaxed as Sawyer's skin warmed hers. She squeezed Sawyer's hand and felt the answering pressure against her fingers. A couple minutes outside of downtown, they navigated through an older, well-established neighborhood. Instead of the tiny lots and identical rows of houses common to most modern subdivisions, these streets fronted large lawns and homes with character and individual style.

"I like this area," Jori said. As a kid in foster care, she'd often imagined what it must be like to grow up in a house like these.

"I know." Sawyer smiled. "You say that every time we drive through here."

Sawyer turned into a driveway. Two large trees stretched bare limbs over the front yard and cast craggy shadows over a quaint stone house. Jori checked the number on the mailbox again.

"Are you sure this is it?"

"Yep. What? You don't like it?" Sawyer popped the trunk release and got out of the car.

"Actually, I do. It's very cute, just not what I expected. I thought someone who merited 'very important' status with Erica would live someplace a bit more extravagant."

"Yeah, well, every now and again Erica still surprises me, too." Carrying the boxes of cookies, Sawyer headed toward the house.

Jori caught up and, as they walked, Sawyer put a hand in the small of her back. Jori smiled at the tender gesture. When Sawyer was a little possessive like this, she felt safe and loved, though she would never admit it to anyone but Sawyer.

They climbed the three steps to the porch and Jori rang the doorbell. When no one responded, she rang again.

"Surely Erica let them know to expect us." Trying another tactic, Jori knocked on the deeply stained wooden door.

"Hm. Let's see." Sawyer handed Jori the boxes and turned the knob.

"Yeah, okay. We'll just let ourselves in."

The door swung open. When Sawyer stepped forward, Jori stared at her in disbelief. She was actually going to go in.

"Sawyer!" Jori bobbled the boxes as she tried to grab Sawyer's arm.

"Whoa. Careful. I'm not going back to the restaurant to make more." Sawyer swept the cookies from her hands and entered the house. "Maybe we'll just leave them on the counter."

"Sawyer," Jori called, but Sawyer didn't stop. She glanced around and, seeing no witnesses, followed Sawyer inside. Was this really a crime if they had no sinister intent?

The foyer opened to a spacious living room—an empty living room. Sunlight from a large window reflected off the dark hardwood floors unobscured by furniture. A pristine white mantel surrounded the fireplace slanted into the far corner. The broad archways separating the various rooms were decorated with the ornate woodwork of the 1940s.

"Check out this yard." Sawyer had set the boxes down somewhere and now looked out the window at the back of the house.

Confused, Jori crossed to her. "We shouldn't be in here. We've obviously got the wrong address."

"Maybe. But it's clearly vacant. Since we're here, let's explore a little." Sawyer's eyes sparkled with mischief. She took Jori's hand and led her toward the hallway.

"I don't think we should."

"Who's going to know?"

"The owner, or a realtor maybe. If we get caught."

Sawyer paused and pulled Jori close, grasping her hips. "Be brave with me. We're alone."

She pressed her lips to Jori's, silencing the protest she'd been about to offer. Sawyer kissed her aggressively, as if she'd been waiting all day and just realized how much she wanted it. Jori followed her, making the transition from teasing to passion quickly. She sucked Sawyer's lower lip. Sawyer squeezed her waist and she threaded her hands into Sawyer's hair, tugging her close.

When Sawyer eased back, they were both panting a little. "Let's check out the rest of the house." She grabbed Jori's hand again.

They went down the hall, and Jori glimpsed two empty bedrooms and a bathroom as they passed. When they reached a closed door, Sawyer smiled, then swung open the door and moved aside. Jori took two steps inside and stopped.

Closed curtains darkened the room and a floor lamp in the corner cast a warm glow. Unlike the rest of the house, the bedroom was completely furnished. Jori immediately recognized the cherry platform bed and matching dresser. She'd helped pick them out for Sawyer's apartment only a few months ago. The simple pattern of the sage and ivory color-block comforter complemented the clean lines Sawyer favored.

"Sawyer?" Jori said. "What is this?"

When Sawyer said nothing, only watched her with a faint smile, she crossed to the dresser and leaned to look at a framed photo of the two of them. Sawyer's arms came around her waist, and Sawyer rested both hands high on Jori's stomach.

"Do you like the house?" Sawyer's cheek brushed Jori's.

"Yes. Are you moving?"

"Maybe. Only if you are."

Turning, Jori draped her arms against Sawyer's shoulders. "What are you saying?"

"I haven't bought the house yet. The realtor is a friend and she let me move a few things in to surprise you." Sawyer nodded toward the bed behind her. "But if you don't love it, we can keep looking." She feathered her fingers down to cradle Jori's jaw. "I love you, Jori. You anchor me in ways that no one ever has. When we're apart, I can't wait to see you again. I want to buy a house with you and build a life together."

They'd been splitting their time between Sawyer's apartment and Jori's for months and rarely spent a night apart anyway. In the beginning Jori had occasionally worried that Sawyer, habitually unable to commit, would become bored or restless. But eventually Sawyer had put her fears to rest and Jori now trusted her completely.

Jori's chest ached as love flooded her. Despite the progress they'd made, she knew this was still a big step for Sawyer. She had just made the biggest commitment of her life and Jori didn't feel a hint of hesitation from her.

"Aren't you going to say something?" Sawyer asked.

"Yes." Jori took Sawyer's face in her hands. "Yes, I will move in with you."

"Good."

"So, hold on, let me get this straight, there's no very important customer."

"Um, no, there isn't. It was my plan to get you here, and Erica played along." Sawyer tempered her words with a lopsided smile that she had to know always melted Jori's resolve.

"I baked all of those cookies for nothing."

"I wouldn't waste perfectly good cookies. We'll drop them by the domestic violence shelter later, an early Christmas gift for the women and children."

"That sounds nice." Jori had just gotten the only gift she needed this season.

Sawyer slid her hand to the collar of Jori's shirt and slipped the top button free, and then the one below it. Jori watched her fingers work downward until the final button was undone.

"What are you doing?"

"Hmm. Well, I came into this bedroom with two goals. The first was getting you to move in with me." Sawyer pushed Jori's shirt off her shoulders and it slid down her arms and to the floor.

"And the second?"

Sawyer kissed the sensitive skin just below Jori's ear. "The second," she whispered in Jori's ear, "I'll have to show you."

Sawyer unclasped Jori's bra and gently removed it. She touched Jori's breast reverently, cupping it in one hand, then stroking her tightening nipple. Jori arched into her touch and sighed. She watched Sawyer's eyes trace a path over her skin, enjoying the arousal flashing across her expression and darkening her brown eyes almost to black in the shadowed room.

While removing the rest of Jori's clothes, Sawyer led her to the bed, both of them nearly stumbling over her jeans when they clung stubbornly to her legs. She pushed back the sheets and guided Jori down. After she stripped off her own clothes, Sawyer stretched out next to Jori.

"I want to go slow. I always want to go slow with you, but I can never seem to help myself."

"You know by now I don't always need slow." Remembering one particular time that Sawyer had nearly taken her on the stairs outside Erica's apartment, Jori felt her body flush. She pulled Sawyer on top of her and slipped a knee between Sawyer's. When Sawyer rose up, she pushed her thigh higher, keeping pressure against Sawyer's center.

Sawyer kissed her, softly at first, leading her, then pulling away just enough to make sure Jori tried to follow before thrusting her tongue inside. Jori moaned, part arousal, part frustration as Sawyer maintained the thread of control. Sawyer drove her fingers into Jori's hair, and when Jori lifted her thigh again, Sawyer tightened her grip. Jori sucked in her breath as the sharp tug against the back of her head drove her to the edge of pain and pleasure.

Sawyer moved down Jori's body, dropping kisses between her breasts and over the slope of her belly. She circled her fingers around Jori's ankle, then trailed her fingernails up the back of Jori's calf.

"Sawyer, you have to touch me." Jori shivered as Sawyer's other hand traced up her leg.

Resting her weight on her arms, Sawyer looked up at Jori. Something about seeing Sawyer this way—supplicant, yet powerful, her shoulders bowed and the muscles in her arm flexing as they supported her—something about this always made Jori want her even more.

"I love you," Jori said.

Lowering herself to the vee of Jori's legs, Sawyer finally touched her, first with one finger, and then with her mouth. She covered Jori, and her tongue slid through wet folds, then withdrew as she drew Jori's clit between her lips.

Jori moaned as pleasure speared through her, her body tightening like a bowstring desperately needing to release a quivering arrow. "Oh, God, I love it when you suck me."

Jori's words seemed to propel Sawyer as she devoured her, alternately sucking and licking, never quite giving her enough of one before switching. Jori grabbed the back of Sawyer's head as she thrust against her mouth.

"Please, don't stop, don't stop, don't stop," Jori chanted when she was too close to go back—too close to let Sawyer shift gears on her again. Sawyer didn't stop, she never stopped giving Jori what she needed. And seconds later, when Jori trembled and bucked beneath her, Sawyer held on until Jori's pleasure ebbed into gentle waves.

Sawyer crawled up the bed and collapsed next to Jori, draping an arm across her stomach. "I suppose now we *have* to buy the place."

Jori smiled. "Of course. You've christened it. It's ours."

Sawyer rose up on one elbow, her gaze on Jori's possessive and passionate. "Say it again."

"It's ours."

CATE CULPEPPER grew up among the luminarias and enchiladas of southern New Mexico. She returns to her Southwest roots in her newest novel, *River Walker*, her sixth title with Bold Strokes Books. She is also author of the four books of the Tristaine series and *Fireside*. Cate is a 2005 and 2007 Golden Crown Literary Award winner in the Sci-Fi/ Fantasy category, and a 2008 recipient of the Alice B. Toklas Readers' Choice Award. She now resides in the Pacific Northwest, where she supervises a residential program for homeless young gay adults, and haunts Taco Bell.

"Luminaria Light" features characters from *River Walker*.

Luminaria Light

Cate Culpepper

The keening wail of a lost infant instinctively captures the immediate attention of any human heart. Grady Wrenn didn't consider her own heart particularly maternal, but a baby was lost out there in the storm, and she had to find it before it died.

She power-kicked through another bank of sodden snow, her face stinging from the wind and icy pellets of the current flurry. She couldn't see more than a few feet through the stark whiteness, which was broken only by the cruel grays and browns of dead trees and stones. The infant was barely audible now, its whimpers weakening in the force of the wind. Lunging toward the sound, she tried to contain the gasping in her lungs lest she miss it. The baby's sobs were breathless and fading.

"Elena!" Calling that name in dire circumstances came naturally to her. "Elena, help me!"

But she was alone.

Grady was the only hope this baby had, her only chance of survival. The weak cry drifted to her again, this time from the opposite direction. She staggered toward it, sobbing now herself.

"Grady." The voice was brushed satin, calm and low and dear—Elena's voice, calling Grady up into the cold and implacable sky.

"Open your eyes, *querida.*"

Grady grasped a pair of familiar arms and felt herself pulled upright on the deep sofa. Cool hands cradled her face. Her eyelids felt glued shut, but she wanted badly to see Elena right now. She forced her eyes open and her lover's pale face, framed in curling dark hair, swam into view. Elena's gentle brown eyes watched her intently.

"And where have you been?" Elena swept Grady's hair off her sweat-beaded forehead. "You went very far away, I think."

Elena was a *curandera,* a healer who dealt with the spirit world, and she took dream-travel seriously. She was also a nurse, and she measured Grady's pulse at the throat with clinical practicality. "Grady? Can you hear me? You're scaring me a little here."

Grady understood Elena's worry. She was sure the dumb shock that infused her dream still fogged her features—she couldn't seem to shake the daze. Elena's expression deepened into real concern before she could string words together.

"Okay," Grady gasped. "That was a little intense."

"I see that it was." Elena frowned. "Your heart is still racing."

Grady swung her legs over the cushions, but Elena held her arms. "I don't think you should get up just yet." She was a good foot shorter than Grady, but she was strong.

Elena was strong, but Grady was embarrassed, or she was getting there fast. She patted Elena's hand until it loosened from her forearm. "It's okay, I'm back. I'm okay."

"All right. I'll believe you." Elena let her go, still studying her with a worried frown. "This dream comes at a strange time, *mi amiga*. I don't think I've ever known you to fall asleep so early."

"It's still Christmas Eve, right?" Details were surfacing through the murk. She had fallen asleep on the sofa in Elena's herb shop below the rooms Elena shared with her mother on the second floor. She was surprised she had dozed off, too—she had never been especially comfortable sleeping in Elena's home, in close proximity to Inez Montalvo. She liked Elena's mother, she had even grown to love the cantankerous bat, but the woman was not exactly a relaxing presence.

"*Sí*, it's still Christmas Eve. About nine o'clock." Elena took Grady's pulse again and seemed satisfied. "Are you going to tell me about this dream?"

Grady shrugged, finding comfort in nonchalance, feigned or not. "A newborn lost in a blizzard in the woods. I could hear it, but I couldn't find it."

"I see." Elena folded her hands in her lap and watched her for an inordinately long time. "A newborn child?"

"Right." Grady rubbed her forehead, glad to silence the lingering echoes of those pitiful cries. "Probably a pretty common anxiety dream. Possibly brought on by the fact that I still don't know what to get you for Christmas, might I add."

"I'm not so sure this was a common dream." Unsurprisingly, Elena didn't seem ready to let the topic go. "I think we should take a walk."

Grady blinked at her. "Right now?"

"Yes, if you're feeling yourself again."

She was, more or less. Her knees only shook for a moment when she rose. Walking with Elena through the streets of Old Mesilla on Christmas Eve would be no hardship, but Elena's insistence puzzled her. "Is there a reason we're taking a walk?"

"Well, this baby is obviously not in here, Grady." Elena slung a heavy shawl over her shoulders, serene in the odd logic of *curanderas*. "Take your scarf, it's cold out."

That much was evident as they stepped out onto the boardwalk fronting Elena's shop. It was one of southern New Mexico's best brands of crystalline winter nights, crisp and frosty. Elena's breath misted from her full lips, but the cold wasn't unbearable. Grady took Elena's elbow as they stepped down off the boardwalk, then flinched at the noisy clack of shutters opening above them.

"Elenita?" Inez purred from the window.

"*Sí*, Mamá?"

"Tell the heathen gringa down there to bring me back my Pepsi. There were three left in this case, now there are only two."

"I didn't take your Pepsi, Inez," Grady called pleasantly.

"Well, then bring me back my ungrateful daughter." Inez perched her elbows on the windowsill and drew hard on her cigarette, wincing down at them through the smoke. "What kind of lousy daughter leaves her poor widowed *madre* all alone on Christmas Eve?"

"My father is alive and well in El Paso, Mamá." Elena adjusted her shawl on her shoulders, unperturbed. "And we'll only be gone a short while."

"Did you turn off the gas in the kitchen?" Inez yelled after them. "The last time the gringa was here, she left on a burner and almost gassed me to death!"

"That wasn't Grady, that was me," Elena called back, taking Grady's arm as they walked down the street. "And we have an electric stove. *Cálmate*, Mamá. We'll see you soon."

This was Grady's first Christmas in New Mexico, and apparently the holiday was a community event. The narrow roads that ran through

Mesilla were beginning to fill with couples walking hand in hand, scrambling children, and shuffling seniors. She heard laughter and splashes of Spanish in the cold air. Elena slid her arm free and stepped further away. Grady looked at her regretfully, and Elena shrugged with an answering sadness. Mesilla was slowly catching up with the rest of the nation, but many Christmases would have to pass before two women could stroll its streets openly as a couple.

Grady was drawn from her glum contemplation of social injustice by the pleasures of watching tradition come alive around her. A cultural anthropologist, she was familiar with Hispanic folklore, but it was still fun to see the *luminarias*—small brown bags, each bearing a single votive candle weighted by sand—being set along the main streets leading to San Albino Church. This was a major project, involving dozens of volunteer groups. The honor of lighting the candles was reserved for the churchgoing teenagers of the village. When all the lanterns were laid and lit, the electric light in the area would be darkened, and Mesilla Plaza would glow with thousands of twinkling candle flames.

"The *luminarias* light the path leading to Midnight Mass, right?" Grady nudged Elena aside as another pickup truck rolled slowly by, carrying more pallets of filled paper bags. "The candles are supposed to guide parishioners to their spiritual home?"

"Yes, but that's not all." Elena waved at a large woman across the street, who called a friendly greeting. "We still lay *luminarias* up our sidewalks, too, right to our front doors. They're also meant to lead the infant Christ Child to our homes."

"Yeesh."

"Yeesh?" Elena repeated.

"Well." Grady frowned. "I respect religious tradition, but all I can picture tonight is a naked, bawling baby crawling on its hands and knees up a cold sidewalk trying to find a house, knocking over *luminarias* as it goes…"

Elena laughed, a musical sound. "Mamá is right, Dr. Wrenn, you are a heathen. Ay, look."

Grady felt the first cold touch of lace on her cheek before she followed Elena's gaze to the clouded sky. She heard a few delighted yelps from a group up ahead. Snow wasn't common in southern New Mexico, and this light dusting was nicely timed.

"I hope it sticks." Elena caught a flake on her tongue. "The kids around here would be so jazzed to wake up to snow on Christmas morning."

The simple happiness on Elena's face made Grady jam her fists in her coat pockets to keep from taking her hand. They wandered toward the Plaza. Grady was content to enjoy the night and leave images of cold babies in snowstorms, or any babies of any kind, well behind them.

"And I have finally decided." Elena walked with her hands clasped behind her, her eyes on the ground, a mysterious smile on her lips.

"You have decided…?"

"What I want for my Christmas gift. I want us to have a baby." Elena walked on for several steps before realizing she was alone and turning back. *"Cálmate, querida,"* she called. "I don't mean this Christmas."

"Good." Grady folded her arms against a sudden chill. "I couldn't possibly have a baby gift-wrapped by morning."

Elena came back to her and touched her arm. "All I'm asking for now is your faith in this matter, Grady. A promise between us, that we'll raise a child together."

"Well, you and I have talked about family." Grady glanced over her shoulder to be sure they wouldn't be overheard. "We both want the possibility of kids, sometime in the future."

"And how distant must this future be?" A dimple appeared in Elena's cheek. "Your womb is getting no younger, Professor Gringa."

"Me?"

"Grady, you know I can't." Elena's smile faltered. "If we're to have a child from one of us, it will have to be you."

"Me." Grady rubbed the back of her neck. "Elena, we've talked about taking in foster kids, or adopting someday, and we're nowhere near ready for *that.* Now you want me to consider getting pregnant, some year soon?"

"Some year soon." Elena nodded. "That's the gift I'm hoping for. And I know it's an enormous thing to ask, Grady. I'll honor your decision entirely if you don't want this. We can still look into fostering, adoption—"

"Or we could start out with a goldfish. Or an iguana." Grady walked on, her shoulders hunched. She wasn't sure why this conversation rattled her so. Elena wasn't suggesting they break into a sperm bank tonight. That damn dream must still be getting to her. Well, that and the sudden and unexpected prospect of grueling labor and episiotomies.

The Plaza awakened around them. Streams of flickering lights came alive, candle by candle, leading toward the dignified edifice of San Albino. Snowflakes fell more heavily now, a drifting curtain of white, lending the scene a timeless charm.

"Feliz Navidad." An older man with a broad smile waited at the corner, balancing a round tray of paper cups that steamed in the brisk night air. He extended the tray gallantly to Grady and Elena, and they accepted cups of fragrant hot cider, sweetened with cinnamon sticks. "Pass by this way again, Señorita Montalvo," he said. "My wife is bringing fresh *biscochitos* soon."

"Gracias, Señor Paz." Elena patted his frail arm as they went on. Grady had noted much of Mesilla addressed Elena with this same friendly courtesy. This community respected their *curandera* as an ethical and highly effective healer. Grady only wished the village where Elena was born and grew up was more willing to truly know her.

Elena walked silently beside her, cupping her fingers over her steaming drink to warm them.

"Elena, if we have a child, where will we raise it?"

"Well, in Mesilla." Elena's smile was hopeful. "Wouldn't we? My mother would welcome a grandchild, even one who came to us through…untraditional means."

"Okay, but would Mesilla welcome me, as this kid's parent?" Grady spoke gently. "I can't move in with you, we can't live openly here as a family. So I'd sleep in my lousy condo in Las Cruces, then try to catch a few hours with you both during the day? I don't want to hide, Elena."

"No. Of course you don't." Elena rested her head very briefly on Grady's shoulder.

They walked together silently, and Grady's heart ached at the new slump in Elena's shoulders. They had circled this topic before, more than once. Long before the subject of babies came up, Grady knew what she wanted. She believed Elena wanted it, too. It was past time they lived together, shared a home. She couldn't resist giving logic one more try.

"Las Cruces is a big city compared to Mesilla, much more open. And I've got a big condo in this big city."

"I know."

"Elena, if you moved in with me, she would still see you almost every day. You'd still spend more than thirty hours a week in your shop, right downstairs."

"Yes."

"Cruces is within walking distance of Mesilla. It's not like we couldn't get to Inez quickly if she needed us."

"I know."

"And there's really nothing wrong with your mother, physically. She's not elderly, or medically frail, or disabled. She's capable of taking care of herself."

"Grady, she needs me. She gets frightened sometimes."

"Elena, the woman has a loaded Remington pump-action shotgun under her bed. I should know, she tried to shoot me with it. Inez is far from helpless, believe me."

"I didn't say she was helpless, I said she was afraid." Elena sighed. "You've known this about her, as long as you've known me. I can't heal whatever is broken inside my mother that makes her so fearful. She feels safer when I'm near, and a daughter should look after her mother."

"For the next forty years?" Grady softened her tone. "Elena, when will it be your turn? When do you get to have a life?"

"I wish I could help you understand, Grady. I grew up so differently than you." Elena frowned at the ground passing beneath their feet, as if hoping to read words there. "I know what you're saying is important, and I worry about these things, too. I don't have all of the answers tonight. I just thought if we made a commitment to each other now, about this child…it would be a promise to work together, to find a way. And it would say something about us."

"About us?" Grady wished Elena would lift her head. She thought she heard tears in her voice.

"It would say what we have between us is strong enough to overcome all of these problems. That we both believe that."

"Elena." Grady turned and stood directly in front of her. If ever there was a moment for looming, this was it. "Look at me, please."

Elena did, and Grady had been right about the tears.

"What we have together is stronger than any love I've ever known," Grady said quietly. "I may not be real clear on motherhood yet. But I know with absolute certainty that you're the woman I want to wake up next to each morning, for the rest of my life. If you need to hear me say that every single day, Elena, it would be my honor."

Beyond Elena, Grady caught a glimpse of a small flame near the ground as another *luminaria* was lit, but all she really needed to see was Elena's slow smile. They stood close, almost touching, the steam of their breath blending. Somehow the sweet intimacy of Elena's gaze was more powerful in that moment than her touch could have been.

"Thank you, *querida*."

"You're welcome." Grady took their empty cups and dropped them into a curbside bin. Beyond Elena, a cloaked woman kneeling in the entrance to an alley used a tapered candle to light the next in a series of *luminarias* leading into the dark passage. "Hmm. What's up with that?"

"What?" Elena asked.

"I thought teenagers usually lit a town's *luminarias.* And she's placing them pretty far from the church, isn't she?"

"Who is?" Elena looked over her shoulder, then studied Grady intently. "You see a woman lighting *luminarias,* back in that alley?"

"Well, yeah, honey. She's right there."

"All right." Elena smiled and bounced on her toes. "I think perhaps we should stroll down this alley."

"Down there? But it's dark." Grady pointed the way they came. "And the *biscochitos* are back there."

"We'll get you some cookies on the way home. Come, please."

Grady sighed and followed Elena down the twisting path. Elena walked past the kneeling woman without acknowledging her. The woman cupped the lit taper with her hand, and its glow gave her porcelain features a reddish cast. She wore an intricate metal crucifix around her neck. She had large, kind eyes, and she smiled up at Grady.

"Evening," Grady said.

The cloaked woman nodded pleasantly, then bent over the next paper bag.

The alley was narrow and apparently deep. A thin, wet trail of melting snow marked the middle of the stony ground, and Grady walked closely behind Elena.

"Watch that broken glass there." Grady detected no sign of other holiday revelers in this dank place, so she took Elena's hand. The passage was crowded with barrels and stacked wooden crates, and they had to wend carefully around them. The cold seemed to have deepened several degrees in the dim corridor. "Do you know what we're looking for?"

"I might." Elena peered around a jag in the alley's wall. "I seem to remember a…ay, there she is. There she still is."

Grady felt an odd prickling at the back of her neck.

As Catholic shrines go, this one was small and looked long neglected. The image of the honored saint stood about waist-high in a wooden square no larger than a shoebox set on an upended barrel. Old, melted candles stood in a half-circle before the image, and long-dried stems of flowers adorned its frame.

"My grandmother brought me here once." Elena slid the shawl off her shoulders and folded it. She lay it on the cold stones at the base of the shrine and knelt on the bunched fabric. "Grady, this is Saint Brigid." She crossed herself and whispered softly in Spanish.

"Saint *Brigid*? Brigid of Ireland?" Grady rested her hands on her knees, fascinated. "I wouldn't think an Irish saint would have a big following in Mesi—"

"Excúseme." Elena opened one eye and pointed skyward. "I am not talking to you."

"Oops. Sorry." Grinning, Grady unbuttoned her coat and slipped it over Elena's shoulders. Crouching on her heels, she studied the icon while Elena prayed.

The pale face wore a generically benevolent expression, interchangeable with most religious portraits Grady had seen. She touched the thick glass square covering the picture and gently wiped the moisture from the pane to see her more clearly. The dark-haired woman wore a cross around her neck and carried a lit candle in her hand. Grady blinked. When she focused on the saint again, the candle had changed into a small lamp.

Grady sensed Elena watching her with an indulgent smile. "Hey. Really. What are we doing here?"

"You tell me. I'm not the one who was drawn to this place."

"Are you kidding? Elena, you all but dragged me in here."

"Grady, of the two of us, who would you say is more Irish?"

"All right, yes, I'm Irish. But I don't pray to—"

"Saint Brigid is always depicted carrying a lamp. Which of us saw a woman lighting *luminarias* leading to this shrine?"

"I thought we both did…"

Elena cleared her throat.

"Oh," Grady said.

"And which of us is having dreams pleading for holy intervention?"

"What?"

"Saint Brigid is the patron saint of babies." Elena nodded fondly at the icon. "Specifically of newborns."

And Brigid began to weep.

They didn't see the saint cry, they heard her. Elena's eyes widened as soft sobs sounded in the freezing alley. They both turned to the icon, but the saint still regarded them with serene detachment, dry-eyed.

"What *is* that?" Grady's heart filled with rising horror. "Jesus, Elena."

"If it's Jesus, we better find Him fast." Elena jumped up and began searching behind the crates and short towers of boxes that cluttered the space.

Grady searched, too, shaking with cold, listening hard for the faint cries. Her stomach soured with fear and disorientation at this jarring return to her nightmare.

"Do you hear it?" Elena sounded shaken, too.

"It's not over here—"

But it was.

Grady lifted a snarl of crumpled newspaper covering a tattered box. Speechless, she could only stare.

"Grady? What is it?"

"Uh, it's a rat." Grady bent and lifted a small puppy carefully by its nape. Its legs kicked the air feebly, and it whimpered again.

Elena gasped. "*Diosa.* The poor thing." She quickly took the little animal from Grady, cradled it against her chest, and wrapped Grady's coat around it. The puppy trembled so hard it seemed to vibrate in Elena's arms.

"Damn, it's just a baby." Grady's pulse began to settle. "Doesn't look old enough to be weaned yet."

"The little *niña* is skin and bones." Elena rested her cheek on the puppy's head. "No one has been looking after her. Hurry, Grady. We need to get her someplace warm."

Elena rushed away and Grady stumbled to catch up She slowed just long enough to snatch Elena's shawl from the ground at the base of Saint Brigid's shrine, taking one last look at the saint's distant smile before bolting after Elena.

The puppy made weak mournful piping sounds as they emerged from the alley. Grady didn't see the woman lighting *luminarias* at its entrance—she didn't even see the *luminarias* now. The path was dark.

But Mesilla Plaza was alight in its full Christmas Eve glory, thronged with people. Snow still fell, dusting the cobblestones of the plaza a ghostly white. *Luminarias* burnished the stately square with carpets of flickering gold-red light. Grady spared a few seconds to appreciate their beauty, but mostly she concentrated on keeping up with Elena and her squeaking bundle.

"I'm glad she's strong enough to cry. She needs food badly," Elena said. "Grady, you're out here in shirtsleeves. Put my shawl on, if it isn't too damp."

Grady did, watching a small black nose poke inquisitively out of Elena's arms. If this was a certain breed of dog, its identification might remain forever a mystery. From what Grady could see, its fur was a motley collection of black and brown and white, and it had outsized floppy ears. The puppy peered up at her with anxious brown eyes, its forehead wrinkled. After a brief glance, it rested its head against Elena's breast again, shivering. Grady understood the comfort of laying her head on that breast. She hoped the puppy would survive.

Elena smiled at Grady and indicated the shadow cast on the ground before them. The faint *luminaria* light outlined their figures—Grady's tall, shawl-cloaked form walking close beside Elena's smaller one, carrying a fragile little life in her arms. They formed an unnerving image of the Holy Family. The light from the *luminarias* faded behind them, and they entered the darker neighborhoods near Elena's shop.

Grady brushed snow off Elena's dark hair. Elena's fine-boned hand cradled the puppy's head as she murmured calm, soothing words to the little dog. Grady couldn't imagine a woman more naturally born to parenting than Elena. Somehow Elena had grown beyond the needy example of Inez Montalvo. She would be a strong and loving mother. And Grady owed her a Christmas present.

"A puppy is a little more appealing than an iguana," Grady said.

Elena looked at her with a question in her eyes.

"A puppy is also a lot more tangible than a promise." Grady saw no one else on the dark street and draped her arm around Elena's shoulders. "If we keep this wee mutt, we'd need to make a home for her. We'd want to start making it now, working together on that. A home that can also welcome our kid, some year soon."

Elena was silent, but the shining in her eyes dazzled Grady's heart. At that moment, they turned a dark corner and were suddenly bathed in a glorious light. Grady stood transfixed.

At the end of the small road, Elena's shop was festooned with shimmering *luminarias*. They stood three deep on the roof, and two perfectly aligned rows of them began at their feet and led directly to Elena's door. By comparison, the rest of the neighborhood dimmed into obscurity. A crew of five or more would be needed to prepare such a display. Many ladders would be involved.

Grady swallowed. "Do you think your mother—"

"Not one chance in hell," Elena whispered.

Frowning, Grady remembered coming upon this wondrous sight just as she voiced her promise to Elena. "Is Brigid known for making cheesy and dramatic gestures?"

"We'll have to Google her." Elena leaned against Grady with a contented sigh and held the puppy up to see the glowing bags. "Look, little one. Holy lanterns lighting your way home. Do you have something to tell us? Like perhaps you are a very special dog?" She touched her nose to the puppy's, looking at her seriously. "Use your words."

As they walked together down the luminous path leading to Elena's home, Grady heard Spanish Christmas carols blaring loudly behind closed shutters on the second floor. She stepped up onto the boardwalk and opened the door for Elena.

"Welcome home, little dog," Grady said. "We're going to call you Inez."

D. Jackson Leigh works as newspaper journalist in North Carolina. She shares her life with her wonderful partner, her Jack Russell terrier, and "the cat" that made herself at home when Jackson and the JRT weren't watchful. Her Bold Strokes novels include *Bareback* and *Long Shot*. This story, "Reindeer Roundup," revisits the characters featured in *Long Shot*. Her third novel, *Call Me Softly*, is scheduled for release in 2011.

Reindeer Roundup

D. Jackson Leigh

Tory cursed when still another string of red and green lights blinked off. She flung the garland in her hand to the floor and turned to get the box of replacement bulbs from the coffee table, groaning at the sound of glass ornaments crunching under her foot.

"I give up," she shouted to the empty room. She flopped down onto the couch and stared out the window at the eight inches of fresh snow.

What the hell was she thinking when she let Leah talk her into buying all these decorations? Oh, yeah. She was thinking they would be sipping warm spiced wine and stringing lights together to celebrate their first Christmas.

Four months had passed since she and Leah admitted their love for each other and openly began their courtship. Three of those months had been the most exhilarating of Tory's life.

They had taken a day-long horseback ride in the Appalachian Mountains when the leaves changed to an autumn palette of red, gold, and brilliant yellow. They'd shared afternoon picnics and candlelit dinners, art exhibits, and shopping trips. For one cozy week, they'd hidden out at a private cabin and skied the slopes at a nearby resort.

What she'd loved the most, though, were the simple moments when they cuddled on her couch to watch a DVD or laughed together at the antics of their overly curious Chincoteague foal, Sure Thing.

Those nights when they opened their hearts and shed their clothes to explore their passion in every soft curve, every sensitive pulse of each other's bodies, were wonderful beyond description.

There wasn't much about them that was similar. Leah was a petite brunette, while Tory was tall, athletic, and blond. Leah was an outspoken steel magnolia whereas everyone described Tory as laid-back. As a journalist, Leah took things apart to expose what was wrong. As a veterinarian, Tory put things back together and made them right again.

Despite their differences, like two polar ends of a magnet, they were drawn together by a force too powerful to resist. That's why the past few weeks, when work had pulled them in different directions, had been pure torture. Leah had recently won a new contract to help shape a new legislative proposal on extended home care and was busy lining up witnesses to testify before the Virginia General Assembly in January. Tory was glad that Leah's new venture—consulting work based out of Cherokee Falls—was already paying off. But damn it, it was hard to be apart so early in their relationship.

Leah had first said she'd only be away a week, and they'd talked on the phone several times a day. When the work took longer than expected, Tory had driven to Richmond for a promised two days of making love and ordering room service in a fancy hotel suite. The weekend of passion had melted away on Saturday morning with the fifth phone call for more information. Tory ended up watching television alone while Leah spent most of the weekend working at her laptop with an apologetic, but very attractive and openly lesbian lawyer.

Tory had returned to Cherokee Falls on Sunday night, clutching to her heart Leah's vow to be back home before the next weekend. But by the end of the second week, Leah's phone calls had become less frequent, and when they did talk, Leah was too tired to carry on much of a conversation. On Thursday, she had called to say they still had not finished their work. To make it home in time for Christmas, she would have to work through the weekend again and most of the next week.

So, here it was Sunday afternoon and no Leah. Tory surveyed her halfhearted attempt to decorate the tree alone, her heart growing heavier with each wink of the cheerful lights. Their last conversation on Friday kept replaying in her mind, awakening every devil that had ever plagued her.

"We're working every minute of the day, honey," Leah told her on Friday night, but she sounded distracted and Tory could hear giggling in the background. She had hung up without the soft sighs and confessions of love and loneliness that usually concluded their phone calls. The real knife in her gut, the ache in her chest, came from the fact that Leah hadn't seemed to notice.

Her depression was a heavy weight. Lugging it around the past two days had exhausted her. Tory leaned her head back and closed her eyes. She imagined Leah calling to say her work in Richmond had reminded her why she liked living in large cities. She imagined Leah saying things just weren't going to work out for her to live in Cherokee Falls.

Those thoughts were her last until cold hands and warm lips feathered across her face and drew her from a troubled doze. She blinked several times to focus on eyes the color of dark honey and realized the weight pinning her legs was Leah straddling her lap.

"There they are," Leah said softly. "I've been missing my leprechaun's green eyes."

"You didn't call me yesterday," Tory said, her voice gruff. *How much have you really missed me?*

"You hung up Friday without telling me that you love me," Leah said, her words more of a question than an accusation.

Tory didn't answer and averted her eyes, ashamed for Leah to see the mistrust in them.

"You hung up before I could tell you how much I was missing you," Leah said, stroking Tory's cheek.

"You sounded busy…and distracted. You sounded like you weren't alone." Tory scowled, still refusing to meet Leah's gaze. "I could hear someone laughing."

"Ah. I see." Leah shrugged. "You caught me. I met another woman in Richmond. She's very cute and blond like you. But her eyes are blue. The prettiest color blue I think I've ever seen. I fell in love with her the first time I met her."

"I don't want to hear about it." She couldn't believe Leah could be so casual about another woman. She couldn't look at her and didn't want to be touching her. Tory tried to push her away.

But Leah locked her hands behind Tory's neck and hung on tight. "And she's ten years old."

Tory stopped her struggle. She blinked back tears and looked up at Leah. "Wha…what?"

"That was Alisha's ten-year-old daughter. We were working at their house because her partner had to attend a fund-raiser and they couldn't find a sitter."

Relief and embarrassment flooded through Tory. She buried her face in Leah's neck. She felt like a big baby, a big jealous baby.

"Oh, sugar. This is my fault." Leah tightened her arms around Tory. "I know there were times when we first met that I pushed you away. But that was before I gave you my heart, darlin'. Don't you know you own me?"

Leah stroked Tory's back. "I've always been able to lose myself in work. But when you didn't call me at all yesterday, I told Alisha that I had to go home. If the snowplows had cleared the roads sooner, I would have been here last night."

"Really?"

Leah chuckled at Tory's muffled voice against her neck. "Really, sugar."

"I was afraid you had changed your mind about us. That maybe you decided Cherokee Falls was too small and dull for you."

"No, baby, never. Christ almighty. I missed you so much I actually had a wet dream about you. It was so real I woke up in the middle of a huge orgasm."

"You dreamed about me?" Her dark cloud lifting, Tory pulled Leah closer.

"Night and day." Leah slipped her hands under Tory's shirt and raked her nails along her spine. "Now, what are you going to do about making those dreams come true?"

Tory nuzzled Leah's neck. "You smell like chocolate."

Leah leaned back and lifted her chin to expose a tiny reindeer tattoo on the pulse point just below her jawline. "Compliments of my young girlfriend. Taste it."

Tory sniffed at the reindeer, then tentatively stroked it with her tongue. "Mmm. Chocolate mint." She couldn't resist planting kisses along the length of Leah's neck. "My favorite flavor on my favorite person. I love early Christmas gifts."

"Oh, no, sugar. This gift is for me." She hummed with pleasure when Tory's mouth found the tattoo again, then gasped as Tory sucked hard. Leah rubbed her crotch against Tory's stomach. "I've got Santa's whole team hidden all over my body. It's your job, lover, to find every one of those little fellers and lick it off before you get me so hot they melt."

Tory growled, her mouth never leaving Leah's neck as she stood and wrapped her arms under Leah's hips to carry her to the bedroom. No one but Leah had ever provoked such an aggressive need to possess and protect.

Dasher was nothing but a lingering bruise on Leah's neck, and when she spied another reindeer nestled in Leah's cleavage, buttons flew across the room. A scrape of her teeth, a lashing of the tongue, and Dancer was a casualty, too.

Leah's body was her battlefield and each tiny reindeer devoured was another doubt conquered. Leah belonged to her. No job, no other woman was going to steal her away.

It took some effort, but Tory slowed her attack when she discovered Prancer covering a puckered nipple. Torture by tongue was to be his sentence for hiding in such a coveted place.

"God, I've missed your mouth on me." Leah moaned as Tory freed her breast of the invader.

She found Cupid prancing low across Leah's soft, lean belly, his antlers poised to guard what Tory came to claim. She attacked swiftly, wielding her tongue with deadly accuracy and moving on.

Vixen was patrolling the inside of a firm thigh and Tory pushed Leah's knees apart to pounce. The sweet mint that coated her lips mingled with the heady scent of Leah's arousal. She nuzzled into that wet heat, painting her lips, chin, and cheeks with the spoils of her campaign.

"Tory, oh, God." Leah's hand was on the back of her head, urging her to engage the final skirmish.

She licked her slick entrance clean, then plunged her tongue inside.

"Yes," Leah hissed, lifting her hips and opening her legs wider. "Please, baby, I need to come so bad."

She laved her tongue alongside but not touching Leah's turgid clit. She loved it when her normally bossy lover was reduced to begging.

"More," Tory growled.

"Anything. Anything you want. Just make me come."

"There are four more."

"No, don't stop," Leah pleaded as a bite to her thigh signaled Tory's retreat. "Oh!"

She gripped Leah's knees and flipped her over to attack the rear guard. She stalked her next victim, nipping and sucking upward from the ankle.

Leah squirmed as Donner quickly surrendered his post behind her knee, then grew still when she felt Tory pause. Hot breath bathed the backs of her thighs and she shuddered.

Comet had been spied.

Tory knew exactly why Comet was stationed on Leah's right butt cheek, inviting ambush. Leah loved Tory's teeth on her sensitive buttocks, relished Tory's assertive tendency to bite when they made love in this position.

"Look what I found," Tory whispered.

"God, I want your hand between my legs, your fingers inside me. I need you to make me come."

Leah jerked when Tory bit down hard on the hapless reindeer and moaned as Comet was devoured in one huge sucking assault. Tory's attack didn't stop with the tattoo. Leah writhed as every inch of both cheeks was licked and nipped.

"God, touch me before I come without it."

Tory stroked the inside of Leah's thighs and Leah reflexively opened her legs in offering. When she stopped caressing her, Leah's hips pumped, as if begging for more.

"Please, baby. I need you. I need you now."

Tory didn't answer, but pushed between Leah's legs and under her thighs. With her face pressed into the bed and her thighs draped over Tory's shoulders, Leah was totally open, totally exposed and dripping wet.

"Oh, please lick me."

Again, Tory denied her. She worked upward to thrust her tongue inside and Leah groaned. Tory inched her tongue higher and Leah's breath hitched.

"I'm gonna come. I'm gonna come," Leah panted.

"Wait." Tory pushed up and covered Leah with her weight. She rubbed her swollen clit against Leah's firm thigh and filled her with her fingers. She stroked her inside and out, pumping her hand in rhythm with the rolling of her hips against Leah's leg.

Tory's orgasm gathered and began to swarm through her belly as Leah matched her movements, pushing backward to meet each thrust.

"I can't wait. I can't wait," Leah cried.

That's when she saw Blitzen, the last reindeer sentry, protecting the juncture of Leah's shoulder and neck—Tory's claiming spot.

"Now. Come now," Tory commanded, biting down hard and holding Blitzen in her teeth as she thrust with her hips and hand.

Leah's cries mingled with Tory's howl as they released together and rode out the waves of pleasure. They collapsed in a heap, their hearts pounding in perfect sync.

Tory lazily licked at the remnants of Blitzen and smiled to herself. Her very creative lover had so many facets to her personality, she looked forward to a lifetime of discovery.

She rolled onto her back and pulled Leah into her arms. They were both sweaty and parts of Leah were still sticky, but Tory didn't care. She kissed her slowly, tenderly. "I love you."

Leah rose up on her elbow, her eyes searching Tory's. "I love you, Tory." She combed damp tendrils of Tory's hair back from her face. "I don't like being away from you. I know we'll probably get better at it after a couple of years, but not now, not yet."

"I don't want to keep you from your work," Tory said. "I'm afraid you would resent that somewhere down the road."

"I've already decided on my next project, and the research won't take me any farther than the Equestrian Center."

Tory frowned. "You're investigating our friends?"

Leah laughed softly. "No, sugar. Alisha told her daughter that I had a baby pony and that's all the kid wanted to hear all about. So I told her a few stories about Sure's adventures and she said, 'You should write a book about your pony.'"

"You're going to write a kid's book?"

"You don't think I can?"

"I think you'd be wonderful at it. You're a natural storyteller." Tory grinned. "And you won't have to go away to do it."

Leah kissed her again. "No, I won't have to go away."

"I want you to move in with me." Tory blurted it out before she lost her nerve. "We can change the house any way you want or we can sell it and build a new one." She stroked Leah's bare back. "I want to lie down with you every night and wake up with you every morning.

When I'm working, I want to be able to think about you in your own office here, typing away on your laptop. I want to cuddle on the couch and watch television with you. I want to do laundry with you, cook meals with you, take naps with you."

Leah's eyes filled and she laid her cheek against Tory's heart. "I've been waiting for you to ask."

Tory attempted to sit up. "Let's get dressed and go get your stuff now."

Leah pushed her back down on the pillows. "We'll go tomorrow. We're not done here yet."

"We're not?"

"No, sugar. I've got a big old red-nosed Rudolph that I saved just for you." Leah pulled the sheet back to expose all of Tory's long, naked body. "I just have to decide where I'm going to stick him."

Tory grinned. "Merry Christmas to me."

CJ Harte grew up loving words. By age four, she was reading to her mother, and by nine she was writing poetry. She wrote her first play in the ninth grade. She has written numerous short stories and poetry, which have been published in regional literary magazines and online. CJ wrote many of the lyrics, including the title song, for the musical *Am I Blue?* She is the author of *Dreams of Bali*, which introduces Madison and Karlie, and *Magic of the Heart*. She lives in Wyoming with her two dogs and enjoys traveling, spending time with family and friends, and writing and reading. She can be reached at www.hartescape.net.

Dreams: A Promise Kept

C.J. Harte

Karlie Henderson stared across the kitchen table at her lover. Madison Barnes had once made her life hell and now made it heaven…mostly. "Okay, what's going on?" She watched Madison push food around on her plate and then play with the glass of wine. *Something's up.* "Neither one of us is pregnant, so that can't be the problem."

Madison laughed. "You're still a smart-ass." She took Karlie's hand and gently caressed it. "I'm sorry." She thought about their argument earlier in the day. "I know I asked you to live with me last year, and this wasn't what I had in mind. The two of us commuting between New York and Miami, catching whatever time we can get." Falling in love with Karlie had been life altering, and now she often found the ground shifting under her and didn't know how to make it firm again. "I just needed time to sell my practice and…"

Karlie pulled her hand away and leaned back in her seat. She was tired of this discussion. "Please, Madison, I don't want to argue." When Madison started to interrupt, she put up her hand. "No, listen. Please. I offered to move, but you didn't think your place was big enough. I said I could get my own place in Miami, and you thought it was ridiculous for us to live in different houses. I suggested I apply for a vacancy at Florida State University in Tallahassee, and you didn't want me living that far away. Madison, New York is a hell of a lot farther. We've been lovers for nearly a year."

She took a deep breath, hating the anxiety that was threatening to drive a wedge between them. "If you're not ready for me to move in, I accept that, but I don't want to spend the rest of our lives like this." She again held Madison's hand. "Now, take me to bed so I will miss you terribly when you leave in the morning."

When she woke up, Karlie found the bed empty. Madison was already in the shower. As much as Karlie wanted to beg Madison to stay, her pride kept her in bed. Only the cries from the puppy Madison had given her finally forced her to get up and get dressed. "Come on, Alice B," Karlie called as she grabbed the miniature poodle's leash. "I think we both need a walk."

By the time she got back, Karlie was calm and ready to say good-bye. Again. Madison was already dressed and packed, her bags at the door. "What time is your case?"

"It's just a preliminary hearing this afternoon, but I need to get there early enough to meet my client." She paused, as if looking for something more to say. "I've already called for a cab."

"Is this a new client, then?"

"Yeah, he's…" Madison stopped. "Karlie, this is a good kid who…"

I will not cry, Karlie thought. "Madison, you are doing what you love." She kissed Madison with a new hesitancy. "Now go, before I start taking your clothes off."

"I love you."

"I know. I love you, too."

"Are you coming down next weekend?"

Karlie looked down at her hands. "I've got a lot to do. End-of-semester stuff." She finally looked up. "Maybe we ought to just focus on work until Christmas break. It's only a month away."

"A month?" Madison sounded shocked.

"I think we both need some time." Karlie quickly hugged Madison one last time, then opened the door. "Now go. The cab must be here."

"Fine! I'll probably be busy anyway." Madison grabbed her bag and stormed off.

Karlie watched Madison walk away, feeling a void opening up. "Why does love have to be so complicated?"

❖

Madison slammed down the phone. "Fuck it," she shouted. She really wanted to throw something. Nothing had gone well in the three days she had been back in Miami. For the first time in her career, she didn't give a fuck about the law. She missed Karlie so much it hurt. "Well, then, do something about it." She turned her chair around and stared out at Biscayne Bay. She had never felt lonelier. She laughed at the realization. "I'm the one who avoided commitments."

Sure, she had changed in the past year, but not enough to make room in her day to day life for the woman she loved. *The only woman I have ever loved.* It was time to do something. She called in her senior legal staff and then called her sister Dee. It took the rest of the week, but she had a plan. Once she made up her mind, she acted.

❖

On Saturday, Karlie got a call from Madison.

"Did you know that my mother is English?" Madison asked.

That was the last thing Karlie expected to hear. "I vaguely remember Dee saying something about that when we were in college. Is something wrong with your mother?"

"Not hardly. She and Dad will be returning to Florida the first of December. As usual, they want to have a big family gathering to announce their return. Anyway, I was wondering if you would like to go to London and Paris with me for Christmas. I need to take care of some things for my mother and I thought it would be a great way for the two of us to spend a month together."

"A month?" They hadn't had more than three days together in over six months. "That's a wonderful idea, but what about Bali?"

"We were there last year and I went to escape. Now I have you, and I want to celebrate the holidays with you."

Karlie couldn't believe Madison would take that much time away from work. Suddenly doubt and worry struck. She was still feeling guilty for the way their last visited ended. "You really mean a whole month?"

"Absolutely. With you."

Madison sounded so assured. "Yes," Karlie said, "I would love to go. What's the plan?"

"I'll fly up there and we'll leave from New York. See you in a couple of weeks." Karlie thought she heard a sigh of relief. "I really do love you."

❖

"I've never flown in first class," Karlie said, impressed with the accommodations so far. She had a glass of champagne in her hand even before they had taken off. The phenomenal success of her first romance novel had given her more money than she had ever hoped for, but she still was conservative in her spending. "University profs are not rich."

"I've spent so little of the money my grandparents left in trust," Madison explained, "and Dee and I will someday inherit my parents' assets, too. I decided it's time to spend some. Besides, you're worth it." For the first time in her life Madison had someone she wanted to have fun with. She and her sister had been raised by a succession of nannies while her socialite parents traveled and led their own lives. She had assumed responsibility for her younger sister at a very early age. As a result, work had always come first, whether it was school, college, or her law career. Now she wanted to play. "And you will just have to wait to see what else is planned."

What's going on? Karlie wondered. This was a new side to Madison, one she had not seen before. "I can do that, as long as we are together."

"I need to tell you that my parents were disappointed you wouldn't be joining them at Christmas. The notorious Karlyn Henderson would be even more stellar this year than you were as just a writer last year."

"I would much rather be known for writing and teaching, not for being arrested for murder or having my lover shot defending me." Unpleasant memories flooded to the surface, and Karlie fought back tears. "Sorry. The thought of losing you scared me. And I would much prefer being known as Madison Barnes's wonderful, beautiful, intelligent, talented lover." She stroked Madison's hand and familiar desire stirred. "God, I want you."

Madison smiled smugly. "Don't worry. We'll have plenty of time."

"Okay, when are you going to tell me what we're going to do?"

"Patience, my dear."

"I can't believe you said that. Miss I-got-to-have-it-now."

"I'm learning. You know, you're an excellent teacher."

"And you are my best student." The leer on Madison's face

negated the need for words. Needing a diversion until they landed, Karlie grabbed her headphones and scrolled through the list of movies. "I am not listening to this. Go to sleep."

❖

Heathrow Airport and customs went smoothly, and during the luxurious limousine ride into central London, Karlie had watched the passing scenery and contemplated the past year. So many changes and challenges for them both. Neither of them trusted easily. Now they were building that trust.

"Madison, this place is beautiful." Karlie turned around in a complete circle, absorbing the beauty of her surroundings. The Dorchester's opulence was far beyond anything she could imagine. She was on visual overload. Almost immediately their bags were whisked off to the elevator. *Lift*, Karlie reminded herself. The lift stopped at the top of the Dorchester and they were escorted to one of three uniquely decorated suites. When they were finally alone, she kissed Madison. "Make love to me right now, in this room and every room."

"Including the bathroom?"

"Every room!"

"Demanding, aren't you?" Madison teased as she began to undress Karlie. She trailed kisses down the side of Karlie's neck, enjoying the change in her lover's breathing. "God, I love you." Madison recognized the heat between her legs and hoped she could last long enough to carefully remove her lover's clothes. *She may want to wear this again. I can't believe how much I want her.*

They made love in every room and sometimes twice in the same room until Madison was too exhausted to move. "We probably should have saved the bedroom for last. This bathroom floor is cold and hard."

"I can't move."

"Neither can I." Laughter soon filled the room as Madison tried to lift Karlie from the floor. "Delilah, you have sapped my strength."

"Well, Samson, just give me your hand and let's see if I can stand up." Once standing, Karlie pulled Madison into the bedroom and quickly fell asleep. It was dark by the time she woke up. "Samson, I'm hungry."

"Room service?"

"No, we go out. I don't want to miss a minute."

"Let me make a call and get reservations, then we'll shower and get dressed." An hour later the phone rang and the reservations were confirmed. "Let's go, beautiful. Too much to see and do."

For the next ten days, Madison had every day planned. They drove to Bath and visited the home of Jane Austen, one of Karlie's favorite authors. Then on to Wales and finally back to London with stops in Windsor and Cambridge. The restaurants and hotels were all exceptional and they never ate in the same place twice. Madison experienced a mix of emotions she often had no name for. Her love for Karlie, at times, was so intense she felt control slipping away.

"Madison, thank you," Karlie said over high tea after a day of shopping at Fortnum & Mason. "For an English major, this has been an incredible trip. You've taken me to museums, which you hate, gone shopping with me, which you find boring, walked with me through Westminister, which you called a tomb. You even walked with me all over Harrods and bought me their Christmas bear. This has been the happiest time of my life. I can't imagine anything better."

"It's so little compared to what you have given me. I'm just sorry I've taken so long to figure this out."

"Madison, you…"

"No, please. You're right. I don't know how to make a commitment, but I'm learning. I do love you. I promise things will be better." She gently placed her hand on top of Karlie's. "Tomorrow we're getting on the Eurostar and going to Paris."

"Paris? Oh, Madison, how romantic."

"I think you wrote a love story set there." She looked at Karlie and her heart pounded with all the love inside. She was learning about love. "I'm glad you're happy."

❖

Madison had arranged for a private guide through the Louvre. She thrilled at the oohs and aahs coming from Karlie as they went through the different halls. She enjoyed the Louvre more than she had imagined because she was sharing the experience with Karlie.

When they stopped in the museum café for lunch, Karlie finally asked, "Okay, how did you arrange all this? I know you have unlimited funds, but I don't think travel agencies make these trips this personal."

Madison leaned back in her chair. *How much to tell? No, the real intent won't be given away.* "My sister discovered this wonderful organization, Privus, that plans personalized trips just for women. I joined and told them the kinds of places we would like to go, our budget and all that, and they arranged everything." She leaned closer and murmured, "I wanted this to be special."

"It is." Karlie hesitated, old insecurities rising. "I just hope you aren't planning to dump me after and this is your way of saying good-bye."

Madison clasped Karlie's hand. "I don't ever want to say good-bye."

The seriousness in Madison's voice was unsettling. Could Madison be ill? She had recovered from the gunshot wound last year. "Are you okay?"

"I'm more than fine. I have you."

Karlie looked carefully into Madison's eyes and saw only love. She trusted that. Trusted her. "In that case, let's find the guide and continue our tour."

For the next three days they strolled the banks of the Seine, visited Notre Dame, and walked throughout the Latin Quarter, stopping in shops whenever something attracted their attention. Karlie was ecstatic. "I feel like I'm on a marathon arts pilgrimage." She pulled Madison closer. "Thank you."

"You're doing my parents proud. They've been trying to get me to do this for years. Instead I learned to box and shoot guns."

"And quite well. Now for more culture."

"Have I told you I love you?"

Karlie looked at her watch. "Not in the last hour."

Madison just smiled and allowed her lover to drag her along on their next adventure.

❖

On Christmas Eve, Madison walked arm in arm with Karlie down to the Seine. A bateau had been chartered just for their evening cruise, and it was almost time to board. Over the last few days, she had been more at peace than ever in her life. She knew she was making the right decision. Once they were seated, she ordered champagne. It was a large boat, one that could easily seat seventy or eighty people, but they were the only guests. "May I propose a toast?"

"To us?"

"Kind of. To promises kept. A year ago I asked you to move in with me." The joy vanished from Karlie's face. "Wait. You were right. I was afraid. I felt comfortable with the way things were—you in New York and me in Miami." Madison reached across the table and took Karlie's hand. "You've made me want things I didn't know I wanted. I do want to live with you—more than I want to practice law."

Karlie gasped. "I thought sex was the only thing you loved more than the law."

"Ouch. That's my old Karlie." Madison smiled, falling more in love every moment. "Only with you, dear."

"I'm sorry. That just slipped out."

"Let's step outside. The view right now is magnificent." Madison held Karlie's coat as she slipped it on. December on the river was generally cold and damp. Outside, the Eiffel Tower was sparkling with thousands of lights.

"It's beautiful," Karlie said. "I've never seen anything so lovely." She turned and found Madison's arms. "Please hold me. I need to be close to you. Let's just look." Madison pulled Karlie tighter and turned them so they both could watch the Eiffel Tower lights. When she felt Karlie shivering in the cold, she led them both inside. A covered plate sat in front of Karlie's seat. "Hmm. Wonder what that is?"

Madison helped Karlie to her seat and lifted the cover, revealing a small burgundy velvet box with the name of an English jeweler embossed on the lid. She sat next to Karlie, opened the lid, and held the box out to Karlie. "Karlyn Henderson, will you marry me? I may not have lived up to my promise in the past, but now I can't live without you. I made a promise to you a year ago and I want to remedy it. Marry me?"

Karlie's eyes welled with tears. "Yes, Madison, if you're absolutely sure."

"More than anything." She removed the ring from the box and placed it on Karlie's finger.

"Alice B and me?"

Madison laughed. "Yes, you and our dog."

"*Our* dog. God, I love the way that sounds, especially when a little voice in me kept warning me that you might be changing your mind." Karlie brushed Madison's thick hair. "I love you so much."

Madison wiped away the tears. Karlie's face was so soft she felt like she was touching love. Her hand trembled on Karlie's cheek. "Two of my junior partners have asked to become senior partners. I've promoted my secretary to executive assistant, so she will run all the day-to-day operations. I'm free of the practice except to occasionally attend some partner meetings."

"You're full of surprises. I do love you, and"—Karlie gestured to the room filled with wait staff, musicians, and crew, and lowered her voice—"if there weren't so many people in this room, I would make mad passionate love to you right here."

Madison raised an eyebrow. "I think there's a private suite on board if you want to avoid dinner, but you'd miss the view as we circle Île de la Cité and Notre Dame."

"Ugh, there's something almost sacrilegious about having sex anywhere within five hundred feet of such a religious symbol. I can wait. Let's eat. Food, I mean."

Madison laughed, happy that everything had gone smoothly so far.

That evening, when they had returned to their hotel, there was a new intensity to their lovemaking. Madison couldn't believe she was capable of the things Karlie made her feel. For the first time in her life, making love brought her near to tears. As the tension built in her body, she whispered, "I love you so much, Karlie," and those words brought her to a magnificent orgasm. She trembled and clung to Karlie. "Hold me. Hold me just like this always."

Karlie did.

Gun Brooke lives and works in her Viking-era village in Sweden, where she divides her time between writing, family, friends, and dogs. She often visits the USA on her travels and is constantly on the lookout for great characters and locations. This short story takes us back to Carolyn and Annelie from *Course of Action*, the very first romance Gun published with Bold Strokes. These characters also make an appearance in Gun's latest romance, *Fierce Overture* (July 2010).

Through the Eyes of a Child
Gun Brooke

Christmas Eve

"But, Carolyn, you're not ready." The reproach in Annelie Peterson's voice was obvious, but the tenderness in her eyes belied her exasperated expression.

"I…I think this might be a mistake, darling." Carolyn Black donned her best version of a convincing smile as she tugged at the belt of her silk robe. Sitting at her vanity, she had begun to put on impeccable makeup, making sure every auburn hair was in place, but she was not dressed. She told herself that she had rehearsed similar scenes in movies and films enough times to make it sound believable.

"You don't fool me for a second," her wife said quietly and took her by the shoulders, effectively vanquishing the illusion that she'd ever be able to fool the stunning, tall blonde whom she'd loved more than life for over five years.

"I don't?"

"No. You're intimidated at what's going on, and you hate that." Annelie pressed her full lips to Carolyn's temple.

"No, I mean, yes, perhaps, but I still think that subjecting Piper to a multitude of friends so soon is perhaps not the best course of action."

"Are you sure that's the real reason?" Annelie didn't break contact, and her bright blue eyes penetrated every single one of Carolyn's defenses, as usual.

"No." Carolyn rolled her shoulders. "I'm not sure of much of anything, but the fact remains, Piper's been with us for less than two months—"

"And she's already dressed in her Christmas dress that you bought her, sitting on the stairs, waiting."

"She is?" Carolyn faltered, unable to remember what she intended to say. "Perhaps because we more or less talked her into this."

"She'll be introduced to family and friends who will be her support network next to the two of us." Annelie was frowning now, a familiar but certainly disconcerting knitting of her perfect eyebrows that could still make Carolyn cringe.

"What if we introduce them to her a few at a time?"

"But, Carolyn, we've done that. Your sister and her family. Jem and the others at Key Line Productions. Now we're extending her world a little more by having our annual Christmas party. I don't see the harm." Annelie pulled Carolyn off the vanity chair and into her arms. "Unless you have a reason you're not telling me about?"

"I don't. I just don't want to do anything that puts unnecessary pressure on her. She's just a child."

"And you're a mother hen." Annelie's narrow features softened as she leaned in for a kiss. She nibbled along Carolyn's lips, coaxing them apart.

"I'm not!" Carolyn insisted after the deep, searing kiss ended. Annelie's mouth usually distracted her no end, but right now thoughts of what was best for Piper took precedence.

"You have about twenty minutes before our guests are here. If we were going to cancel, it's a tad on the late side."

"All right, all right," Carolyn muttered and sat down at the vanity again. "I'll be ready in two minutes." Carolyn snorted at Annelie's expression of doubt. "I promise. Two minutes." She pulled her shoulder-length hair into her trademark twist and pushed bobby pins into it without even looking. Perfecting the already applied mascara and blush took twenty seconds, some dark berry red lipstick took another ten, and then she slipped into a black cocktail dress and black pumps. "There."

Annelie looked impressed and quite shocked. "You're telling me that you could've moved that fast at any given time during our years together and you've kept it a secret?"

"Funny." Carolyn stood and gently but insistently pushed Annelie up against the door leading into their walk-in closet. She held Annelie by her waist and pressed her lips against her neck, inwardly blessing whoever invented her smearproof lipstick. Annelie's familiar scent of citrus and vanilla made Carolyn dizzy and she had to remind herself they were running late. She reluctantly let go, but was pleased to see Annelie's eyes darkened with the same passion. *Five years, and she can still take my breath away. And I hers, apparently.* Carolyn thought back to the time when it had just been the two of them. A few months ago, their lives had changed forever, but most of all it changed irreversibly for a little nine-year-old girl named Piper.

Two months earlier

Annelie looked at the sleeping child next to her. The plane was only thirty minutes from landing at Miami International. It had been a long flight, more than five hours, and the little girl had already been exhausted before they left Los Angeles.

Finding an unusually rain-drenched City of Angels utterly depressing, Annelie had spent most of her forty-eight-hour stay indoors. It had been an eerie sense of continued déjà vu when she'd sat in the social worker's office, trying to wrap her brain around the fact that she had a little family member she'd never known existed. So used to being alone until she met Carolyn, Annelie had sometimes envied the people around her with large families. A place to feel safe, where you could be yourself among people who actually knew you. The real you. Annelie saw that when Carolyn spent time with her younger sister Beth and her family, she was far from the famous iconic actress who couldn't go anywhere without being recognized. She would tumble with the kids and joke with Beth and her husband Joe. Nowadays, they all regarded Annelie just as much a part of their family, which had taken some getting used to.

Glancing down at the white-blond head resting against her shoulder, Annelie sighed. *I'm going from no living relatives to having a little sister.* It was so surreal, it wasn't even funny. Suddenly blinking away persistent tears, Annelie thought of the haunted look in Piper's eyes when the social worker introduced them at the temporary foster parents' house. Her first impression was a pair of huge, porcelain blue eyes in a triangular little face, looking at her with a dulled expression. The unreal feeling was reinforced by the fact that her little sister looked exactly like Annelie at that age. Unexpected, since Annelie was the very image of her mother. *Perhaps my father fell for a certain type of woman. Blond, tall, and curvaceous.*

Annelie's father had only lived with Piper's mother for a year, then left before the little girl was born. He had never paid any child support or taken any interest in Piper whatsoever, something that didn't surprise Annelie in the least. She remembered many birthdays and Christmases when she'd waited by the phone and the mailbox, hoping to hear from him. It hurt her to imagine this elfin girl doing the same, and pained her even more to think of Piper losing her mother less than a week ago. The social worker had sounded relieved to find a relative so soon, and had been quite perplexed when the half-sister turned out to be a famous Hollywood producer and publisher. At first this seemed to bother the conscientious woman, but she mellowed when she realized Annelie was also a prolific philanthropist who generated enormous amounts for programs for women and children, as well as HIV/AIDs victims of any age.

"Piper, this is your big sister Annelie." The social worker carefully made the introduction together with the foster parents. Piper had not spoken a word for the first hour, but when it became apparent she was going to stay with Annelie, she had whisperingly asked if Annelie's trailer park was far from where she had stayed with her mother.

"Oh, Piper." Annelie sank to her knees, taking both of Piper's hands in gentle grip. "I don't live in a trailer park. I live in a house in Miami, Florida. I have plane tickets for us to go there tomorrow. I'll be back here tomorrow morning to pick you up."

"I can't go with you now? Please?" Piper asked and clung to Annelie's fingers, her own hands ice cold.

"No, sweetie. Not yet. Tomorrow."

"You promise to come back?"

It broke Annelie's heart to hear Piper plead. "I promise." Annelie acted on impulse and pulled the little girl into her arms. She felt how thin Piper was, how she trembled. Annelie rocked her, wanting to infuse some of her own warmth. When she let go, she dug in her purse for a business card. "Here. If there is anything you need, or you just want to say hello, you can call this number." Annelie pointed at the number at the bottom. "That goes to my cell phone."

"Okay." Piper pressed the business card to her chest.

"Ladies and gentlemen, we've started our descent to Miami International and expect to touch down in fifteen minutes…" The captain's voice made Annelie flinch and return to the present. Piper still slept soundly, and considering this was her first flight ever, it was no doubt a sign of her exhaustion that she hadn't been able to keep her eyes open.

"Piper? Sweetie? We're about to land."

Piper stirred and then sat up, wide eyed when she noticed she had slept leaning against Annelie. "Will Ca-Carolyn be there?"

"I know she will. She's so eager to meet you."

"She won't think I'm in the way?"

"Far from it." Annelie knew that Carolyn was probably pacing the VIP section of Miami International as they spoke, impatiently waving off the staff as they tried to cater to her. "She's been really busy getting your room ready."

"My room." Piper suddenly had that dazed look from yesterday when Annelie first met her.

"Shh. Everything will be fine." Annelie hoped she sounded more convincing that she felt.

Christmas Eve

"You thinking about what Santa might bring tomorrow?" Carolyn asked and sat down next to Piper halfway down the landing.

"Santa?" Piper blinked repeatedly. "I don't think he knows I'm here. He thinks I'm still at the trailer park with…with Mama."

"Oh, honey." Carolyn hugged Piper close. She kissed the top of Piper's head. "I think Santa knows exactly where you are. And he knows you lost your mom as well, sweetie. He knows these things."

"Really?"

"Absolutely," Annelie chimed in, sending Carolyn a grateful nod as she took a seat on Piper's other side. "Santa is a clever guy."

"Not always," Piper murmured.

"What do you mean?" Carolyn asked.

"He didn't always come to the trailer park. He forgot me and my friends." Piper sighed.

"Oh, honey, I understand." Annelie briefly touched Piper's cheek, but the girl pulled back suddenly.

"No, you don't." Piper sounded angry and glowered at Annelie and Carolyn. Her small body was tense and she trembled. "You don't know *anything*. You never came to see us. You never saw how sick Mama was."

"Piper, sweetheart." Carolyn spoke softly. "We didn't know. If anyone had contacted Annelie, we would've helped, I promise."

"Nobody could help Mama." Piper stood up, but her legs buckled beneath her and she slumped down on the plush-carpeted step again. "Mama was always afraid that social workers would take me away from her. I tried to tell her that she shouldn't worry. I wouldn't let them take me, but…then she left *me*." She wiped furiously at her eyes. "That's not fair."

"God almighty, it's not fair at all," Annelie muttered.

"You know what? You're right." Carolyn extended a hand to Piper. "We have only some idea what you've been through. I lost my mother when I was twelve, just a little older than you. I had to take care of my sister, who was one, and my brother, who was six, because my father had to work."

Piper sobbed, but her eyes had softened marginally. "Really?"

"Really." Carolyn motioned for Piper to move closer. "And one thing I can promise you, you're going to be okay. You will think of your mama many times and cry, but you'll be fine in the end."

"How do you know that?"

"We just do." Annelie wrapped her arms around Piper and Carolyn. "And there's one more thing I know for sure." She waited until Piper's curiosity made the girl scoot closer. "Your mama wouldn't want you to be sad forever. She wanted what was best for you. Always. That's what mothers do."

"Yes." Piper nodded and finally relaxed into Annelie's arms. "I just want her back so bad."

"Of course you do. That's only natural." Annelie looked through tears at Carolyn. The thin arms around her neck obviously choked her in more ways than one. "I can make you another promise, Piper. You're not alone. We're not going to abandon you."

Trembling and crying quietly, Piper hid in Annelie's arms long enough for her legs to go numb and her back to ache, but Annelie kept her gentle hold on the little girl. Eventually Piper's tears ceased and she accepted a tissue from Carolyn.

"Let's go downstairs and make sure everything is ready for the party." Carolyn rose. "I think I can hear cars pulling up outside."

❖

The house glittered and sparkled like a treasure chest. Not one but three Christmas trees stood tall and abundantly decorated in the living, family, and dining rooms. Illuminated garlands adorned the doorways and staircase railings, and Mary's efforts at the stove added to the holiday spirit as their aromas wafted from the kitchen. Carolyn stood in the wide doorway leading into the living room, where all their guests gathered around the fireplace. Outside, Miami was quite cool, which in turn added to the illusion of a winter season. The skyline across the water was a jewel in its own right, reflecting in the calm water. A few illuminated boats glided silently across the bay, making it picture perfect.

"The last of our guests are arriving, Carolyn. Noelle and Helena are walking up the driveway as we speak."

"Oh, so that's actually Noelle singing 'Silent Night'? I thought you put her new Christmas CD on." Carolyn smiled and tilted her head. In the distance a strong, blues-inspired voice could be heard singing. "Can you believe that voice?"

"Can anyone? Noelle has shown the world that she can sing *anything.*"

"And Piper?" Carolyn looked around, suddenly alarmed.

"She's playing with Pamela. Beth is keeping an eye on them, and she says it's like they've been friends forever."

"I think we should take turns staying close to her, at least for now," Annelie said, still looking concerned. "She looked a bit shell-shocked at first at the sight of this many people. Perhaps you were right and we should've canceled our plans?"

"Actually, I think *you* were right." Carolyn brushed her thumb across Annelie's lower lip. "This way she sees that life goes on. It will become part of what's normal for her from now on. Piper will be fine."

"All right." Annelie took a deep breath. "Oh, look, I think Chicory Ariose are arriving."

"Oh, good, they made it." Carolyn smiled at the thought of the famous all-women group. "Tell them I'll be there in a little bit."

Annelie took the time to kiss Carolyn softly on the lips before she walked toward the cheerful voices, calling out "Merry Christmas" to everybody.

Carolyn hid halfway behind a column next to one of the Christmas trees, spying on the two girls sitting on the stairs together, one auburn head and one blond close together while looking at something Piper was holding. The sudden thought that Pamela looked so much like her, and Piper being the spitting image of Annelie, brought tears to Carolyn's eyes. Piper was the image of an angel in white leggings and a crisp light blue cotton dress that went almost to her knees. Carolyn knew Annelie hadn't expected her to pick up something quite so stylish for a nine-year-old, but Carolyn had claimed that this outfit was much more Piper than a regular red or green Christmas dress that would make the child cringe. The fact was, this looked entirely right on Piper, and the girl's pink cheeks spoke volumes when she tried it on before the party.

"Helena and Manon are asking for—oh…" Annelie stopped behind Carolyn and wrapped her arms around her, resting her cheek against her wife's temple. "They look like us."

"They do, don't they?"

"Are you crying, Carolyn?" Annelie's voice took on a tinge of worry.

"Not really."

"Liar." Annelie dipped her head and kissed Carolyn's cheek.

"Trying to save face at our party." Carolyn laughed and wiped quickly at her cheeks where a few errant tears clung to her skin. "She's really going to be okay in time, isn't she?"

"You and I are doing pretty well, and we had similar things to deal with. I think I can say we have a good insight into what she's going through, and that's half the battle."

Carolyn agreed. She listened to the two young girls whisper, and suddenly Piper laughed out loud. "Oh, my. I don't think I've ever heard her laugh before."

"Neither have I." Annelie's voice caught. "Having Pamela in her life will make just as much of a difference for her as having access to either of us."

"All the better that Beth and Joe are moving to Miami after the holidays." Carolyn turned within Annelie's embrace. "It was brilliant of you to offer him and Beth the chance of a lifetime."

"Are you kidding? Key Line Publishing is lucky to get our hands on Joe's talents within the IT sector. Remember what happened when it was time for the first Diana Maddox convention? We drowned in e-mails from readers. Our system nearly crashed. Not to mention that Jem nearly had a heart attack before it was sorted. It seems to happen every time you are involved, be it conventions or movie releases. Your brother-in-law will be our secret weapon to make sure that never happens again."

"He's over the moon about it, and Beth can't wait to go back to nursing."

"Nurses are always in high demand."

"It will be easier for both their kids and Piper to acclimatize in a new school when they already know each other." Carolyn absentmindedly rubbed the small of Annelie's back. "I don't go on location for another two months."

"Your third Diana Maddox movie. Getting tired of it?" Annelie was teasing her, but Carolyn knew every single nuance of her wife's voice and easily detected a faint concern.

"Tired of Maddox? Are you kidding? Playing her is the role of a lifetime, and you know she brought me to you. How could I ever be tired of her?"

"I second that." Annelie kissed Carolyn softly, making her tremble at the thought of having her completely to herself later.

"They do that all the time. Kissing." Pamela's clear voice interrupted the embrace, and Carolyn turned to look at her.

"You spying, little Ms. Pam?"

"Hardly," Pamela said with a grin. "You're standing here smooching in the middle of the party."

Carolyn gazed around her, and it was true. Their guests were all within sight, and there was more than one indulgent smile flashed their way. "Oh, great."

"That's what married people do," Piper said, her little voice matter-of-fact. "They smooch all day and have babies."

Faint laughter traveled through the crowd of friends.

Even Annelie laughed. "You're more right than you realize, Piper." She pulled Carolyn close with one arm and Piper with the other. "Smooching all day, and then we had a baby. You."

Now the sound of laughter escalated and even Piper grinned broadly. "I'm hardly a baby."

"No, not a baby, but a child, at least." Carolyn cupped Piper's thin neck. "And a child who is showing more and more signs of being a true rascal, I might add."

This turned out to be a most pleasing comment for Piper, judging by the brilliance of her smile.

"I propose a toast for this new little family, and to all of us, family and friends," Beth said and raised her glass.

"Family and friends," the guests echoed and raised their glasses in return.

Carolyn couldn't imagine ever being happier than she was in that instant. Standing in Annelie's embrace with both their arms protectively around Piper, and only seeing love and acceptance in everybody's eyes—surely this was what "utter bliss" meant?

"I love you, Annelie, and I love you, too, Piper," she murmured after sipping some champagne.

"I love you, Carolyn." Annelie quickly kissed her temple.

"Me too, Carolyn." Piper's voice was barely audible. "I think I'd like some smooches, too."

Overwhelmed by tenderness and hardly able to breathe, Carolyn bent forward and kissed Piper's forehead. "Sweetheart."

A husky voice interrupted the emotional moment. "Merry Christmas, everybody!"

"It's Jem!" Pamela jumped up and ran over to the brunette who had just entered the scene. "And she's got a big bag of Christmas presents. How come, Jem?" Pamela's eyes glittered.

"Ah, you see, I ran into Santa, who said that he was really busy and needed some help. There are even more presents than these. Santa says he's bringing the rest over tonight when we're asleep."

"There's *more*?" Piper's wide eyes showed her disbelief.

"You bet. Now, should we place this under the tree, or…?" Jem looked around, smiling broadly.

"Why don't you do the honors and hand out some to the kids?" Annelie walked over to Jem. "I'll help."

Carolyn sat down with her glass of champagne, thoroughly enjoying the scene before her. The children squealed and alternated between hugging their presents, Annelie, and Jem, who apparently enjoyed being "Aunty Claus."

"Isn't this amazing?" Beth came to join Carolyn. "You're a mother again, Carolyn."

"Guess I am."

Annelie and Piper looked so much like mother and daughter, Carolyn had to blink several times to keep the tears away.

"Carolyn—?" Annelie tilted her head questioningly. "Are you all right?"

"Never better." Carolyn stood and let Annelie wrap her close. "And there are even better days to come."

PJ TREBELHORN was born and raised in the Pacific Northwest, having spent the first twenty-eight years of her life in the Portland, Oregon, area. She currently resides in eastern Pennsylvania with her partner of fourteen years and their menagerie of pets—six cats and one extremely neurotic pug/Jack Russell mix dog. PJ enjoys movies, sports, writing, and reading, though not necessarily in that order. The characters in this story are from the romance *From This Moment On*. Her next novel, *True Confessions*, will be released in 2011 by Bold Strokes Books.

A Christmas Wish

PJ Trebelhorn

Katherine Hunter glanced at her watch as she pushed the car door shut and headed for her porch. *Shit, we're never going to get everything ready in time.* She faltered in the doorway of the living room, smiling at the cozy site on her couch.

Her lover, Devon Conway, appeared to be sound asleep, one arm cradling Kat's one-year-old granddaughter Cathy protectively against her chest. The baby was sleeping, too, and Buddy, the beagle, was curled up next to Dev's feet. Baxter, the gray and white fuzzball Dev had rescued, had stretched out on Dev's thighs, as cats often do. Kat tiptoed over to them and knelt down so she could study Dev's face.

A year ago at this time, Dev had just been released from the hospital, and those few weeks right around Christmas had been rough for both of them. She'd talked Dev into staying with her so that Dev's godmother, Sheila, wouldn't have to bear all the burden of Dev's care. She'd taken time away from her veterinary clinic to take Dev to her doctor's and physical therapy appointments.

PT had been the hardest part of Dev's recovery, and more often than not after those appointments, Dev had been in a foul mood, and in much more pain than she would ever let Kat believe. But Dev had slowly recovered, and they'd made her move into the house a permanent one.

And now, a full year after that horrible night Kat had spent in the hospital worrying about the two women who were everything in her life, she and Devon were living together and babysitting little Cathy whenever they had the opportunity. They were both happy, and life was finally good again.

As Kat glanced at Cathy, she felt her throat constrict at the memory of her premature birth and the risk it posed to her daughter, Vanessa. Vanessa and Josh had tied the knot three weeks earlier and were due to return from their honeymoon in just a few hours. It was Christmas Eve, and Kat was looking forward to having her family with her this year. Having everyone in her family healthy was only one of the wishes she had made for this Christmas. Another was that Dev would answer in the affirmative to a question she intended to ask before the night was over.

"Hi there," Kat said, smiling when Dev's bright blue eyes opened.

Dev cleared her throat. "I'm sorry. I really didn't mean to fall asleep. She was crying, and I just wanted to lie down with her for a few minutes."

"It certainly appears as if you figured out a way to make her stop." Kat gently smoothed the baby's hair. The two of them together were so beautiful her heart stuttered. She stroked Dev's cheek. "Do you have any idea how incredibly sexy you are?"

"Grandmas aren't supposed to think things like that." Dev displayed the slow, sexy grin that had drawn Kat in from the moment they met.

"Are you trying to tell me you don't think things like that?"

"I'm not a grandma." Dev's arm tightened around the baby when she stirred slightly. "I'm not old enough to be a grandma."

"Honey, this right here"—Kat motioned toward the two of them—"pretty much makes you as much of a grandmother as I am, and believe me, you're old enough. My mother was only thirty-seven when Vanessa was born. And besides that, you've apparently bonded with this little girl more than I have."

"Jealous?" Dev smiled.

"Not at all. In fact, I'm in awe."

Kat stood and gently picked Cathy up. Dev stretched, and Buddy jumped down with an annoyed huff. Baxter, however, simply shifted his position and stretched out on his back between Dev's legs. Kat put Cathy in her crib on the other side of the room, liking the way Dev's gaze followed her. When she returned, Dev grinned and put her hands behind her head. "You're great with her, you know. I'm not quite sure what I ever did to deserve you, Devon."

"I've often wondered that very same thing myself."

Dev moved over and Kat sat next to her on the edge of the couch, chuckling. "Modest much?"

"Not usually, no." Dev snaked an arm around Kat's waist and pulled her close. "What time is it?"

"After three." Kat knew she shouldn't indulge herself in the arms of her lover because it always led to other things. Things they didn't have time for right now. But she couldn't help it. She kissed Dev's cheek. "We have a lot to do before everybody gets here. You still need to run to the store and get beer, and I need to get the food ready."

"Cathy and I went to the store right after you left for that emergency at the animal clinic." Dev's voice turned husky, and she moved her hand up to cup Kat's breast. Dev's grin told Kat that her quick intake of breath had been the response she was after. "We have enough beer, wine, and assorted alcohol to last us more than a year."

"I suppose it's too much to hope that you got the food ready?" Kat laughed at Dev's fearful expression.

"You know better than to suggest I do anything in the kitchen other than fix a leaky faucet."

"Sweetie, we're just having cheese and crackers and other assorted munchies. The only thing that has to actually be cooked are the cookies."

"Trust me, I'd probably drop the cheese on the floor and Buddy would have the runs for the next week."

Dev smiled when Kat couldn't help but laugh at the visual. Kat let herself be coaxed into stretching out on the couch. Baxter scrambled away as quickly as he could, obviously knowing that things could get heated whenever the two humans got together like this.

"It's better for everyone involved if I just stay out of the kitchen," Dev said.

"What do you think you're doing?" Kat's breath caught in her throat when she felt Dev's hand sliding down the front of her jeans.

"Trying to show you how grateful I am to have you in my life," Dev whispered, her breath hot in Kat's ear. "Baby, you have no idea how much I want you right now."

"Jesus, Devon," Kat gasped when she felt the undeniable rush of arousal course through her. "Honey, it is *so* not a good time for this. The baby is here, and we have eight people coming over in a couple of hours."

"Then promise me we'll continue this later tonight, after everyone is gone."

"I promise. You and me, bedroom, the very *second* the last person leaves."

❖

Dev scanned the room for Kat. A minute ago she'd been just a few feet away, talking to Rick and his wife. Now she was nowhere to be found. The party was in full swing and everyone seemed to be having a good time. Hostess duties taken care of, she walked through the downstairs looking for her lover, but couldn't find her. Finally, she went up to their room and stopped just outside their bedroom door. Kat was at the sliding glass doors, looking out at the falling snow. Dev leaned against the doorjamb and took a moment to simply watch her. The lights were out, and she only had the moonlight to see her by. Dev's fingers found their way around the small jewelry box in her pocket, and she felt her heart speed up as the nervousness set in.

It didn't surprise her when Kat spoke. It was a kind of sixth sense Kat had developed in the past year. If Dev was anywhere near, Kat knew it without even looking.

"Are you just going to stand there, Ms. Conway, or are you going to come hold me?"

"You never need to ask me twice," Dev said as she crossed the room. She slid her arms around Kat's waist from behind and pulled Kat against her chest, breathing in her faint citrus smell as she closed her eyes and sighed with contentment. Kat tipped her head back to rest on Dev's shoulder.

"You feel so damn good," Dev murmured, kissing the side of Kat's neck.

"I really can't wait until everyone finally leaves."

Kat turned in Dev's arms and rested her forearms lightly on Dev's shoulders. Dev's thigh muscles clenched when Kat's eyes darkened with desire.

Kat pushed one hand through Devon's hair and she pulled her in for a kiss. Dev parted her lips for Kat, and she couldn't stop the groan from escaping when Kat's tongue slid slowly along hers.

"God, you are sexy as hell." Kat was breathing heavily. "You take my breath away."

"You do incredible things to me, too," Dev said, her voice hoarse. She had wanted to give Kat her gift later that night, when they were truly alone in the house, but this seemed like the perfect time. It really didn't seem to matter that there was a house full of people downstairs. "I love you."

"I love you, too. With everything that I am."

"Come sit down with me." Dev pulled away and took Kat's hand, leading her to the bed. They both sat, and Dev smiled at the look of unease on Kat's face. "Relax. I just want to give you something."

"We said we weren't going to exchange gifts until Christmas morning."

"I don't want to wait." Dev took a deep breath to steady her nerves. What if Kat said no? She didn't think she could deal with that. Before she could talk herself out of it, she went on.

"After Jo died, I had convinced myself that she had been my only chance at love. Before I met you, I was resigned to spending the rest of my life alone. I don't know what you did to me, but you somehow managed to steal my heart when I wasn't paying attention. You've made every second of the past fourteen months wonderful."

"Even the times when you were cursing a blue streak because of the pain the physical therapist was putting you through?" Kat smiled, a tear sliding down her cheek.

"Yes, even then, because you were there with me, through every miserable second of it." Dev gently brushed the tear away with her thumb, but another followed. "I don't ever want to make you cry, baby."

"They're happy tears, Dev. You make me so happy." Kat placed a hand on Dev's cheek, and Dev closed her eyes as she leaned into the touch.

"You make me happy, too." Dev caught Kat's hand and kissed the inside of her wrist. After another deep breath to calm the butterflies, she stood and pulled out the jewelry box from her pocket. "Bear with me, Kat. I've never done this before."

"Dev—"

"Shh," Dev interrupted, "please let me do this." She dropped to one knee and opened the box, holding it so Kat could see the ring it contained. She gained the confidence she needed when Kat placed one hand on her chest, fingers splayed, and the other covered her mouth. There were more tears, but Kat just let them fall. "I can't imagine spending even one day without you for the rest of my life. Katherine Hunter, will you marry me?"

Kat laughed, and Dev's heart dropped at the sound. Kat's expression indicated she regretted the reaction, but as far as Dev was concerned, it was too late. She got to her feet and snapped the box shut. When Kat grasped her wrist, Dev pulled it away, stuffing the box back into her pocket. She headed for the door, not entirely sure where she intended to go.

"Devon, please," Kat said.

Dev was almost to the hall, but she hesitated long enough for Kat to reach her. Kat gripped Dev's shoulder and pulled her around.

"I am so sorry I laughed," Kat said. "You have to believe I wasn't laughing at you. I was laughing at the situation."

"That makes me feel a lot better." Dev's tone was sarcastic, and Kat winced. "You were laughing because I proposed."

"If you'll let me explain, you'll laugh, too. I know you will."

Dev finally walked back to the bed and sat waiting for the explanation.

Kat hurried to the dresser, pulled out a small box wrapped in festive green and red holiday paper, and held the gift out to her. "I was going to give you this tonight anyway. This just wasn't the way I pictured doing it."

Dev slowly took the box and unwrapped it. "Is this what I think it is?"

"Open it and find out."

Dev opened the lid and gasped when she saw the ring.

"Now do you see why I reacted the way I did?" Kat asked.

"Yeah." Dev smiled and wiped away a tear. "And you're right. I probably would have laughed if you'd given me this before I gave you mine."

"Is it safe to assume your answer is yes?" Kat took the ring and held it, waiting for Dev to offer her left hand.

"Yes." Dev smiled when Kat slid it on her ring finger. "My answer to you will always be yes."

Dev pulled the box out of her pocket again, removed the ring, and put it on Kat's finger.

"I love you, Devon."

"And I love you."

"I was so worried you'd say no."

"*You* were worried?" Dev snorted. "I think Nessa was convinced I was going into shock when I finally decided on a ring."

"Nessa knew you were doing this?" Kat somehow managed to stop the laugh this time. *Wait until I get my hands on that kid.*

"I needed her help. I wasn't sure what kind of ring you would want because you don't wear much jewelry. I also needed her to convince me you wouldn't say no."

"She helped me pick your ring, too." Kat chuckled. "I've got one hell of a sneaky daughter. If I didn't know better, I'd think she planned all of this."

"*We* have one hell of a sneaky daughter." Dev held up her left hand to wave the ring in Kat's face. "She's started calling me *mom* when you aren't around."

Kat put her arms around Dev's neck and pulled her closer for a kiss.

"Jesus, Kat," Dev said breathlessly. "I can't believe the things you do to me."

"You ain't seen nothing yet, baby." Kat began to undo the buttons on Devon's shirt.

Dev covered Kat's hands and laughed. "We have guests downstairs."

"How can you even think about them right now?" Kat gave a pretty good imitation of a pout. "They'll never know we're gone."

"Yeah, well, I don't know about you, but I would really hate it if your little niece walked in here thinking it was the bathroom, only to find us naked and writhing around on the bed."

"*Our* niece."

"That's all you have to say? You aren't worried about things like that?"

"No one's going to walk in on us. Everyone's gone, Devon." Kat resumed unbuttoning the shirt when Dev's hands dropped away. "I talked to Nessa before I came up here. I told her that when she saw you come up the stairs looking for me, to make sure everyone left. She knew I was going to propose to you tonight. She was happy to do it—because she's exhausted from the honeymoon. I told her she shouldn't have planned to come back on Christmas Eve."

Dev backed away and looked out the window. Dev slowly returned, letting her shirt fall to the floor. "There are no cars in the driveway. Everyone really is gone. You tricked me, Katherine."

"True." Kat raised her arms, allowing Dev to remove her sweater. She groaned when Dev's mouth found her nipple and bit it lightly through her bra. She held Dev's head against her with one hand while reaching back with the other and unsnapping her bra. "Are you complaining?"

"Never." Dev watched Kat's eyes darken with desire.

Wishes really do come true.

LESLEY DAVIS lives with her American partner Cindy in the West Midlands of England. She is a die-hard science-fiction/fantasy fan in all its forms and an extremely passionate gamer. When her Nintendo DSi is out of her grasp, Lesley is seated before the computer writing. *Truth Behind The Mask* was her first publication with Bold Strokes Books. She has short stories in *Erotic Interludes 2: Stolen Moments*, *Road Games: Erotic Interludes 5*, and *Romantic Interludes 2: Secrets*. A novel entitled *Playing Passion's Game* is forthcoming in 2011. "Christmas in Chastilian" revisits characters from *Truth Behind The Mask*.

Christmas in Chastilian

Lesley Davis

Poised atop the stepladder, Pagan Osborne leaned with her arm outstretched.

"Hey! Be careful!" Erith Baylor stood below, her hands wrapped tightly around the stepladder's legs, her foot resting on the bottom rung to hold the steps steady.

Pagan stared down in amusement. "Excuse me? I spend most of the night traversing up and down buildings suspended only by wire, and you're worried I might lose my balance on a stepladder?" She grinned at the sharp look Erith shot at her.

"I have the utmost confidence in you when you don your Sentinel suit and watch over the city at night. And I remember all too clearly how marvellous you are at flying through the air after that time you jumped off a building with me in your arms." Her eyes got a faraway look in them as she obviously recalled that night. Shaking her head, she gave Pagan a firm look.

"But right here, right now, the fact you are perched upon a stepladder trying to drape tinsel garlands around the biggest tree I have ever seen is giving me cause for concern."

Pagan snorted at Erith's unusually polite choice of words. "Cause for concern?"

"You're freakin' the hell out of me! There, satisfied?" Erith grumbled. "Just drape the damn stuff and be done up there."

Laughing, Pagan carefully fixed the bright gold piece of tinsel around a high tree branch, then wrapped the rest around the lower branches. "You can't just drape the tinsel any old how, sweetheart. Every piece has to be positioned just right. Believe me, I learnt that from the master."

"Says who?" Erith asked, tugging gently at the cuff of Pagan's jeans.

"So will say the Master herself when she appears," Rogue Ronchetti announced as she walked into the room. She stopped in her tracks, taking in the sight before her. "Great job you're doing there, Pagan. Have you untangled the lights yet?"

"No, I thought I'd leave that job for you." Pagan reached over a little bit more, conscious of Erith's sharp intake of breath from below her, and just tweaked the tinsel into place. She caught Rogue mutter thanks for getting left with the worst job and then heard a faint tinkle as the mass of lights was lifted out from the box. Pagan twisted a dial on her hearing aids so she could hear every single sound. She loved the tiny noises that the lights made when tangled up with the string of bells Rogue had tossed in there last year when they had taken down the decorations. Once again she was grateful that Rogue had fashioned the aids that helped her hear when her world was usually so silent. Smiling at the contented feeling spreading through her, Pagan sat down on top of the stepladder and gazed down at Erith. "You could be decorating the lower branches, you know."

"Yeah," Rogue added, "at least you'd be able to reach those." With her back turned, she missed Erith's glare.

"Just because I'm not as tall as all of you are," Erith grumbled as she climbed up a few steps to rest her hands on Pagan's knees. "Or as handsome, or dark haired, or so totally gorgeous it blows my mind." She caressed Pagan's cheek and smiled when Pagan planted a kiss in her palm. "Tell me, why the need for such a big tree? And a real one at that? It's going to shed like a bitch!"

Pagan brushed her fingers through Erith's bright red hair and thrilled to the softness that tickled her fingertips. "Because it's just not Christmas without having a proper tree. You need that pine scent to fill your nostrils, have to see the lights shining through real branches. Artificial trees are all well and good, but nothing says Christmas like a real tree."

Erith leaned her cheek into Pagan's hand. "Well, just don't expect me to clean up after it when it's shed its needles all over your floor." Her gaze returned to the tree. "I can't remember the last time my family had a tree," she admitted softly.

Pagan's hand stilled in Erith's hair. "Did you not celebrate?"

Erith shrugged. "Not really. Dad didn't like to spend money on anything other than himself, and any decorations we did have usually ended up being used as a weapon when he'd gotten enough drink inside him. So I don't really remember having a Christmas where there wasn't some sort of trouble." She must have read Pagan's sadness in her face. "Hey, there's to be no sad eyes. This year is going to be different."

"Yes, it is." Pagan pressed her lips to Erith's forehead.

Melina Osborne, Pagan's older sister, walked into the living room and Pagan whispered into Erith's ear, "The Master has arrived."

"Wow, I have to admit I didn't think that tree would have fit in here but it has. When you and Pagan brought it home, Rogue, I was certain you were going to have to cut a hole in the ceiling for it to fit."

Rogue left the lights and swept Melina into her arms. "I cut a hole in the floor. We can always cover it with the carpet after." She stilled Melina's gasp with a kiss and grinned at her. "We picked a good one. It's going to look beautiful when Pagan gets off her butt to finish decorating it."

Taking the hint, Pagan rose and gestured for the lights. "Let's get this thing covered, then. Melina, please show Erith how you like your tree to look."

Melina guided Erith over to a large box full of all manner of baubles. "Some of these are years old. We add a few new ones every year when the older ones start to fade or get broken. Mom and Dad used to take us to pick new decorations and Pagan would always pick the biggest and brightest. On our first Christmas without them I wasn't sure I wanted to even bother putting up a tree, but Rogue took Pagan to pick out her new baubles and they came back with a tree. The pleasure on Pagan's face made me realise I couldn't deprive her of Christmas, too." Melina gave her lover a tender look. "Rogue told me life goes on regardless, and family traditions are what keep family together even when we're separated." She wrapped an arm around Erith's waist and drew her close. "Later we'll go shopping for this year's baubles to hang on the tree, your baubles, because you're a part of our family now and the tradition includes you."

Pagan's heart clenched at the joy that coloured Erith's face. Erith had suffered under the hands of a tyrannical father and a mother who had been too scared to keep her only child safe. Erith's father had chosen the wrong side of the law to fight on, and just a few months previous, Pagan and her fellow Sentinels had gone up against the Phoenix, the man Erith's father had put before his family. Fighting the Phoenix and his followers had devastated the city of Chastilian and cost too many lives, but it had brought Erith to Pagan. With the Phoenix dead and his followers imprisoned, the city was starting to rebuild itself and the Sentinels had returned to watching over the city at night in relative peace.

Pagan was grateful that this year would soon be over, closing the book on what had been a terrifying chapter in Chastilian's history. Melina and Rogue unfurled the tiny strings of lights together and surreptitiously watched Erith carefully wrap a tinsel bower over and around the tree's branches, her entire concentration on getting it just right for Melina. Pagan loved how her family had welcomed Erith. She couldn't imagine a better place to be at Christmas than with her family here in the home they shared. She smiled wryly at herself. Home. A security specialist shop beneath them, and hidden away in the lighthouse tower, the eyes of the Sighted who guide the Sentinels in their tasks.

"You'd get the job done a lot quicker if you'd stop staring at your girl," Rogue commented, waggling the lights before Pagan's face.

Pagan hastily grabbed at the lights, but not before she saw Erith wink at her. Pagan willed her face not to flame, but Rogue's snicker announced that hadn't worked.

"Pagan, there's a star in here. Do you want to put that on while you're up there?" Erith asked as she dug through the box.

"No, that doesn't go on until Christmas Eve," Pagan replied.

"Let me guess," Erith said. "Another Osborne/Ronchetti tradition?"

Rogue answered her. "Yes, when everything else is decorated, lit up and tinselled to within an inch of its life, only then can the star be placed. It's the crowning piece to signify the lighting of the star in the sky. You'll get used to our strange ways, I promise." Rogue unobtrusively held the stepladder still as Pagan worked her way down, then patted her on the back for a job well done. Pagan beamed at the silent praise.

"I'm finding I like your strange ways." Erith wrapped her arms around Pagan's waist and hugged her close. "Though," she tugged Pagan's short hair, "some of you are stranger than others."

"I am not strange." When Pagan pretended to pout and looked to her family for support, they hastily busied themselves with anything to hand. Rogue even whistled a Christmas carol off-tune. "Thanks," Pagan muttered and picked Erith up off the ground and held her captive in her arms. "For that, you are so cleaning up the needles when this tree sheds!" Captivated as always by the bright lights that shone in Erith's green eyes, Pagan dipped her head and kissed her soundly. "You're going to have a great Christmas," she promised when she finally drew back for air.

Still dazzled by the kiss, Erith just grinned at her. "With all the mistletoe I know Rogue has yet to hang, yes, I think I am."

❖

The weeks before Christmas flew past. Melina gathered reports from the Sentinels that spoke of Chastilian seeming finally free from the Phoenix's chokehold. The police reported that crime had dropped to its more normal level. The Sentinels didn't relax their vigilance, however. Crime bosses didn't remain dormant for long when one had been toppled from his seat, but for now, Chastilian was ready to celebrate the holidays and ring in a very welcome new year.

"Are you actually willing it to snow?" Erith asked softly.

Embarrassed to be caught doing exactly that, Pagan turned away from the dark sky and regarded her love. "It has to snow tonight, it would make everything perfect."

Erith cuddled into Pagan's side and slipped an arm about her waist. "Tell me, Sentinel, what could be more perfect than you and I out in the cold night air—you masked and dressed in some serious sexy leather," Erith's eyes drifted over Pagan's suit, "and me wishing that Rogue's jacket didn't make me feel like I am wearing oversized hand-me-downs." She flapped her arms to show just how long the sleeves were.

Chuckling, Pagan fingered a stray piece of red hair that had escaped from beneath the black knit cap covering Erith's head. "I won't keep you out of the warm for long, I promise. I just wanted to share something with you. It's one of my favourite holiday treats."

Erith stayed close at Pagan's side as she led them out from the back of Ronchetti Security and onto the streets, all the time keeping to the shadows until the shadows from tall buildings provided huge pools of darkness where they could walk comfortably. Pagan checked around her then spoke quietly.

"Heading topside, Sighted."

"We'll keep the home fires burning." Melina's voice was soft in Pagan's ear.

Pagan fastened the clip from her utility belt to a corresponding one on Erith's borrowed jacket. Satisfied they were secured together, Pagan pulled Erith close and aimed her wire gun at the building above them. The soft sound of the wire shooting out barely broke the silence of the night. Pagan felt the wire grip high above her, and with a quick warning to Erith to hold on, she pressed a button and they quickly flew up the side of the building.

"Flying like this with you never gets old," Erith said, grinning at Pagan in sheer exhilaration. "Just like so many other feelings I have with you that I love to relive over and over and over…"

Pagan warmed at Erith's seductive tone. "You know the Sighted can hear every word you're saying, right?"

"She knows all too well how I feel about you. It's written all over my face every moment of every day." Erith snuggled into Pagan's chest as the top of the apartment building neared.

Slowing down their ascent, Pagan expertly found the foothold that would help boost them up onto the rooftop. "Hold tight," she muttered. She easily lifted herself and Erith over the small ornate ledge that ran along the length of the roof, retracted the wire back into her gun, and unfastened Erith's clasp. She noticed that Erith kept close to her even though they were separated. "Are you afraid to be up here?" Pagan asked, concerned. "I know I don't usually bring you up this high."

Erith shook her head. "No. I mean, I'm a little nervous, tall building, long drop, sudden stop and all, but I know I'm safe up here with you. I'm safe wherever you are."

Holding out her hand, Pagan guided Erith over to the far side of the building. "I know you don't really celebrate Christmas, and that the religious pageantry, as you call it, goes right over your head." She lifted Erith's chilled hands to brush a kiss across her knuckles. "I understand all that. For me Christmas is all about family, and you know how important my family is to me."

"They're your world."

"And you are my everything, now and always." Pagan took a deep breath. "You know I love you and that I will protect you until my last breath."

"Pagan," Erith murmured, putting her fingers to Pagan's lips, "don't talk like that."

Kissing her fingertips, Pagan continued, "I have a present for you, something I want to share with you here. Before we exchange gifts with Melina and Rogue tomorrow. This is between you and me, my gift to you if you'll accept it." Reaching inside her jacket, she withdrew an envelope and handed it over to Erith.

"What? You didn't have time to wrap a bow around it?" Erith joked as she opened it up and removed the thick papers. She scanned the sheets by the light of the moon.

Pagan's chest hitched at Erith's startled look.

"Land deeds?"

Nodding, Pagan wrapped her arms about Erith's waist and read over her shoulder. "These are the deeds to the vacant lot next door to Ronchetti Security. I believe it's crying out for a house where you and I can live. That way, we can move out of my room above the business and have our privacy, but we'll still be just a stone's throw away from the lighthouse when duty calls."

"You're giving me a piece of land?" Incredulous, Erith's mouth opened in surprise. "A piece of land to build a home on?"

"We have family members who can work out the plans to design it, and ones to build it exactly how we want it."

In the dark of the night Erith's sudden tears lit up like diamonds, sparkling as they fell upon her cheeks. Spinning around, she flung her arms around Pagan's neck and hugged her tightly, laughing and crying all at the same time.

"Do you like it?" Some of Pagan's nervousness over the enormity of the gift finally eased.

Drawing back, Erith gave her a watery smile. "It's only the best present ever!" She tugged Pagan's head down to kiss her soundly. "A home of our own, you and me." She stilled as a thought struck her. "How the hell are we paying for this?"

Pagan grinned. "The land is paid for. I used my money from the inheritance I got from my parent's deaths. I never needed to touch it before now. Now we just need to mortgage ourselves to the hilt for the building and then we can wrestle with the payments while we grow old and grey together."

Erith laughed delightedly. "God, I love the sound of that. It's a good thing I've gotten a job with your family now, isn't it? We're going to need steady wages coming in if we're going to be homeowners." She reverently folded up the documents and put them safely back inside Pagan's pocket, patting them where they lay. "A home to call my own, somewhere I can be safe and sound. You've just given me the best Christmas present of my whole damn life."

"I hope it's the gift that keeps on giving because I doubt I'll ever be able to top it." Pagan swung Erith's hands in her own. "So, do you want to spend forever with me?"

"Yes." Erith's answer was swift and sure. She shivered a little as the chill night air breezed past. "But you could have given me this surprise at home and gotten the same answer, very likely followed by lots of kissing where I wasn't afraid our lips would freeze together."

Pagan drew Erith along with her to the roof's edge. "I could have, but then I wouldn't have been able to share this with you." She turned Erith around so she could see what Pagan wanted her to witness.

Below them the whole city was alight with the golden glow of homes interspersed with the bright flashes of a multitude of Christmas lights. The city's seasonal decorations were all lit up, framing the buildings in the city centre, edging the parapets, some flashing to a silent rhythm while others blazed their trails around tall trees as focal points in every street. Pagan never failed to find the multicoloured display a delight, not since that first Christmas Rogue had brought her up this same building and shown her the city alight in celebration.

"Oh my God, it's so beautiful," Erith whispered, her gaze searching as far as the horizon where the lights flashed with tiny pinpricks of coloured sparkles.

"Merry Christmas, Erith." Pagan gently kissed her cheek and

held her close as they marvelled at the lights sparkling in the darkness of Christmas Eve. Pagan blinked as something floated past her eyes. Slowly, silently, the first flakes of snow began to drift across the city. Content, Pagan hugged Erith closer and watched the city at rest, ever the Sentinel watching over Chastilian and ever the lover keeping her sweetheart safe.

Clifford Henderson is the author of three novels, including *Foreword* magazine's Gold Medal Book of the Year and Lesbian Fiction Readers' Choice Winner *The Middle of Somewhere*. The characters for "Holiday Gnomosexuals" originated in this novel. Clifford lives and plays in Santa Cruz, California, where she runs The Fun Institute, a school of improv and solo performance, with her partner of nineteen years. In their classes and workshops, people learn to access and express the myriad of characters itching to get out. Her other passions include gardening and twisting herself into weird yoga poses. Her third novel, *Maye's Request*, will be published in 2011. www.cliffordhenderson.net.

Holiday Gnomosexuals

Clifford Henderson

Jameson looked over the rims of his glasses at Buddy Bud down on all fours by the small refrigerator in the corner. He was trying to coax a spider into his custom-made spider catcher, a pickle jar covered in colorful bug stickers. "Come on, you big Bo Bo!" he said, drumming his stubby fingers on the floor behind the spider. "I'm going to take you outside so nobody will kill you."

The tiny black spider didn't move.

Buddy Bud heaved a frustrated sigh. His thick-framed black glasses held in place by a neon green sports strap interrupted the slope of his forehead, and he wore his favorite Dolly Parton T-shirt, so tattered it really should be tossed into the rag bucket. His jeans rode low on his hips, revealing the elastic strip of his BVDs.

Lily wouldn't let him go out looking so ratty, Jameson thought. *She would have found some creative way to get Buddy to make another choice.* Like he'd tried to that morning, only Lily's method wouldn't have ended in Buddy Bud throwing one of his tantrums.

It was the fifth anniversary of Jameson's wife's death. The small upstairs office of Jameson's Market was covered in Christmas cards. Left to himself, he wouldn't flaunt the cards—too painful a reminder—but Lily's death had left him the sole parent to their twelve-year-old son.

Jameson hunched over the oak desk that had once been his father's and went back to paying the pile of monthly bills, unable to shake the feeling that he wasn't doing right by his son. *A grocery store is no place for a kid to hang out.* He tossed his pen on the desk and ran his fingers through his thinning hair. *But what else can I do with him?*

The small town, smack in the middle of the Texas Panhandle, had few opportunities for normal kids, let alone ones with Down Syndrome. And Jameson couldn't move. The market was his life.

"Dad!" Buddy Bud whined. "The spider's not doing it right!"

"You might need to try like I showed you." Jameson didn't have it in him to sound patient. He was too damn tired. "Put the jar over the spider, then slip a card underneath."

"Nooo!"

Jameson removed his wire-rimmed glasses and pinched the bridge of his nose. Did Buddy Bud remember his mother's death? Was that what was making him so cranky? More likely, he was picking up on Jameson's brooding.

"Maybe the spider doesn't want you watching him. Maybe if you leave the jar on its side next to him, he'll climb in all by himself."

"He's a she!"

The back of Jameson's throat tightened. Was all this spider stuff really about Lily? "Maybe *she* doesn't want you watching her."

Buddy Bud rocked back on his checkered sneakers as if considering this. "Like yesterday when I didn't want you watching me tie my shoes? When I was being a handful?"

Jameson smiled. It was amazing to hear what Buddy Bud retained. "Exactly. And I'm sorry I called you that."

Buddy Bud shrugged. "S'okay." He leaned back over, his face just inches from the spider, and crooned, "I'm not looking, Mrs. Spider. You can climb in the jar if you want to."

Kitty, the youngest of Jameson's cashiers, poked her hairdo-ed head into the office, gaudy ornament earrings dangling from her earlobes. "Mail call."

Buddy Bud looked up, his face glowing with delight. "More cards?"

"You bet." Kitty stepped into the room, revealing an even more gaudy holiday sweater over creased jeans. "A pile of 'em."

Buddy Bud reached for the clutch of mail, inadvertently knocking it from Kitty's manicured fingertips and scattering letters and circulars all over the floor. Buddy Bud's eyes grew wide and his hand flew to his mouth.

"It's all right, son," Jameson said. "But you need to apologize."

"Sorry, Kitty!"

Kitty laughed. "No prob, Bud, you was just excited." She bent down to help gather the spray of mail.

Buddy Bud picked up a large red envelope. "Hey! Look at this one! It's got bugs!"

Kitty took the envelope covered in creepy-crawly stickers. "Well lookie here. If it isn't from you-know-who."

"Who?" Buddy said, looking bewildered.

"Them two what breezed through last summer." Kitty scowled at the return address. "Living in California now. Both of 'em. Together."

"Who?" Buddy Bud repeated, his timbre rising with frustration.

"I think she's talking about Eadie and Cadence," Jameson said.

"Eadie and Cadence!" Buddy Bud snatched the letter from Kitty and held it to his chest. "I love Eadie and Cadence. I'm gonna marry Cadence when I grow up. Ain't I, Dad?"

"Aren't I," Jameson said.

"Aren't you what?" Buddy Bud said.

Jameson gave Kitty an apologetic look. He knew it was time to quit humoring his son's obsession with Cadence, but he hated to upset the boy. Still, he should—

"You can't marry her," Kitty blurted, then scooped up the rest of the mail. "She's a homosexual."

"A what?" Buddy Bud said.

Kitty glanced briefly at Jameson as if to say, "If you won't tell him, I will," then went on in a schoolteachery voice, "She's a homosexual, and you don't want to mix yourself up with a homosexual. The Bible tells us they are sinners."

Buddy Bud stared at Kitty as if she were speaking in tongues, his face contorted in confusion.

Jameson, annoyed more with his own passivity than Kitty's audacity, deliberately shoved his chair back and stood. "That'll do, Kitty."

"I just think he should know—"

"I *said,* that'll do."

Kitty got up off the floor where she had been kneeling and handed Jameson the mail. "Sorry if I spoke out of line."

"I appreciate your concern…" Jameson cleared his throat. "But I'm not sure we see eye to eye on this. Now, I think it's time for you to get back to work."

Kitty sniffed her disapproval before parading out of the office.

Jameson, unsure what to do next, just stood there. Buddy Bud, clearly troubled, was turning the card round and round like it might somehow help him make sense of Kitty's words. Jameson examined his motives for not speaking with Buddy Bud about this matter sooner. The problem was, he was unsure of his own heart. He'd taken a shine to each of the girls before they'd gotten together; then, once they became a couple, well, quite simply, their returning to California took away any burning necessity to think further on the subject.

A weak man's excuse.

He walked over to the couch and sat. "Let's take a look at that card, Bud. See what your friends are up to."

Buddy Bud crawled up onto the couch next to him.

Jameson took the card and opened it.

"Look, Dad. It's hand-drawed!"

It was one of Eadie's pen-and-inks: she and Cadence riding a lavender reindeer through a sky full of shooting stars. Eadie had drawn herself wearing forest green slacks and a flowing white blouse. A Santa hat, pulled low on her head, forced her black mop of hair to stick out comically on all sides. Cadence was in a red dress trimmed in white fur, blue cowgirl boots, and a holly wreath with a tail of ribbons atop her copper-colored hair, and, of course, her lime green cat's-eye glasses. Riding behind, she had her arms tightly wrapped around Eadie's waist, her head on Eadie's shoulder. They looked happy.

Jameson read the caption for Buddy Bud. "May your Holidaze be full of love and magic."

Buddy Bud ran a finger lightly across the picture. "It's sparkly."

Jameson sighed. He missed the two of them. They were so different from the young women of Rauston. So spirited. Feisty. He opened the card and read it out loud.

Dear Buddy Bud,

Santa Cruz doesn't have near as many bugs as Rauston, but there are other things here you would like. Seals for one thing, and lots of fish. Including dolphins. You should see the way they jump out of the water! I put the rubber snake you gave me on the dashboard of my car. It looks cool.

Miss you, Needy Eadie.

Beneath this, Cadence had written:

Hey Buddy Bud,
No sick or injured birds so far, which is lucky.
Who would fix them up?
Miss you. XXXOOOO Cadence

At the bottom in Eadie's handwriting was a note to Jameson.

Hey Jameson! Miss you, too.
We're planning to get back out there one of these days.
Maybe around April? (Before it gets too hot. Ha. Ha.)
Love you. E

Jameson decided against reading this part aloud. No use getting Buddy Bud worked up over a tentative plan.

Buddy Bud grabbed the card. "I love Eadie! I love Cadence!" His tone was defiant, as if warding off Kitty's words.

Jameson ruffled Buddy Bud's short brown hair. "Me too, son, me too." He had to address the topic that Kitty had broached, but how? Her judgmental stance made such a difficult jumping off point.

Lily would have known how.

Buddy Bud let the card drop to his lap. "Um. Dad?"

Jameson braced himself. "Yes?"

"What's a gnomosexual?"

Jameson couldn't help but smile. "The word is homosexual, Bud."

Buddy Bud rubbed his fists on the sides of his pant legs. "Um... well...what is one? Is it bad?"

"Nope. But it might be kind of hard to understand."

Buddy Bud groaned. "O-kaaay."

Jameson felt like groaning, too. Where to begin? The logistics weren't all that difficult to describe, girl loves girl or boy loves boy. Thankfully, Buddy Bud wouldn't know enough to ask the harder questions, like how they consummated their love, which Jameson himself would be hard-pressed to describe. When it came to Eadie and Cadence's sexuality, he simply chose not to think about it. He didn't think about other people's bedroom activities, why should he think about theirs? But now, with Kitty casting this negative light on the girls, he was going to have to broach the morality of their love, and this got trickier, because, quite frankly, Jameson had no idea where he stood on the topic.

He wrapped his arm around his son and forged ahead like a truck driving with no headlights into a pitch-black night. "The thing is, sometimes instead of a girl and a boy falling in love, two girls fall in love, or two boys."

Buddy Bud stuck his finger up his nose. "Uh-huh."

"Don't pick your nose, Bud."

Buddy Bud wiped his finger on his pants. "Sorry."

"And when that happens, say, two girls fall in love, like Eadie and Cadence, well then, they don't want to marry a boy."

"Because they want to marry each other?"

"Sort of. Only they're not allowed to get married."

"Why not?"

"Well, some people don't think they should."

"Why not?"

"Because some people think it's wrong."

"*Is* it wrong?" Buddy Bud asked, his fingers twisting into a knot.

Jameson stared across the office to the picture of a five-year-old Buddy Bud sitting on his beautiful Lily's lap. *What do I do?* he asked his wife, as he often did when he was flummoxed by parenthood. *Tell the truth*, was what he heard her say, although he was never really sure if it was her sending him the messages or just his idea of her.

"I'm not sure what I think, Bud. But I do know it's unchristian of us to wish ill on someone just because they're different."

Buddy Bud stretched out his legs and then let them drop back against the couch. "Like Kitty?"

"Well, yes, like Kitty." The last thing Jameson wanted to do was turn Buddy against Kitty. She was just young, and narrow in her thoughts, a product of her upbringing. "The thing you need to know is, there are many who pass judgment on people they don't understand." Jameson said this definitively, praying it would be the end of it, that Buddy Bud would get bored with the conversation and want to go back to his spider, but Buddy Bud wrinkled his nose, a sure sign that he was far from done with the topic.

"But, Dad, that's stupid!"

Jameson massaged the back of his neck. "How do you figure?"

"Well," Buddy Bud said, using his grown-up voice, "Mom always told me that God lives in people's hearts, right?"

Jameson nodded. "Right."

"And when you fall in love, that comes from your heart, right?"

"Right."

"So how could God be mad at a girl falling in love with a girl, when he's the one making the love?"

Jameson let out a short, audible exhale. "That's some quality thinking there, Bud."

Buddy Bud held up a thumb. "Quaaaality!" Then he knit his eyebrows. "But you still haven't told me what a gnomosexual is."

"A homosexual is what we call a girl who falls in love with another girl, or a boy who falls in love with another boy."

Buddy Bud slipped from beneath Jameson's protective arm and stared at him incredulously. "So Cadence won't want to marry me because she's in love with Eadie?"

"Yup."

Buddy Bud fell over sideways on the couch and grabbed his head as if he were trying to loosen a giant vise grip. "That's crazy!"

Jameson wasn't sure what to make of this declaration. He gave Buddy Bud's pant leg a tug. "You okay?"

Buddy Bud giggled then pressed his hand to his mouth and spoke through his fingers. "Want to know what I just thought of?"

"I can tell you're fixin' to tell me."

Buddy Bud shot back up to sitting. "If Cadence loves Eadie, and Eadie loves Cadence, and I love them both, then we could all three get married!"

Jameson pulled his son back into his embrace. "Now you're being silly."

Buddy Bud snuggled into Jameson's chest. "You're the bestest dad ever!"

Jameson's heart swelled. "I hope so, Bud. I hope so." He found himself once again glancing at the picture of Lily. This time it was to thank her. *For giving me this beautiful boy.*

"Hey!" Buddy Bud said, twisting around in a panic. "Where's the card?"

Jameson whipped the card from beneath Buddy Bud's leg. "Ta-dah!"

Buddy Bud studied the drawing on the front. "I'm glad they're in love."

"You sure?"

"Yup. 'Cuz I have you to love—and you're a handful!"

Laughing, Jameson gave his son a bear hug.

"Not so tight!" Buddy Bud squealed.

Jameson released him and straightened out the now skewed thick-framed glasses. "You can still love them, you know."

Buddy Bud rolled his eyes. "No duh, Dad." With that, he slid from the couch to check on Mrs. Spider.

MJ Williamz is the author of over twenty-five published short stories, mostly lesbian erotica with a few horror and a couple of romances thrown in for good measure. Most recently she had a short erotic story, "Guard Duty," in the *Women in Uniform* anthology, which was released earlier this year. Her first novel, *Shots Fired*, was released in 2008. Kyla and Echo from "Making New Memories" first appeared in that novel. Visit MJ's website-in-progress at www.mjwilliamz.com.

Making New Memories
MJ Williamz

"I think now would be a good time to open this."

Echo handed the rectangular package to Kyla, who was sitting next to her on the bearskin rug. Kyla smiled and shook it.

"Don't worry. It won't break," Echo said.

Kyla reached under the tree and pulled out a long, narrow package. "And this is your special present from me."

"Open yours first," Echo urged.

Kyla started to untie the ribbon, then paused. "Can you believe it's been a year?"

"Some days, it seems forever ago, and some days, it feels like it just happened. I'm so thankful you came out of it all unscathed in the long run."

"Overall."

Echo remembered the horrible day the prior January when a deranged child molester had shot Kyla in the head and caused her to roll her car, resulting in short-term amnesia, broken ribs, and a broken leg. She gestured to the package. "Open."

"Yes, ma'am." Kyla took off the ribbon and carefully unwrapped the present that Echo had obviously had someone else wrap for her. Echo's skills did not include gift-wrapping. When she removed the top, she smiled broadly at the red satin teddy with black lace trim that lay in wait for her.

"Go try it on," Echo encouraged.

She didn't have to ask twice. Kyla disappeared into the downstairs half-bath and quickly changed. She swept her dark blond hair into a clip and walked out of the bathroom to the appreciative look in her lover's dark blue eyes.

"Dear God, you're beautiful."

Kyla stepped into Echo's waiting arms and welcomed a soft, tender kiss. The kiss soon grew more passionate as their tongues tangled, dancing in a rhythm perfected during years of practice.

"Thank you for putting your hair up," Echo murmured as she kissed Kyla's exposed neck.

"I know how much you like it." Kyla tilted her head to the side to allow Echo easier access to the spot at the base of her neck.

"And I know what this does to you."

"Remember last Valentine's Day?" Echo kissed the smooth slope of Kyla's shoulder. "You didn't even want to have dinner with me."

Kyla pulled Echo on top of her on the bearskin rug. "We've come a long way since then."

"Mmm-hmm." Echo moved the black lace strap down Kyla's arm and kissed the area left bare. Despite having been together almost twenty years, after the attack they'd had to go back to the beginning and relearn each other's bodies. It hadn't always been easy with Kyla's ribs and leg to consider, but finally, they knew each other's desires and weaknesses again like they knew their own.

"God, I hope Colton doesn't come home," Kyla said.

"Babe, we have nothing to worry about. He's fifteen and has spent the last three Christmas Eves at his cousin's. We're the last thing on his mind. Now relax."

Echo kissed along the edge of the teddy, slowing when she reached the area just above Kyla's half-exposed breasts. She licked and nibbled the pert tops, reveling in the softness of her woman.

Kyla guided Echo's head to the valley created there, but Echo gave her one last kiss before biting her way down Kyla's satin-clad stomach. When she got below Kyla's belly button, Kyla was mewing in anticipation. She spread her legs and gently pressed the top of Echo's head, urging her onward.

Echo licked long and hard over the satin that covered Kyla's mons, occasionally teasing lower. When neither woman could take it any longer, Echo rested her head on Kyla's inner thigh and undid the snaps that separated her from where she wanted to be. She took a moment to admire the glistening pussy that called to her, already so wet with need. She separated the swollen lips and lazily ran her tongue between them, eliciting a low moan from her partner. She traced Kyla's shaft and circled the head of her clit with her tongue, causing Kyla to raise her hips and move against her.

Echo laughed, her warm breath caressing Kyla's clit.

"Easy, baby. We've got all night."

She pushed the teddy over Kyla's soft belly, trailing kisses as she did, knowing how tiny kisses right there aroused her. She moved the teddy up and over Kyla's waiting breasts and bent to take one erect nipple in her mouth while twisting and tugging on the other with her finger and thumb.

Kyla's fingers were laced through Echo's hair, her grip holding her mouth firmly in place. Echo had no intention of moving as her teeth gently held the upright nub and her tongue flicked across its tip. She sucked the nipple deeper, taking the tip of Kyla's breast in her mouth and running her tongue over it.

"You're going to leave a mark," Kyla whispered.

"Who's going to see?" Echo released her grip and sat up, pulling Kyla with her. "Help me with this." Together they got the teddy over Kyla's head, and Echo kissed Kyla hard on the mouth. She didn't bother to remove her sweatshirt or jeans, but laid Kyla back down and covered her body with her own. She pressed her knee between Kyla's legs, and wetness soaked through her jeans as they moved together, never breaking the kiss.

Echo propped herself up and caressed Kyla's body. "I can never get enough of you," she whispered.

"I hope you always feel that way." Kyla frantically pulled at Echo's sweatshirt. Once she had it off, she kneaded and fondled Echo's breasts as they kissed.

Kyla writhed against Echo's leg, her frantic movements signaling she was getting close. Echo nibbled and kissed back down Kyla's neck and chest until she reached a hardened nipple once again. She closed her lips around it and circled the tip with her tongue, causing Kyla to move faster against her knee.

She slid her hand lower, over Kyla's belly and down to her smoothly shaved pubis. Tantalizingly slowly, she dragged her hand back up to Kyla's belly button and back down again, stopping just above her clit.

As her hand began another upward path, Kyla said hoarsely, "I swear to God, Echo, if you don't touch me soon, I'm going to do this on my own."

"As much as I'd like to watch that…" Echo gave in and slipped her hand between her leg and Kyla. She stroked her clit as Kyla closed her eyes and let out a moan. Echo found Kyla covered in juices and couldn't resist dipping her fingers inside. Two fingers slid in easily, and she moved them in and out quickly several times before adding another.

"Yes. God, Echo. Please."

Echo moved between Kyla's legs. "Put your legs over my shoulders."

Kyla happily obliged, and Echo bent to lick her while she thrust her fingers deeper. She squeezed them together as she drove them in, then separated them as she pulled them out, all the while sucking Kayla's clit and glancing over it with her teeth.

Kyla writhed on the floor, pressing into Echo.

"God, I'm so close."

Echo began lapping at Kyla's hardened clit in the same rhythm as her fingers moved in and out. Kyla bucked her hips against Echo, keeping time, each buck harder than the one before.

It wasn't long before Kyla shook from head to toe, screaming Echo's name.

When Kyla's orgasm subsided, Echo held her and whispered, "Merry Christmas, baby."

Kyla smiled back. "And now it's time for you to open your present."

Originally from Cuba, Ali Vali has retained much of her family's traditions and language and uses them frequently in her stories. Having her father read her stories and poetry before bed every night as a child infused her with a love of reading, which carries till today. She has discovered that living in Louisiana provides plenty of material to draw from in creating her novels and short stories. Ali currently lives outside New Orleans, Louisiana.

A Ghost of Christmas Past

Ali Vali

"Are you free later?" Julia Johnson watched her lover Poppy Valente put on socks. After six months of seeing Poppy dressed casually with bare feet, she still wasn't used to this corporate side of her.

Poppy slipped her feet into her loafers and stood brushing off her dark navy pinstripe pants. "I'll be happy to reschedule anything for you, so give me a time and location, and I'll be there."

Going to work was easy now since they'd moved into the penthouse suite in the Piquant after returning to New Orleans from Carly's Sound. For Julia, the move had been a whirlwind that had separated her from her brother Rayford, who was thriving in his job on Carly's Sound, and from her grandmother Tallulah, who'd returned to Texas. Arriving back at the Piquant made her think of the first stay there, when her future had appeared so limited and bleak. Of course, a trip for coffee with a colicky baby had changed her entire landscape.

"If you're busy, don't worry about it," Julia said, smiling when her daughter Tallulah came crawling in and pulled herself up when she reached Poppy, who immediately picked her up. Of all the changes in her life, the most welcome was how much she loved seeing Poppy with Tallulah.

"I'll never be too busy for you," Poppy kissed Tallulah's hand, "or for this beautiful girl."

"It can keep. I just remembered Elizabeth said you two were finalizing the contracts on the Nice property."

Tallulah squealed when Poppy tickled her stomach. "You okay?" Poppy asked as she put Tallulah back on the floor.

"I'm fine." She slid her arms around Poppy's waist under her jacket. "Your mom's coming over later so I can help the crew finish up the Christmas decorations in the lobby and outside."

"Are you bucking for a management job?"

"More like I'm trying to wrap up that girlfriend job." She smiled as she said it and felt the weight of the ring Poppy had given her, but the wonderful cocoon of Carly's Sound was gone. Now she was living in the city where Poppy's great love affair with her deceased partner Carly had started, and everyone in Poppy's life remembered the "golden couple."

"That one you can forget about." Poppy framed her face before kissing her. "You've been put under long-term contract." She took her time on the next kiss and Julia's concerns melted away—at least until their lips parted and Poppy left for her office on the third floor of the hotel.

"I know you love us," she said to the empty room as she picked Tallulah up, "but Carly has left a long shadow." One she figured she'd live in if she spent her life with Poppy. "But a life without sunlight is better than one without her. Right, baby girl?"

She spun Tallulah around, getting her to smile, and wished she could chase her own sadness away as easily.

"Are you sure about this?" Elizabeth Johnson, Carly's daughter and the CEO of Valente Resorts, placed a stack of papers in front of Poppy.

"Not really, but I can't ask Julia to live in the house I shared with your mother." Poppy stared at the address at the top of the page, her mind reeling through the memories she and Carly had made in that home. Carly's presence, Carly's incredible love, had made it home. "I'd rather it go to you than put it on the market."

"I want you to be happy." Elizabeth hugged Poppy from behind. "And I don't want to take something you love away from you."

"I'll visit when I miss our furniture, and remember that I'm giving it to you, so stop feeling guilty. Who knows," she took a deep breath and signed in all the required places, "maybe with a bigger place, you'll have room for Susanna and all your shoes."

"We're not to that point yet," Elizabeth said softly. "I don't want to rush anything since we work together as well."

"Lizzie," she said, putting her pen down and opening her arms to hold her. "You're brilliant at what you do, but you need to separate the different parts of your life."

"What do you mean?"

"You can structure the business so it eliminates problems before they arise, but you can't do that in your personal life." She led Elizabeth to the leather sofa in the corner of the office and sat with her arm around her. "The only things you can do to avoid total catastrophe is to be faithful and love with total abandon."

"Is that why Mom always looked so happy?" Elizabeth's eyes shimmered with unshed tears. "She never looked happy until you came into her life."

"Your mama was a unique woman who loved your father, but eventually her trust in him was broken, and sometimes, no matter the time and effort, that can't be repaired." She combed Elizabeth's hair from her face. "When she lost that trust, she found her happiness in you and your siblings. Carly Valente was a magnificent partner, but her legacy is you. The happiness you saw was always there even before I came into her life. She always told me motherhood nurtured her soul."

"You can admit you had a lot to do with what brought her joy."

"I'm not a genius, but I was smart enough to know what a gift she was." Poppy stared at the picture on her credenza next to the one of Julia and Tallulah—Carly sat on a bar stool in the bar she regularly played in. The expression on Carly's face was to her the definition of love. "She filled my life so completely that I couldn't imagine my life without her in it."

"I never could figure out Daddy's behavior, but Mom got what she deserved before she died."

"Thanks for saying that. I want you to feel that way about yourself. You deserve someone who'll make you happy and fill all those empty places in your heart, but to get that you have to be willing to take a chance." She kissed Elizabeth's forehead and hugged her. "Take your mom's example in that. Even if it doesn't work out, fate gives you more than once chance. If Susanna is it for you, we'll figure out something so work doesn't become an issue. And if she hurts you, I'll find some place in Siberia for her to transfer to."

"Sus hates the cold," Elizabeth said, laughing.

"She'll be fine as long as she's sure about what she's doing, and what the consequences of hurting you are."

"Don't threaten her." Elizabeth pointed at her. "Promise me she's not going to make this decision based on fear."

"If she's smart, she'll work hard to get this right because of the girl, and how lucky she is you're interested. Just remember to set your heart free and it'll make all this worthwhile. The job, the real estate… all of it is better enjoyed when you share it with someone you love."

"Thanks for the pep talk," Elizabeth said, giving Poppy a squeeze. "I love you."

"I love you, too, and your mom was right."

"About what?"

"She left behind a beautiful legacy who now brings me joy. And if you want my advice, I think Susanna is a good choice."

"Remember your promise, though. No threats."

"As long as she behaves, I swear," Poppy said, tapping over her heart.

❖

Julia hurried to the elevator, needing to get away after unintentionally overhearing Poppy discussing Carly with Elizabeth.

She filled my life so completely that I couldn't imagine my life without her in it.

She couldn't pretend to be surprised. She'd said yes without hesitation when Poppy had proposed, with full knowledge of Poppy's past. Hearing Poppy describe Carly like that didn't change her mind about staying, but Poppy's feelings cemented her fear of always being the runner-up. She thanked the doorman when he opened the door that led out to the valet car entrance.

"Julia."

Julia stopped and regarded the elegant older woman standing next to the open door of a Town Car with a smile that made her smile back.

"I'm sorry," she said when she didn't recognize the woman right off.

"Nothing to be sorry for, sugar, since it's me who should apologize for taking so long to come and introduce myself. I'm Emily St. Claire, and your Poppy did a wonderful job of describing you. She's right, you are beautiful."

Emily St. Claire, the grande dame of New Orleans society. The story of Poppy and Carly's tango and the start of Poppy's long and close relationship with Emily popped into Julia's head. One too many memories of Poppy and Carly, and in the next instant, she was crying.

"I think lunch is in order." Emily slid her arm around Julia as if she wasn't sobbing and guided her into the car.

Fortunately, Emily's driver headed uptown past the mansions of St. Charles Avenue at a pace that allowed her to try to get over her embarrassment while focusing on the great craftsmanship most new construction didn't have.

Julia wiped her eyes with the tissue Emily had given her and said, "Mrs. St. Claire, I'm so sorry—"

"Julia, call me Emily, and don't apologize for giving your emotions an outlet." The driver took a left and stopped in front of Commander's Palace restaurant. "I spoke with Poppy after you three returned from Carly's Sound. One thing I heard in her happy tale was the absolute lightness of her voice. Poppy Valente is happy again, and it's because of you." The driver stood outside the car but Emily made no move to get out. "It's been a long time since I've heard that happiness that she always had in abundance."

"She was in love then."

"She's in love now," Emily said, tapping on the window. "Come on, let's take a walk first."

Julia buttoned her jacket, feeling considerably underdressed next to Emily.

"The place we're going, they won't care about the jeans, trust me," Emily said.

Julia took the arm Emily offered and followed her across the street to the entrance of a cemetery that was full of what looked like small brick houses all painted white. Emily led her down a few rows, stopping at a modest grave topped with a family name she didn't recognize. The newly added bronze plaque had Carly's name on it with the appropriate dates, and the words, "Wife and Mother."

"Her ashes are where she wanted to be." Emily sat on the bench across from the tomb and patted the spot next to her. "On that island and in the waters she shared with Poppy is where her spirit will live on, but Elizabeth wanted something more permanent to mark her mother's memory. She buried that little tin Carly found for herself."

Sitting beside Emily, Julia looked down at her hands, her focus on the ring Poppy had given her. "I didn't know."

"Neither does Poppy. Elizabeth did it before Poppy came home. She put the last physical link to her mother in with her grandparents and hasn't wanted to tell Poppy. I imagine she thinks Poppy has borne enough pain for ten lifetimes."

Julia gazed up at the plaque again, and it made Carly as real as she'd ever been to her. "Why are we here? Do you want me to tell Poppy about this?"

"Poppy is important to me, so I want us to become friends. Since you're important to her, I assume you must know about Carly."

"I asked Poppy about her," Julia said, not knowing how to continue.

"The other woman, huh?" Emily teased.

Julia laughed at how perceptive Emily was. "The *perfect* other woman. There's no way to compete." Mortified, she stopped talking. If Emily's intent was to set up a trap for her, she'd walked into it effortlessly. "I'm sorry. You must think I'm a horrible person, talking ill of the dead."

"You're honest, my dear. Never apologize for that. It'll be the only way to keep Poppy, and from our friendship all these years, I know she isn't one for games. But don't waste your time thinking about Carly and what was. That will drive you mad. Think instead of what a special person you must be to have driven the hermit from her cave." Emily took her hand as if to be of comfort.

"What did you think of Carly?"

Emily took so long in saying something, Julia thought it was the most polite way not to answer the question. "I'm sorry, you don't have to—"

"Carly was a woman who for too many years just went through the motions of her life—daughter, wife, mother, and volunteer. As if she knew what was expected of her, and that's what she delivered. She did it with such ease and grace that some envied her life. They envied the window dressing, but I dug deeper because she was my friend. Carly was one of those rare individuals who people gravitate to, and it was unfortunate that for someone who could've had her pick, her first choice was Thomas."

"Matlin and Kelly told me a little about him," Julia said when Emily stopped to take a breath.

"Now that you're here, I'm sure you'll get around to meeting Thomas. Myron and I attended their wedding all those years ago and it seemed like a perfect match. He was charming, ambitious, and good looking."

The parallel between the man Emily was describing and Poppy jumped out so she couldn't stay quiet. "Sounds like the perfect mate. Actually it sounds like someone I know and love."

Emily laughed and shook her head. "Don't make that mistake, dear. It's true your love is all those things, but her ambition is different from Thomas's. Poppy's ambition is for everyone she comes in contact with, whereas Thomas's drive is fueled by finding ways to enrich only himself. Carly's first marriage became a struggle for control, and he tried every trick he could think of to break her."

"Doesn't sound very pleasant," Julia said softly.

"It wasn't, and I'm sure Thomas will have much to explain for his actions when he meets his maker. But he didn't control her as much as he thought. There was never any fire in Carly's eyes, and her smile never went past her lips. She was good at pretending she was happy, but she never really was. Then the impossible happened. She left him, and the reasons why made the rumors epic even in a town like New Orleans. The stories were dying down and then the real golden couple came back to town." Emily made air quotes for the moniker. "Carly came home to prove the stories true, a young lover with a passion for life and an even bigger passion for her. As a bonus, it didn't hurt that Poppy had become successful in the resort business."

"I heard about the tango and your party."

"Ah, Matlin and Sabrina. The part I'm sure they left out was the guts it took to face those who'd had so much fun talking about her. The elite had only heard Thomas's side of the story, but that night Carly Valente showed those ninnies who she really was. Even the mask couldn't hide it."

"What?"

"The fire in those green eyes. The only thing brighter in the room that night were Poppy's when she looked at her."

"Thank you, Emily. I feel so much better now," she said, laughing.

Emily joined in as if knowing what she'd found so humorous. "Believe it or not, there's a point to telling you all this besides answering your question."

"What, to prove my assumption Carly was perfect is right on target?"

"Julia, an old friend called on me a few weeks ago, and there was something very different about her but also something familiar. The eyes, Julia, those gorgeous blues never lie when it comes to the way she feels. For Poppy, her eyes are truly the windows not only to her soul but to her heart. I'm so happy my prediction was wrong."

"What's that?"

"I always figured Poppy would eventually find someone she could spend her life with. But while you spend time and money, you share a life. There's a difference. My father was a bit of a gambler, and he was fond of one saying: It only takes losing everything once to make you wise to the games of chance. Smart gamblers always hold something back so they never truly get burned, and Poppy's smart. When I looked at her I saw the hand she was holding."

"I guess I'll always get to hear about how she was and settle for that." Julia tried not to show how much that hurt but couldn't stop her lips from quivering.

"Julia, in my opinion, you're sitting at the table with someone who's pushed all her chips back into play. There is no woman alive or dead who can beat your ante now, girl."

"Thank you," Julia said softly. Maybe, maybe it was time for her to step out of Carly's shadow.

Poppy, holding Tallulah in her arms, watched the Town Car pull up in front of the Piquant, grateful the doorman had overheard Emily and Julia say they were going to lunch earlier. She opened the door for

Julia, kissed her cheek as Julia climbed out, and passed the baby into her arms.

"You look like you had a good lunch," Poppy said. Julia seemed more relaxed than she had earlier.

"I did," Julia said as Emily's car drove away. "Are you busy now?"

"I'm all yours for whatever you have in mind." Poppy took Julia's hand. "And I do mean that…I'm all yours."

"I know, and I'm sorry I've been acting like a nervous cat lately. There's something I'd like to show you."

"Then lead the way."

"We'll need to take the Jeep."

Poppy drove, following Julia's directions, and pulled up in front of the pinkest house she had ever seen. She rested her elbows on the steering wheel and just stared. *Please God, let pink not be her favorite color.* The sound of Julia unbuckling Tallulah's car seat snapped her out of the visual stimulation overload.

"It has four bedrooms plus a great master suite, and wait till you see the yard," Julia said enthusiastically as they walked across the lawn.

Poppy regarded the large flock of plastic pink flamingos in the side yard, thinking of the papers she'd signed that morning giving Elizabeth the house that was only a block away.

A very cheerful real estate agent waited on the porch. "Ms. Valente, I'm Georgia Easel with the Western Group. Want to step inside and take a look around?"

Not really, but I think my vote is severely limited here. Poppy shook Georgia's hand and smiled, hoping it looked sincere. "I'd love to."

Julia stopped right inside the door. "I know you already have a house here, but when we talked about what came next, you said maybe we could start fresh in someplace that would be ours. If you're not ready for that, I'll be okay with staying at the Piquant as long as you need to, so don't think this is something I'm forcing on you."

Poppy blinked. The deep purple of the foyer made the outside color look good. The adjacent living room was a shade of red that only looked good on cars and lipstick. Not the response Julia was after, apparently.

"Is something wrong?" Julia asked.

"You love this place, huh?"

Julia handed the baby over as if trying to decipher her question. "You can't hate it already, we just walked in."

"I don't hate it. I'm just asking if you like it."

"Are you kidding? This place's great. Come on and I'll show you why I think so."

The back room Julia led her to had been used by the owners as a family room. Large windows afforded a great view of the pool surrounded by what appeared to be thousands of cactus plants. Beyond that was a large overgrown patch that led out to Audubon Park.

Poppy stopped blinking and squinted, since she was now having a hard time adjusting her eyes to the combination of sun streaming in the windows and screaming bright yellow walls. Even the baby buried her face against her shoulder for relief.

"Ms. Easel, could you excuse us a moment, please?" Julia asked, prompting Georgia to head to the front of the house. "You hate it, don't you? You can be honest, honey. I don't want you to be miserable for the next sixty plus years."

"It's just that it looks like Sherwin Williams threw up in here. I don't know if you've noticed, but white's my favorite color. And all those prickly plants out there wouldn't be safe for Tallulah."

"What's the matter, honey, pink's not your color?" Julia turned Poppy away from the windows and looked her in the eye. "Honey, I'm not moving into a house that has more colors than a crayon box, and you're not acting any differently than I did when I first walked in here. My one salvation is Susanna was with me to point out the potential buried under the rainbow—like the great floors and molding the original builder put in. As for the yard, imagine a canopy starting from the house extending over half the deck. The shade would make this room bearable in the mornings. And a big bulldozer to knock down all the cacti. You have to remember you're getting a landscape architect in the bargain, and I'm not a big fan of cactus either."

"How about the outside color?"

"White happens to be my favorite color, too, in houses anyway, and we'll have a party to set the flamingos free if we decide on this place. Since I'm so nice I'll let your lack of faith in my tastes pass this one time." Julia reached up and kissed Poppy until a small pudgy hand slapped the top of her head. "Now stop looking at the walls and let's go upstairs."

Julia's choice wouldn't require near the work Poppy's first house had needed, so they signed a contract of intent and gave Georgia a check along with their bid. Just the look on Sabrina's and Matlin's faces when they saw the decorating nightmare would almost make the purchase worthwhile.

"Thank you," Julia said on their way back to the Piquant. "You sure made that easy."

"Buying's easy, but the easiest part is making it a home with you and Tallulah. I should be thanking you for giving me everything I didn't even realize I needed. And a house was high on my priority list since I gave one away this morning."

"You gave your house away?"

"Elizabeth will be happy there, or at least I hope she'll be as happy as Carly and I were when we lived there. You and I deserve some place where we can start making our own memories."

"I love you."

"I love you, too, baby, but I know a group of people who'll adore you maybe as much as I do."

"Who?" Julia asked.

"Think how much the neighbors are going to love you when the paint crew arrives carrying buckets and buckets of white."

❖

A week later Julia stood in front of the full-length mirror in their bedroom at the Piquant checking the fit of the formal gown she'd picked for the annual Christmas Ball, a charity event to benefit the Carly Valente Trust Fund. In only a short period of time she'd learned to ask, and had received much more than a house. It was like Poppy had come alive making plans for the future, a future she wholeheartedly wanted with her and Tallulah.

Emily had been right in that Poppy would never forget Carly, but the only one who'd had a hard time separating the past from the present was her. A wasteful mistake she wasn't about to repeat.

"I'm so sorry we never met," she said to Carly, moving to the main room. "Though if you were still here, Poppy wouldn't have given me the time of day." She laughed but knew how true that statement was. "I owe you a debt for teaching her how to love as completely as she does, so the part of her heart that'll always belong to you will be taken good care of by the part that belongs to me."

The verandah door flew open just as the elevator doors did and she could've sworn she heard the words "You're so very welcome" in the wind. The voice sounded a lot like the one in her head when she'd picked Carly as Tallulah's middle name.

She shook her head as she closed the verandah doors and turned at the sound of Tallulah's laughter. Smiling, she took in the mutual admiration society made up of her partner and daughter. Tallulah was in her reserved spot in Poppy's arms listening to her sing, laughing when long fingers would tickle her as she finished up a verse.

"Mama," Tallulah said when she saw her.

Poppy stared. "Wow."

"You like it?"

"I love it, but looking at you may make me forget how to dance." Poppy put Tallulah on the floor and stepped closer to Julia.

"Let's hope not because I've been looking forward to this, and it's for a good cause."

After they arrived and were seated with their closest friends, Julia started to relax and enjoy the event. No one was dancing yet even though the band was playing.

"Darling, care to get the evening rolling for us?" Emily asked Poppy. "I've been resting my knee for long enough, and while our usual waltz is a few months away, I thought you'd give me an early Christmas present and dance with me."

Trying not to look disappointed, Julia watched Poppy walk toward the bandstand to make her request. Poppy looked fantastic in her tuxedo with a red vest and bow tie that matched her dress. She had thought about Matlin and Sabrina's story and had hoped to share her own special moment with Poppy when the opportunity presented itself, but couldn't begrudge Emily her fun.

"May I have this dance?" Poppy's question interrupted her spiraling self-pity.

"Aren't you going to waltz with Emily?" Julia realized they were now the center of attention.

"In a little while, but now I want to dance with you. It's considered rude to dance the first and last dance with someone other than the lady you came with. It's the rule of the South," Poppy said. The band continued playing the soft background music as if waiting for her and Poppy to step onto the dance floor. Poppy sat next to her and leaned in to continue their talk when she didn't take her hand. "You know what else is rude?"

Julia shook her head and tried to control her emotions.

"To have you live one more minute with a picture in your head of me doing something but with a different woman in my arms, even if I loved her with all my heart, especially when I'm in a position to do something about it. Would you like to make new memories with me?"

"I'd love to."

Standing again, Poppy bowed at the waist and offered her hand. "May I have this dance?"

Dancing the tango with Poppy was like a musical seduction. Feeling Poppy's body pressed up behind her made her completely forget she didn't really know how to dance the tango. Poppy's lead was easy to follow, and she gave silent thanks that the bodice of her dress was a little snug, effectively hiding her response to her lover's embrace. When Poppy splayed her fingers on her stomach and pulled her closer, her nipples got hard and she was ready to head upstairs. By the end it was a godsend Poppy was strong, since she was the only thing keeping her upright.

"Promise me we'll do that again real soon."

As an answer Poppy dipped her head and kissed her.

❖

Two days later on Christmas morning Poppy watched as Tallulah ripped open presents, laughing whenever she was able to tear another piece off the pile of boxes Poppy had gotten her.

"Mama!" Tallulah waved a scrap of wrapping at Julia.

"Your mama needs to open her gift." Poppy handed Julia a flat present.

Julia removed the wrapping and laughed when she saw the calendar. "A gag gift?"

"If you open it to the day we met, you'll see why you'll need that this coming year." Poppy leaned back against the sofa.

Julia flipped to the right month and stared at what Poppy had written. "Honey, you don't have to do this. What we have, and what you've given me already, is enough."

"The property in Nice comes with an adjacent estate that's about six hundred years old. Along with the house, there's a chapel the family owned, and on our first anniversary that's where we'll get married. We're going to do that with all our friends and family in attendance so they can hear me tell you before God how much I love you and how I intend to grow old with you and our children. I also promise I'll wear shoes, and there'll be no sand until we start the honeymoon."

"Thank you for loving me." Julia held out her gift to Poppy. "And thank you for opening your heart to the possibility of sharing your life again. Merry Christmas."

The ring inside was similar in width to the one Carly had given her, but very different in design—the bark of a palm tree appeared to be etched into the platinum. She held it up to the light to see the inscription inside: *With all that I am, until the last sunset.*

When she looked at Julia again she couldn't get a word out around the lump in her throat but it didn't matter. Julia moved to her lap and kissed her. They were celebrating their first Christmas together, but they'd already shared the best gift when they'd fallen in love months before.

Carly stood on the terrace, watching Poppy share the special day with her family. This time she left the doors closed, not wanting to disturb the moment, feeling a sense of peace that had eluded her from the moment she died. That serenity came from knowing that Poppy was healing and that Elizabeth was waking up in her new home with Susanna. Both her lost lambs had found a home and people who would love them as much as she had.

"Merry Christmas, Poppy. I'll love you always," Carly whispered.

She waved at Tallulah, who was looking right at her. "Take care of them both, Tallulah, and enjoy the life your parents will give you and the little brother who's waiting to join you. I'll visit from time to time and will always be looking out for you all."

LISA GIROLAMI has been in the entertainment industry since 1979. She holds a BA in Fine Art and an MS in Psychology. Previous jobs included ten years as a production executive in the motion picture industry and another two decades producing and designing theme parks for Disney and Universal Studios. She is also a counselor at a gay and lesbian mental health facility in Garden Grove. This short story revisits characters Mary and Beth from her novel, *Run To Me*. Her other novels include *Love on Location*, *The Pleasure Set*, and *Jane Doe* (forthcoming, 2011). Lisa currently lives with her partner, Susan, in Long Beach, California. Her website is http://LisaGirolami.com.

Beautiful Burden

Lisa Girolami

Two loud yelps sounded from the station alarm. Mary Walston and Tomas Quinones dropped their wooden spoons and Mary turned off the oven. The Christmas Eve cookies would have to wait.

"Attention, engine five. Respond to a fire at one-seven-zero-zero Mariposa Street."

Mary sprinted down the stairs, two at a time. Tomas was right behind her as they joined the rest of the crew on the first floor. Most of their squad was already pulling on the gear that was positioned, as always, in a neat row along the floor in front of their lockers.

"Attention engines six, ten, and fourteen. Respond to a fire at one-seven-zero-zero Mariposa Street."

Their fire engine started up, its loud rumble reverberating off the walls of the garage as the roll up door lifted rapidly. Mary stepped into her pile of gear, pulled it up, and buckled it quickly. A cold, sharp gust of December wind caught in her lungs and she gasped. She grabbed her helmet from the shelf above and threw on her bulky, protective jacket.

The captain rushed by Mary as she climbed onto the fire engine.

"Shit," he said in his usual controlled tone, but his underlying anxiousness hung in the air like strong cologne. Mary's pulse accelerated. This multiple-engine call was not going to be for a small cooking mishap or an overheated space heater.

❖

Beth knew it was silly to have the Chipmunks Christmas CD playing while she cooked dinner, but it always put her in a cheery holiday mood. Mary would walk in the door after her shift was over and tease her about it. She smiled. Mary was off work at six and they'd have Christmas Eve as well as Christmas Day together. After opening presents the next morning, they planned a five-mile run through Golden Gate Park and could hopefully spend the rest of the holiday in bed. The television was on in the family room, tuned to the five o'clock news so she could catch the weather report for their run.

While Alvin sang of wanting a plane that loops the loop, Beth mixed the salad and checked the steak that was marinating. Over the harmonization of Chipmunk voices, the television news anchor said, "five-alarm fire in Potrero Point."

She dropped her kitchen towel and hurried to the family room.

News cameras were already on the scene, and the television images showed an industrial building completely engulfed in flames. The news station switched to their helicopter's aerial view and the true, immense involvement of the fire became terrifyingly evident.

Beth's heart lurched painfully. Since they had been together, Mary had rarely gotten home late from her shifts. Sometimes she had to stay over to wrap up a fire call or to attend a station house meeting, but Beth had never worried much. This fire, however, was enormous; its hunger overwhelmed the old-looking structure that was already buckling from the assault.

The ground camera panned across the line of fire engines. Number fourteen, number six...maybe Mary's engine wasn't...number five. An ominous dread spread through Beth, paralyzing her where she stood. The love of her life was somewhere in the midst of an all-consuming firestorm.

❖

Mary and Tomas attained access to the roof on the eastern side of the building. They needed to ventilate the building of smoke, heat, and any gases so the interior team could better search for any occupants. She found the scuttle hatch that was farthest away from their ladder. They'd start there and work their way back.

The roof access room, a small shack only as wide as its door, was close to their entry point. Mary checked for heat and, not feeling any, turned the doorknob. She cracked the door open and a light amount of smoke filtered out. She opened it wide and looked down the stairs. Seeing no fire, she and Tomas made their way to the far hatch on the western side of the roof. When Tomas radioed and got the go-ahead, they opened the hatch.

A vertical column of searing smoke jetted through the opening and Mary jerked her head away from the singe of radiated heat. "I don't see any flames."

Suddenly, an enormous explosion behind them shook the roof. They dropped to their knees and shielded their facemasks.

The cover of the middle scuttle hatch had exploded and a five-foot spiral of fire erupted from the opening. A surge of adrenaline rushed through Mary's veins. The fire could be right underneath them.

Tomas grabbed her arm. "Let's go."

They had taken four steps toward the ladder at the other end of the warehouse when the roof around what was left of the middle hatch cracked loudly. The fire seemed to have arms that reached up through the opening, flailing around, looking for something to grab. There were two more loud cracks and the hatch collapsed into itself, falling quickly into the blazing hole. The center of the roof shuddered and groaned.

"Fuck," Mary yelled.

Tomas ran to the closest edge. "It's too far to jump."

"We're going." Mary cocked her head toward the ladder.

Tomas nodded.

❖

Frozen in front of the television, Beth switched back and forth between the two local stations covering the fire. They kept showing the same damn footage of the commotion around the building and kept repeating what little they knew about the contents of the warehouse and those inside. Her future and her life were being played out on fifty-two inches of high-definition plasma.

"Talk to the goddamned fire chief! Get a report of what the hell is going on!"

Tears of fear and frustration burned the corners of her eyes. "Report what the fuck is going on!"

Her cell phone rang and she grabbed it from her waist holster. A bolt of fear ripped through her. The call might be from the station about Mary.

"Beth." It was Alder, the woman who had introduced her to Mary.

"Alder, are you watching TV?"

"That's why I called, honey."

"Shit. I don't know what to do."

"You're doing exactly as you should. Stay right where you are, right where Mary can contact you when this is over."

"But what if she doesn't call? What if it's because…"

"She'll call. You need to take a deep breath."

"I'm scared to death, Alder."

"I know. And it sucks. You know this is part of being the wife of a firefighter."

"I just want her home with me."

"She's trained for this. It's her job, Beth."

"I know. It's her career, actually. And that's what makes me love her so much. She's so passionate about firefighting and every time I see it in her eyes, I fall in love with her again. But I'm freaking out a little here."

The newscaster reported a firefighter had been injured, but no details were available yet as to the person's identity.

"Oh, God, Alder." She gasped and began to cry. "I love her so much."

Beth wanted to close her eyes and block out the fiery images but couldn't.

❖

"Go, go, go!" Tomas was right behind Mary as she ran toward the ladder.

She kept her eyes on the giant hole ahead of her, which looked like the hideous mouth of a subterranean monster gulping at anything nearby. In five more strides, she was upon the hole, staying far to the left to avoid the unstable roof fragments at the edge of the breach.

That's when she felt shaking underneath her feet.

Another explosion threw Mary to her knees. A second scuttle hatch, the one closest to their ladder, had just ripped apart. Fire shot from its mouth as well.

"Tomas, are you okay?"

He was also on his knees. "Yeah, but this is some shit."

"Come on." She stood and moved toward the edge of the roof.

"I'm right behind you."

Her radio crackled to life. "Walston, Quinones, copy?"

"We're okay, Captain."

"Get the hell off the roof."

"That's what we're trying to do."

The structure had been compromised so much that the next footfall could drop them straight down into the deadly inferno below them. But there wasn't time to call for a truck's ladder to be raised to them.

They were fifty feet from their ladder.

They had to make it.

"Turn to channel six," Alder said.

Beth's hand shook as she clicked over.

"Doesn't seem that the engine companies are having much success keeping this fire at bay." The reporter paused before continuing. "We have now confirmed that the warehouse contained some kind of combustible material and possible canisters of compressed air, accounting for the explosions on the roof."

Columns of ominous smoke belched upward, cutting ugly swaths across the cloudless azure sky.

"There have been two explosions on the roof of the warehouse," the helicopter news reporter said as the images switched to the aerial view. "We've got reports of two firefighters up there. It looks like they are trying to make it to the far end."

The helicopter video images showed the two figures as they dodged a gaping hole in the roof. Their bulky uniforms and helmets made it difficult to distinguish men from women, let alone if one was Mary.

The station reporter chimed in, "And it looks as though this fire has engulfed all floors of the building. This may be a total loss, and for some, will certainly be a Christmas Eve fire that won't be soon forgotten. Let's hope those brave firefighters get to safety."

"I can't stay here, Alder."

"You really need to."

"I'm ten minutes from Potrero Point."

"You won't be able to—"

"I'll call you later." Beth couldn't watch the television anymore. She needed some word from Mary, or just some word about her. The police might block her from getting close, but she had to try.

❖

From her left, Mary saw water from a hose hitting the side of the building just below her. The hissing sound as the water vaporized sent an unsettling chill through her. The temperatures were extremely high, which meant that the building was probably fully involved.

Twenty feet to their ladder. All they had to do was move from the building's edge, toward their right, and reach their means of escape. The hole from the second explosion was not more than ten feet away. She slowed her pace, concentrating on the feel of the roof under her feet.

Tomas must have been doing the same. "Feels sturdy here."

Mary looked into the hole and suddenly grabbed Tomas's sleeve.

She pointed, through the fire, to four large metal canisters lying on their sides. Their usually concave bottoms had popped out, swollen from over-pressurization. Those small bombs were dangerously close to blowing up.

"Get to the ladder," Tomas yelled.

Angry, black smoke billowed out of the roof access room that she had opened up for ventilation not ten minutes earlier. The smoke covered the top four feet of the access room, racing toward open air. On the floor of the doorway, strange back-and-forth movement from something brown caught her eye.

She stopped and squinted, trying to focus on what could be moving.

"What are you doing?" Tomas pushed her. "Come on!"

Suddenly the brown object took a step out of the doorway. It was a soot-covered puppy.

She pointed. "Tomas!" And ran toward it.

"Hurry!" Tomas yelled as she scooped the scared little puppy into her arm and turned.

Tomas was already at the ladder, swinging his leg over the side.

A third, deafening blast shook the building and Mary dropped down, cradling the puppy against her jacket. The explosion came from the opening they had been looking into. The canisters had detonated, ripping the hole even wider. The roof between them was now on fire. She couldn't get to the ladder now.

"Climb down," Mary waved to Tomas, "and then move the ladder over here, closer to me."

Tomas's head disappeared over the edge. She crawled to the side of the roof access room that faced the edge of the building. For now, she was alone with the terrified puppy, shivering against her. She prayed that the roof underneath her would hold up.

❖

Beth followed the clouds of smoke and turned down a side road toward Mariposa Street.

Christmas Eve. This would be their first. She burst into tears. *Please let it be our first.*

Mary had become everything to her. It had been so easy, after she had finally given in to Mary's loving nature and kind spirit, to fall in love deeper than she ever had. A warm memory of their first run together washed through her. Beth had escaped to San Francisco to lose herself in unfamiliar surroundings but had found instead a familiar heart. Mary had been escaping her own pain and, through running, they had grown closer and eventually realized that their paths were destined to join.

She'd lived with Mary less than a year and now she couldn't imagine a life without her. But as she turned onto Mariposa Street and saw the army of fire engines, hoses, police cars, news vans, and chaos, she let out a cry of anguish.

Please let her be safe.

She gripped the wheel and drove until a police officer waved her to a stop. She backed up and parked in the driveway of a closed-down warehouse.

❖

Mary looked up at the news helicopter that circled overhead. Beth's exquisite face flashed before her. She prayed Beth was unaware of the fire. These were the calls that brought firefighter's partners to panic and dread.

How she wished she were home by now, kissing Beth in the kitchen and getting ready to sit down to their first Christmas dinner. How lucky she had been that Beth had given her a chance. They had come from different backgrounds, but they were more similar than she had originally admitted. Mary had been patient and so very thankful that she had pushed through her own fears of commitment. Beth had rescued Mary from pain, from her hidden sadness, and from her fear of giving her heart away again.

Overwhelmed with love, she gulped in a deep breath, feeling the sharp twinge from too much smoke.

The puppy began to whimper.

"I'll save you, little one." Like Beth had saved her.

❖

"I'm looking for Mary Walston. She's with engine five." Beth had found a fire lieutenant at the perimeter of the fire containment area.

"You have to stay back, ma'am. This area is too dangerous."

Beth moved away and found other firefighters half a block away, all facing away from her looking upward at the building. As she got closer, she saw the big patches on the backs of their uniforms. SFFD Engine 5.

She scanned the last names emblazoned above their patches. Blake, Rodriguez, Giovanni, Cooper.

"Coop," she called.

The firefighter turned around. "Beth," he said, but his eyes weren't squinting, happy to see her.

"Where's Mary?"

His lips pressed tightly and then he looked down.

"Coop?"

"She's on the roof."

Her eyes followed his gaze upward.

"The explosions." It was Mary she had seen on television. One of the firefighters fighting to stay alive was her lover. Her head went dizzy and her ears began to ring.

Something gripped her arm and she saw Coop's face. His mouth was moving but all she could hear was the ringing. Her arm was forced down and her body followed until she was sitting on the ground. She shook her head and the sound of the commotion all around her slowly returned.

"They're getting her down, Beth."

❖

The roof had turned hot under Mary's knees and rolled insolently around her.

A clunking noise at the edge of the roof was followed by the sight of the ladder dropping against the building close by. Mary crawled toward it and a few seconds later, Tomas appeared.

"The windows below were spewing fire," he said, "so they've got the hoses on them. Be prepared to get wet on your way down."

She tucked the puppy inside her jacket and climbed over the top rung.

❖

A voice came over the radios of all the Engine 5 men. "Walston's on her way down."

The men erupted in cheers and Beth blew out her breath.

"Didja hear what he said?" Coop asked.

"He said," Beth clasped her shaking hands together, "that my life is on its way back to me."

❖

Mary found the captain and quickly debriefed him on anything that might help them fight the fire. She also asked him if the owner was present and he pointed her to a man standing with a few others by engine ten.

She gently extracted the puppy from her jacket. With her hand under it, she could tell that it was a little girl. A lucky little girl. She walked up to the owner and presented her to him.

"We got the puppy out. She was all the way up on the roof."

"Must have gotten in sometime today or yesterday. The mom's a stray that stays in the warehouse yard next door."

"This isn't your puppy?"

"No, but I imagine it's yours now."

The puppy looked up to Mary and opened her mouth, yawning until her tongue curled.

❖

Beth jumped up when she saw Mary walking between the fire engines.

"Mary!"

Mary smiled and Beth's legs wobbled in relief.

"I love you, Beth."

"I love you, too."

Mary threw an arm around her. When Beth hugged her, Mary said, "Ooh, be careful babe. I want a big hug soon, but we have to be gentle right now."

Mary pulled away and showed her the puppy.

"Oh my gosh, is she okay? Are you okay?"

"I'm fine. And she was on the roof. She's a stray."

"You rescued her."

Mary smiled and kissed her. "I know this was hard on you."

"I was scared to death."

"Loving a firefighter can be a burden."

"Yes." Beth looked into the eyes that would be looking back at her forever. "But it's a beautiful burden." She reached over to pet the pup. "What are we going to name her?"

"You'd like to keep her, too?"

"Seeing what you two went through, I believe she just has to come home with us. She's our Christmas present."

"It's only Christmas Eve."

"Eve." Beth grinned. "Let's call her Eve."

The puppy, seeming satisfied with the situation, laid her head against Mary's jacket and closed her eyes.

They kissed again, Beth thankful for Mary's safe return. She knew there would be more days like this. She would just have to love the heck out of her every moment she could.

"I want to start celebrating. Soon."

Mary handed her the puppy. "Will you take her home while we finish up here?"

"Don't be long. I've got a great dinner planned."

Mary smiled her perfect smile. "We've got a great life planned."

CARSEN TAITE works by day (and sometimes by night) as a criminal defense attorney in Dallas, Texas. Though her day job is often stranger than fiction, she can't seem to get enough, and spends much of her free time plotting stories. She is the author of three novels: *truelesbianlove.com*, *It Should Be a Crime* (Lambda Literary Award finalist), and *Do Not Disturb*. She is currently working on her fourth novel, *Nothing but the Truth* (January 2011), which, like *It Should Be a Crime*, is a romance with a heavy dose of legal drama, drawing heavily on Carsen's experience in the courtroom. The characters in this story first appeared in *It Should Be a Crime*.

Love Is the Key

Carsen Taite

"Stay." Morgan slid her hand down Parker's naked, muscled thigh. She loved waking up next to her. She'd spent the past ten minutes admiring every inch of Parker's body as she slept, from her tousled black hair to her long, sleek legs. Now she wanted a glimpse of Parker's piercing blue eyes.

Parker groaned in response to the touch. "It's Monday morning, right? Study. I have to study." Parker rolled over and pinned her to the bed. "Baby, I want to stay, but I can't study in a hotel room, especially not with your naked self distracting me."

Morgan pretend-wrestled against her lover's restraining hold. "Seems like it wasn't that long ago I was the early riser and you would do anything necessary to keep me in bed." She assumed an uncharacteristic pout. "Stay now. Study later." She nipped at Parker's chest. "You deserve a break."

Parker brushed her hard nipples against Morgan's soft, wet lips. Thoughts of the looming bar exam faded fast against her arousal. She surrendered to the ecstasy of Morgan's touch and the want in her emerald green eyes. She wanted to get a head start on the arduous work ahead, but she gladly devoted herself to Morgan's pleasure first. The intensity of Morgan's orgasm signaled just how much her lover had needed the release.

Until a month ago, their encounters had been restrained by their respective roles: Parker as law student and Morgan as her professor. Even after Parker dropped out of Morgan's class, their crazy schedules had restricted their ability to fully explore each other's minds and bodies. Since her graduation from law school on Saturday, she and Morgan had spent every moment in this bed, with only short bouts of sleep and room service to break up the marathon of celebratory love-making.

"Wow." As the tremors ebbed, Morgan could manage only the one word.

Parker leaned down, kissed the corners of Morgan's barely open eyes, and brushed aside her auburn waves of hair. "Wow, yourself. I can't believe you can still come so fiercely after we've made love nonstop all weekend."

Morgan curled onto her side and pulled Parker into the nook of her embrace. "Speak slower. My brain's numb from sex." She slid her hand down Parker's hip and traced her pelvis. "I'm willing to bet I can reduce you to one-word sentences."

"Hold that thought." Parker eased herself out of Morgan's arms. "Study first. Sex later."

"Killjoy."

"I know, I know." Parker didn't want to leave, but now that a new week had arrived, she knew she had to put in some hours of study toward the bar exam or she wouldn't relax enough to enjoy another lovemaking session. "As much as I want to stay here with you, I need to get a jump on that stuff." She pointed across the room at a stack of bar review books.

"All right, I'll let you go. I have plenty to do anyway."

"Lots of new business, huh?"

"Actually, this week's usually pretty slow on the business front." At Parker's puzzled look, Morgan added, "Christmas is in three days."

Parker paused from pulling on her clothes. "Oh, yeah. I guess it is." For the past several years, Parker had tended bar at a friend's club on Christmas Eve, slept in Christmas morning, and was back at the bar that evening to pour cocktails for all the family day escapees. She had no family of her own and she'd never had a relationship coincide with this holiday. Until now.

Morgan observed the glazed-over look in Parker's eyes. She knew enough about Parker's past to conclude Parker hadn't given holidays a second thought for a long time. Now that they were together, she wanted to change that. "Let's get a tree."

Parker looked around the room and laughed. "A tree? Um, I'm thinking a hotel room is not a good place for a tree. There's a big one in the lobby," she offered as a compromise.

"Not the same. Do Kelsey and Erin have a tree?" Morgan referred to Parker's roommates at the large house they shared in East Dallas.

"Nope, but it's a perfect place for one. Kelsey's never home and Erin's moving in with her boyfriend after the first of the year. She's too busy packing to worry with holiday decorations. Irene has one up at the bar."

"Again, not the same."

"I think you need a house to have a tree."

"No such festivities for room renters and hotel dwellers?"

"You got it."

"Are you still up for spending the holiday with my folks?" Because Parker seemed to have forgotten the holiday altogether, Morgan wasn't sure Parker remembered they had planned to drive down to Morgan's parents' home in Wimberly on Christmas Eve.

"Day after tomorrow?" Parker's tone was semi-hysterical. "Sure, although I have to admit I'm a little nervous about meeting them. Didn't you say your father is a judge?"

"Used to be a judge. He's just a retired country dweller now. You'll love their place. It's just a few miles from town, but it's set in the middle of about fifty beautiful wooded acres." Morgan pondered a moment before she spoke her next words. "I don't suppose this would be a good time to talk about us becoming homeowners."

Parker shook her head. "Not with the bar exam around the corner and your new law practice. Besides, Kelsey's already stressed about Erin moving out. She can't afford the upkeep on the house on her own. If I told her I was moving out, too, I think she might lose it." Parker saw Morgan's disappointment. Hell, she was disappointed herself. She'd love to wake up in a place they could call their own, where they could sneak to the kitchen in the middle of the night, naked, without worrying about roommate sightings. Where they could sleep until noon without the sound of other hotel guests going about their day. As much as she wanted to own a home with Morgan, now was definitely not the right time.

Morgan smiled. "I understand. I won't bug you about it. Oh, and it's *our* new law practice. When I advertise that we have a former police detective on the team, we're going to rake in the clients."

"Gotta pass the bar for that to happen." Parker leaned in and kissed Morgan.

Morgan held her close. "I have an idea. Can you pull yourself away from your studies long enough to have a private, pre-holiday dinner with me? We can exchange gifts, just us, the night before we leave." She could feel Parker's rising panic, and acknowledged it with a tight hug, holding her until she felt the anxiety fade. When a much calmer Parker pulled away, she offered a final squeeze. "Go. Study. I'll make all the plans."

"Okay, babe. That's sounds great. Now I have to grab a shower and head to the library."

Morgan grinned as she watched Parker walk away. Parker's singular focus on her studies would make her holiday planning much easier than she could have hoped.

❖

After six hours huddled in a cubicle, Parker decided studying on her own sucked. Throughout law school, she had been part of a study group populated by the best and brightest students. The result of their combined efforts was a Gestalt certainty they would all score excellent grades on their exams. Because she had chosen to graduate early, she was preparing for the bar exam on her own. She missed the synergy of the group. *Why are you so worried? It's not like you need a job.* It was true, her career path was already set. She and Morgan were going to practice law together, but she didn't want Morgan to cut her any slack because they were lovers.

As much as she wanted to pack in more study time, the words were fuzzy on the page. She packed up her books and trotted out to her car. A few minutes later she pulled into the long driveway of the house she shared with her best friend, Dr. Kelsey James. She was surprised to see Kelsey's car parked in the drive.

She wound her way through the stacks of boxes in the foyer, and found Kelsey in the kitchen. "Hey, Dr. James, I thought you worked twenty-four/seven."

Kelsey dropped the mug in her hand and yelped. "Dammit, Parker, don't sneak up on people. I thought you were holed up in a hotel room, making mad, passionate love to a certain professor."

"She's not a professor anymore." Parker scooped the miraculously unbroken mug off the floor. "You're pretty jumpy. Guess you're used to having the place to yourself?"

"Hell, I haven't been here enough to enjoy anything. I just stopped by to change. What are you doing here?"

"I live here, remember?"

"In rent only. I kind of figured you and Morgan had taken up permanent residence at the hotel."

"No, the hotel's only temporary. Now that the office is up and running, she wants to resume her house search and include me, but I told her this wasn't a good time."

"Hopefully not on my account. You know I'll figure out a way to manage if you want to move in with her."

Parker grinned. "I don't see how. Judging by all the boxes, I'm guessing Erin's taking all your worldly goods. My meager belongings may be all that stands between you and civilization."

Kelsey shrugged. "I guess she had more stuff than I realized. But back to Morgan. Don't you want to live with her?"

"Sure I do, but not in a tall building with daily maid service. Seriously, James, I can't really focus on anything except the bar exam right now. I didn't even realize Christmas is this week."

"Oh, so now you have to add shopping to your list."

"Yep. We're supposed to exchange gifts tomorrow night. What do you buy the woman who has everything? She wants a tree. Don't think I'm going to find one that will fulfill her expectations and still be appropriate for a hotel room."

"Hardly." Kelsey glanced at her watch, her expression anxious. "Well, you better get a move on if you're going to get any shopping done. Come on, I'll help you." She grabbed Parker's arm and steered her toward the door. "Go start the car, I'll be right out."

"Hang on a sec. I thought you were between shifts. I just stopped by to pick up some clothes. I didn't plan on a shopping trip."

"I've got a little time, and you need the help. We'll run over to Northpark. When's the last time you bought a gift for a woman you're madly in love with?" Parker gave her a blank look, and Kelsey shook her head. "Go on, I'll be right there. You can pick up clothes when we get back." Without waiting for an answer, Kelsey picked up a pen and started scribbling a note.

The last thing Parker wanted to do was take an impromptu trip to a mall crowded with frantic shoppers, but she did need a present and the thought of selecting one on her own was daunting. She shook her head and went outside to get the heat going in her car. Mere moments later, Kelsey slid into the passenger seat and rapped her hand on the dash. "Let's go."

Parker took her at her word and roared the big engine in her '68 Mustang fastback to life. As she turned onto the main street, she noticed a large Lexus SUV turning onto Kelsey's street. She did a double take, but the SUV wasn't the same color as Morgan's Lexus. Before she could focus on the occupants, Kelsey punched her on the shoulder. "Come on, quit dawdling. I thought you called this a muscle car for a reason. Let's get to the mall."

Parker tore her attention away from the passing SUV. "The mall it is."

❖

"Well, that was rotten timing. I guess I should have figured she'd be around. I mean technically, she still lives over here." Morgan slid down in her seat even though she knew Parker's Mustang was well out of sight.

"I doubt she saw you. It's not like we're in your car." Aimee Howard dug through the console between the seats as she steered her Lexus into a broad driveway next to a beautiful three-story house. "You should introduce us."

"Yes, definitely. I'm thinking of opening lines now. 'Parker, I want you to meet the woman I dated briefly when I was trying to forget about you. Remember that time you saw us together and became insanely jealous?'" Morgan shuddered. "I think I'll pass." She pointed at the house in front of them. "Can we just go in?"

Aimee dangled a key before her eyes. "You bet. Come on."

Morgan paced the hotel room. She was sure it grew smaller with each lap. It was nine p.m. Maybe Parker had decided to return to the library after she finished whatever she'd been doing with Kelsey. *Or*

maybe she saw you riding around town with another woman and she doesn't plan on coming back. She shrugged away the thought. Parker might have been insecure about their future a couple of months ago, but they'd survived a lot since then, including a near-death experience. They were a committed couple now, and nothing could tear that apart. Not even pre-holiday, pre–bar exam stress. Still, after spending the previous forty-eight hours naked, tangled in each other's embrace, Morgan couldn't help but feel a sharp sense of separation since she had last held Parker close.

She glanced at the clock again. The law library had closed ten minutes ago. Morgan reached for the phone and dialed Parker's cell. As her call went to voice mail, she heard the familiar sound of a key card being pushed and pulled out of the door slot. She strode to the door and swung it open. Parker's smile was the first thing she saw.

"Hey you, I was starting to worry." Morgan drew Parker into her arms.

Parker landed a quick peck on Morgan's cheek, then edged away from Morgan's embrace. "Sorry. I lost track of time. Have you eaten? I'm starving, but I need a shower first. If you've already had dinner, I can order something." She kept up a steady stream of rambling as she made her way to the bathroom. She knew she sounded manic, but she needed to get out of the room before Morgan noticed the huge bulge under her jacket.

Morgan struggled to hide her disappointment at Parker's distance. "I waited for you. I'll order something for both of us."

"Great, thanks." Parker disappeared into the bathroom and seconds later, Morgan heard the shower running. She picked up a phone and ordered a festive meal she had no appetite for. While she waited for dinner to be delivered, she sprawled on the couch and closed her eyes.

"Baby, dinner's here."

Morgan looked up to see Parker, wearing an animal print robe, steering a service cart across the room. She yawned large and shook herself awake. She must have fallen asleep; she hadn't even heard the knock on the door. "I'm sorry, I didn't mean to snooze." She noticed Parker's bare feet. Her hair was still damp. "Did you answer the door like that?"

"Yep. I think he slipped us some extra condiments. I should flash my robe more often."

"Tease."

"You got it."

Morgan felt a rush of want. She scooted over on the sofa. "As long as you're giving it away, I have first dibs. Come sit by me."

"In a minute." Parker extended her hand. "Come here. I have a surprise for you."

Morgan placed her hand in Parker's and followed her to the bedroom. She immediately noticed the addition. On the nightstand closest to her side of the bed a tiny rosemary bush, shaped to look like a Christmas tree and decked with tiny white lights and miniature multicolored glass ornaments, lit up the corner of the room. Beneath the boughs was a small box wrapped in shiny silver paper.

"I see someone did something more than studying today."

"Guilty. Kelsey insisted on a shopping trip. She said waiting until Christmas Eve was suicidal at best."

"So you went by the house today?" Morgan waited for a mention of Parker having spotted her.

"Yeah, I needed to pick up some clothes." Parker pointed at the box. "Aren't you even going to shake your present?"

Morgan scoured Parker's face for hints of realization until she was satisfied none were there. Maybe Parker hadn't seen her with Aimee after all. "Don't get me wrong. I'm highly interested in what's in that box, but," she tugged at the tie on Parker's robe, "I'm focused on unwrapping this present first."

"It's just a little something. A token of my affection."

"It may be small, but I recall it creating quite a stir last night." Morgan continued her efforts to disrobe her lover until Parker stilled her hands.

"I'm talking about the present. Under the tree."

"Oh, that present."

"Be serious, Morgan. I'm warning you, it's not much, so don't go buying me something extravagant for Christmas." Parker's expression became earnest. "Promise me."

Morgan's stomach clenched with guilt. If only Parker had known what she'd been doing all afternoon. The last thing she wanted was to do anything that might wreck their newfound love. She decided extravagance was a matter of perception. "I promise."

❖

The next morning, faced with the prospect of another long, lonely day of studying without even a dreaded shopping trip to break the monotony, Parker found it even harder to get out of bed. She rolled toward the middle of the king-sized bed, and was surprised to find Morgan missing. She forced her eyes open and slowly focused on a sharply dressed woman brushing her hair.

"And here I was, thinking about playing hooky. Where are you going, looking like a lawyer?"

Morgan glanced over her shoulder. Parker was adorable, wrapped in the sheets. She wanted to toss her hairbrush down and join her under the covers. "I have a little shopping of my own to do."

"You look more like a working woman than a shopping one."

"I may run by the office and take care of a few things before everyone shuts down for the holiday."

"What if I came by and did my studying there?"

"Well, you could, but I only planned to be there for a few minutes," Morgan said, hoping to dissuade her. If Parker spent the day at the office, she would be too distracted to focus on what she had planned.

"So, you're wearing your hottest suit on the off chance a wealthy new client happens to drop by at the same moment you happen to be there?"

Morgan knew Parker was teasing, that the undercurrent of guilt was entirely self-inflicted, but she couldn't ignore the feeling. Not that it mattered. She had an appointment she couldn't miss, and taking Parker along wasn't part of her plan.

She sat on the edge of the bed. "I have a meeting outside the office." She thought quickly, making a mental note to place a couple of calls as soon as she was out of Parker's presence. "Remember, we're meeting for dinner. How about we make it an early one?"

"Sure. Here at the hotel?"

"Actually, I was thinking I would pick up a dinner for two from Central Market, and we could eat at your place."

Parker scrunched her brow. "My place? Oh, you mean Kelsey's house."

"You look disappointed."

"I guess I imagined a romantic dinner for two."

"We can light lots of candles and have a picnic in your room. It'll be like the first time we were together."

"Except there was no food at that particular picnic."

"I don't recall going hungry," Morgan purred.

Parker smiled at Morgan's sexy expression and decided a romantic dinner in her room at the house where she'd first made love to Morgan would be the perfect end to a boring day of studying. "Meet you back here at six?"

"Perfect." Morgan paused on her way to the door. "I love you."

"I know. I love you, too."

❖

Morgan flinched when the door to Kelsey's house flew open before Parker could fit her key in the lock. She shrugged when Parker shot a surprised look her way.

Kelsey spoke first. "Hey, you two. My shift changed, but don't worry, I have plans, but not here. I had to take care of a couple of things before heading out." She waved them in. "I'll only be a few minutes."

Parker walked into the living room, but Morgan hung back. She whispered in Kelsey's ear, "Are you alone?"

Kelsey answered quietly. "Nope. She was running late. You're going to have some explaining to do."

Morgan rushed to catch up to Parker. She found her lover in the living room, standing in front of Aimee Howard. Parker wore a puzzled expression and Aimee looked like she wanted to vaporize herself.

Parker placed the grocery bag on the coffee table and shoved a hand toward Aimee. "Parker Casey, nice to meet you." Morgan approached them and took over the introductions.

"Parker, this is a friend of mine, Aimee Howard." Morgan watched Parker's expression slowly morph from puzzled to perturbed.

Parker pointed at Aimee. "Wait a minute, I know you." She turned back to Morgan. "Didn't you two date? What's she doing here?" Parker swung around and delivered a piercing stare in Kelsey's direction. "Would someone like to tell me what's going on?"

Kelsey was the first to speak. "Aimee and I were just leaving." She grabbed Aimee's hand and pulled her toward the door. Aimee dropped a large white envelope on the coffee table as she passed by. Kelsey paused long enough to look Parker squarely in the eye. "Morgan bought you the perfect Christmas gift. Get her to show it to you."

Parker flinched at the crack of the slamming door. She looked at Morgan.

"I can explain."

Parker raised her eyebrows.

"We didn't date. Well, not really. She's my realtor. I briefly considered dating her, before you and I…well, when you and I were still trying to figure out what we wanted from each other. There was no spark between us. I mean between her and me. She's my realtor." Morgan, who was paid handsomely for her ability to persuade, found herself unable to stop babbling.

Parker placed a finger on Morgan's lips. "Shh." She grasped Morgan's hand, led her to the couch, and settled in beside her. "It's okay. I was disappointed, but mostly because I expected us to be alone and it was disconcerting to see her again, especially here. I'm not jealous. I wonder if she's dating Kelsey. Sure looks that way."

Morgan decided this wasn't the time to correct Parker's assumption. "We're alone now."

Parker made a show of looking around. "You sure? Your accountant or banker isn't lurking around here, too?"

Morgan punched Parker in the ribs. "You're funny." She cuddled close. "Dinner first or presents?"

"Sounds like someone wants her present."

"More like I want to see your face when you open yours."

Parker shook her head. "Morgan, I thought we agreed. Nothing extravagant."

Morgan waved her arm. "You see anything extravagant here?" She reached into her purse and pulled out a small box wrapped in shiny silver paper. She shook it. "Doesn't sound like much to me."

"Hey, where did you get that?" Parker reached into her jacket pocket and pulled out an identical package.

"The store." Morgan grinned and shoved the box toward Parker. "Open it."

Parker traded packages with Morgan. "You first."

Morgan didn't hesitate. She tore through the wrapping. After a quick "oh yeah" when she saw the box, she opened the lid. "Parker, it's beautiful." She held up the lone key it held. "What's this?"

"I made a copy of the office key. I thought you'd like a brand-new fancy key ring for *our* brand-new office. It's an eternal circle. You like?"

"I love." Morgan tapped the other package. "Your turn."

As Parker pulled back the wrapping, Morgan reached for the envelope Aimee had left behind. She held it and waited.

"This box looks very familiar." Parker held a pale blue Tiffany's box. She lifted the lid and pulled out a key ring, identical to the one she'd given Morgan. She smiled. "Obviously, I love the key ring. You have great taste." Parker examined the single key. "What does this open?"

"Part two of your gift." Morgan handed Parker the envelope. "Here's the rest of your present." Parker opened the flap and pulled out a sheaf of papers. She was used to reading legalese, but it still took her a moment to take in what she was holding in her hand. *Deed of Trust.*

"You bought me a house?"

"Well, kind of. I bought *us* a house." Morgan pointed to the key in Parker's hand. "I have a key, too. The key ring was Kelsey's idea."

"She was with me when I bought your present. That girl can't keep a secret."

"I don't know about that. She helped me with both parts of your present."

"How did she—wait a minute…" Parker looked back at the papers and read past the first few lines. She read her name next to Morgan's, and a property description that contained a very familiar address. "You bought *this* house? Kelsey's house?"

"You love it, you're too busy to look for a new place, and your stuff's already here. Kelsey wants to downsize. It seems like the perfect solution. I'm cheating in a way, since we'll *both* be working our tails off to maintain it, but I hope you don't mind. Merry Christmas, baby." Morgan waited anxiously for Parker's reaction.

Parker held the papers to her chest. "It's perfect. I love it. I love you." She dangled the key in front of Morgan's eyes. "But just so you know, our love is the only key I need."

Nestled in the foothills of the Berkshires, Bobbi Marolt happily writes, constantly thinks "what's next?" for her work, and strives for a difference with each of her stories. Her first Bold Strokes publication is *Between the Lines*, a romance. "Merry Christmas from Down Under" is her first short story and introduces Marty Jamison and Liz Chandler. They will make their full-story debut when Marty and Liz star under the neon lights of Broadway in *Loving Liz*, due in 2011. Meanwhile, they wish you a Merry Christmas!

Merry Christmas from Down Under

Bobbi Marolt

It's Christmas Eve in the Big Apple. Snow falls quietly and carolers crowd street corners that aren't already manned by the Salvation Army cauldrons. Somewhere, chestnuts roast and children dream of morning's presents.

It's all good, or so I hear. I don't get to experience holidays in the same way regular New Yorkers do, although I often wish I could do a little figure-skating at Rockefeller Center. Not one to participate outside of my humble dwelling, I do hear all things, which helps set my moods. Songs of Santa and Rudolph fill the air, and I especially like when Marty sings "Silver Bells." This Christmas is especially thrilling for me, but first things first.

I must apologize. I'm not from Australia. Although the temperature outside fluctuates between hot and bitter cold, my climate averages 98.6 degrees and is continually damp. I nestle within soft folds of flesh that keep me well hidden and protected from the world, and I'm subject only to the touch of someone special and to that of my owner, Marty Jamison. I'm Marty's clitoris. I have a date on this eve filled with joy and giving, and you'll hear more about that soon. I think it's appropriate that I tell you some things about Marty and me first.

Few have met me, and that isn't always a lonely existence. When Marty's single, she gives me the attention I need. Marty has a gentle touch and understands how much I hate the tumultuous flesh burn and ungodly buzz of a vibrator. Marty treats me with slow massage and a cute little side-to-side ride with her hips. It's fun for both of us. I'm not particularly needy, but there are times when Marty's anxious hormones find their way to me.

You see, Marty is a stage actor, singer, and dancer. It isn't uncommon for her to excite me while she's onstage strutting and teasing the general public. Her audience isn't aware, but while she's giving up the goods with a song or dance, Marty sexes me up with constant leg motion that stirs and awakens me. Her randy little hormones surround and tease me, and I make my desire known by pinging her with a constant rhythm of delicate throbs. Sometimes I think she deliberately teases me when she tightens her legs and swings her hips side to side. Those hips simply are not limited to the delight of the audience. I can say that with knowledge because Marty always gives me a little lovin' when we're home again.

Well and good, but also boring at times. Nothing beats the touch of another woman who loves Marty and treats me with some of the happiest moments of my life. I mean, if that touch is all I have, I deserve the best. A gentle glide from a woman's lips, a warm blanket from her tongue, oh yeah, those things I do miss. Now Marty, she doesn't sleep around, and I can appreciate that choice because…well…you know the old question: "Where were those fingers last?" I shudder to think. It had been two years before another woman piqued our interest, and Marty's new lover is my date tonight. She's the someone special I mentioned earlier.

Her name is Elizabeth Chandler, Liz for short. God, just saying her name makes me take a breath of contentment and yeah, I quiver. I like Liz.

Liz arrived in Marty's life about four months ago. Although I had doubts about her initially, I couldn't help but do a little happy dance every time Liz came near Marty. To show my delight, I gave Marty a little nudge now and then, just to let her know I was interested in Liz. Marty, she waited. I throbbed while she waited. And waited. And waited.

Marty nearly killed me with her no-rush policy, and I firmly decided the hell with that attitude. I put up a fight for Liz. I knew what I wanted and made sure I got it more readily than Marty would have normally liked. In one sense, though, I give Marty credit. I feel good about having to wait, even for the slightest amount of time, because Marty thought with her brain and didn't give me full control. Some days I damned her, of course.

Before Liz, I had a string of nicknames. One woman called me a happy button and another called me rosebud. I might have tolerated rosebud, but even in these dark crevasses, I'm savvy to the sled. Who wants that thought in bed with them? Rubyfruit was a silly name, too, and then there was a woman who dared call me the little man in the boat. Nuh-uh. No men here. I quickly deflated and Marty promptly discarded the purveyor of those words. I think Marty's words were close to "Get the hell out of my bed." Whatever her words of choice, I agreed.

Ah, my Liz. Can you hear me sigh? Liz calls me Kitten. How cute is that? No one has ever called me anything so charming. Charm. That's what Liz is about in my book. She's charming and possesses the perfect combination of sensual arousal. Her perfume is to die for and I think she uses a hint of peppermint mouthwash. Couple those with a soft voice and the silkiest tongue—Liz makes me purr.

Tonight is Christmas Eve. Liz promised me a special evening, and I hear Marty softly singing "Silver Bells." It's Liz's favorite, too. I know Liz is near. While city sidewalks have been bustling, Marty's hormones have been gathering and swirling around, ready for me to make my entrance.

Wait, I think Liz is coming closer. The anticipation kills me and I tremble at the thought of her next move. Liz will use her delicate, warm fingers to push away the lips that keep me hidden and—yes! Cool air pelts me and Liz is here with lips to warm me again.

Ah, bliss. Liz's precious lips surround me. Marty's hips move slowly, taking me along on her gentle ride. A surprise touch from Liz's tongue sends a shock so strong that I drive it throughout Marty to ease my pleasure and pressure. Otherwise, I know I'll explode.

What? No! Liz stopped. Please come back Liz. This isn't…I'm not—

Suddenly the ride stops and I feel Liz's cheek against me again. She's nuzzling me, loving me in the gentlest way. I purr.

"Merry Christmas, Kitten," Liz barely whispers to me. "I'll return in a few minutes." She kisses me ever so softly.

Sigh. Merry Christmas, Liz.

MEGHAN O'BRIEN is a web developer and author of four lesbian fiction novels. Her third, *Thirteen Hours*, was a winner of the 2009 Golden Crown Literary Society award for Lesbian Erotica. She lives in Northern California amongst the redwood groves and vineyards, a far cry from her native Michigan, where she grew up in a suburb of Detroit. "The Afterparty" features characters from the 2009 contemporary romance novel *Battle Scars*. Her newest work, a paranormal romance/thriller titled *Wild*, is scheduled for publication in 2011.

The Afterparty
Meghan O'Brien

Ray McKenna stood in the doorway of the North Coast Veterinary Clinic and watched with pride as her partner and owner of the practice, Dr. Carly Warner, bade the receptionist good night. Joyce was the last of Carly's employees to leave the annual Christmas party, which had been a well-attended and utterly exhausting affair. For Ray, at least. Carly was positively glowing even after having spent the past four hours being the most charming, funny, and engaging host Ray had ever seen. It was clear that her employees loved her, almost as much as Ray did.

"I guess it's true what they say about opposites attracting," Ray said as she watched Joyce load her Pomeranian into the car. "You're great at parties. Which is good. Helps compensate for me."

"Don't be silly. You were wonderful tonight." Carly wrapped an arm around Ray's waist and pulled her closer, giving Joyce one last wave as she drove out of the parking lot. "I was so proud of you."

"I barely spoke." Ray knew that as far as Carly was concerned, her willingness to attend the party at all was enough. Having struggled with PTSD, agoraphobia, and crippling social anxiety after returning from Iraq almost three years before, she'd pulled off a minor miracle by surviving a raucous White Elephant gift exchange, eating with people she barely knew, and participating in general holiday cheer. Still, she wished she could have been half as amiable and outgoing as her partner. "I had a nice time, I just never know what to say to people."

"You were fine." Carly pulled Ray inside the clinic, closing the front door behind them. "Every time you did speak, you were funny, and warm." Leaning close, Carly gave Ray a gentle kiss on the lips. "And sexy."

Ray giggled, still a little self-conscious after an entire evening of feeling awkward. "I'm pretty sure you were the only person who thought that."

"That you were funny and warm? Doubt it."

"The other part."

Carly nipped at Ray's lower lip gently. "The sexy part?"

Ray's face heated. "Yeah."

"I better have been the only one to think that." Carly drew back from their embrace and winked. "I'll fire anyone who even looks at you sideways."

"Whatever." Laughing, Ray stole another kiss and eyed their attentive audience.

The waiting area was decked out with strings of colorful lights and seasonal decorations. A small Christmas tree sat in the corner of the room with wrapped packages—donations for the local animal shelter—piled beneath. The most festive things in the room, however, were the two dogs that stood side by side behind them, wagging their tails. Jack the shepherd mix was still wearing the antlers Carly had slipped onto his head at the beginning of the party, and Ray's therapy dog Jagger—a blue Great Dane—had a bell-covered collar around his neck.

"Those poor abused animals." Ray shook her head.

Carly snickered as she walked to Jack and removed his antlers. "They're good sports."

"Indeed they are." Ray eased the jingle bells over Jagger's massive skull. "It was Mommy's idea. Not mine."

"Oh, sure. Blame me." Carly scratched Jack behind his ear. It was clear from his beaming doggy grin that he wasn't holding a grudge. "Playing good mommy, bad mommy, are we?"

Ray glanced sideways, sharing a smile with Carly. "It's just that you're so good when you're being bad."

Carly's grin turned positively wicked. "Well, that's true."

Ray broke eye contact first. She had made great strides as far as getting used to flirting so brazenly, but after such a socially intense evening, she slipped back into old habits without meaning to. Sometimes sharing such boldly sexual energy with a woman as beautiful as Carly was still overwhelming.

"Hey," Carly murmured, her smile gentle when Ray finally met her gaze, "you really were amazing tonight. Thanks for coming to the party."

"Are you kidding? I wouldn't have missed it for the world." At Carly's raised eyebrow, Ray chuckled. "Okay, so maybe that's overstating a bit."

"Maybe a bit."

"Seriously, I wanted to come. It was your first office party since buying the practice. Kind of a big moment and everything." Ray moved closer and touched Carly's lower back. The connection centered her immediately. "It was important to you. That meant it was important to me."

Carly laced her fingers behind Ray's neck. "Have I mentioned lately how brave you are? And how lucky I am?"

Ray encircled Carly's waist and drew Carly tightly against her. Now that they were alone, her nervous energy dissipated, replaced by familiar desire. "Yeah, but I like hearing it."

Carly gave her a slow, soft kiss. "I am *so* lucky."

"Damn right you are." Ray dropped her hands to caress Carly's bottom, exhaling as some of her newly discovered confidence came flooding back. Being around other people was getting easier, but nothing would ever feel as good as the time she spent with the woman who held her heart. Alone with Carly, Ray was at her best.

"There she is." With a sigh, Carly trailed her fingernails up Ray's flanks, along the sides of her breasts. "There's my sexy, confident, in-control Ray."

Ray kissed Carly's neck, her skin tingling everywhere Carly caressed. She squeezed Carly's buttocks and pulled her hard against her thigh. "Here I am."

"You may not be comfortable with crowds, darling, but you're *incredible* in one-on-one situations." Carly stroked over Ray's stomach, then sneaked a hand up under her shirt. She palmed Ray's breast through her bra, turning Ray's legs to water. "Maybe we should go in my office and exchange presents."

"I love presents." Ray released Carly with effort, not trusting herself to stay on her feet through much more teasing. "You don't want to do presents at home?"

Carly shook her head, giving her a smile that dripped with pure sex. Clearly the season brought out the naughty girl inside. "I've got something for you to unwrap right now. In my office."

Ray raised an eyebrow. "Is this a *planned* seduction, Dr. Warner?"

"Maybe." Carly grabbed Ray's hand, pulling her past the dogs into the back room. "Let's just say that I've always fantasized about being fucked in my office."

Ray stumbled slightly, clumsy with arousal. Being with Carly had opened up a whole new world as far as lovemaking was concerned. She had no idea whether sex was just plain better between two women or if the chemistry between her and Carly was theirs alone, but she had never experienced pleasure like Carly brought her. Each time was better than the last, and as far as Ray was concerned, there was no safer, happier place in the universe than between Carly's thighs.

Carly opened her office door and gestured Ray inside. "After you, my love."

"You're in rare form tonight," Ray said, zeroing in on Carly's desk. The room was messy as usual, but the desk, normally cluttered, was pristine. "And you cleaned."

"I did." Carly sat on the edge of the broad walnut desk, beckoning Ray closer. "Come here."

Ray obeyed, pushing Carly's thighs apart so she could stand between them. She rested her fingertips on Carly's throat and kissed her, sweeping her tongue deep into the soft heat of Carly's mouth. When she drew back, she murmured, "You like in-control Ray, do you?"

Carly hummed her agreement. "I adore her."

"Good." Carly always said she liked it when Ray took charge, and Ray could finally admit that she liked it, too. A lot.

Ray fingered the top button of Carly's shirt. "Is this what I'm supposed to unwrap?"

"It is." Carly bit her lip, wrapping her legs around Ray's hips and tugging her closer. "Go ahead."

Ray undid the top button, holding Carly's gaze. "I think I'm going to like this present."

"I know you will." Carly batted her eyelashes as Ray got her shirt fully unbuttoned. "It's new."

Dropping her gaze to Carly's chest, Ray sucked in a deep breath.

Carly's creamy breasts were encased in a red, lacy bra that Ray had never seen before. Except possibly in her dreams. "Oh. Wow."

"Festive, isn't it?"

Ray licked her lips and eased Carly's shirt off her shoulders. "Please tell me you bought matching panties."

"Why don't you find out?" Carly's finger traced a line down the center of Ray's chest.

A shot of hot dizzying lust rid her of all the day's inhibitions. Alone with Carly in her office, she wasn't afraid of anything. Ray's focus narrowed to the two of them, to the pleasure they were about to bring to each other. She found the button on Carly's pants and thumbed it open with one hand, the other hand exploring the swell of Carly's breast where it rose above the lacy bra cup.

Unzipping Carly's pants, Ray pulled the material down just far enough to reveal a strip of crimson lace and grinned. "You *are* bad."

"I hope that doesn't mean I'm getting coal this year." Carly played with the neck of Ray's shirt, curling her finger under the edge of the fabric. "Maybe if I promise to be *very* good for the next couple hours or so?"

"Good is overrated." Ray eased Carly's pants down the length of her legs, taking her shoes off as she went. Then she stood, hungry at the sight of Carly in her revealing lingerie. "I can't believe you were wearing this the whole time. I watched you during the entire party with no idea."

"You watched me?" Carly planted her hands on the desk behind her and leaned back, showing off her supple curves. "Really?"

Ray brushed her hand over Carly's bare stomach, enjoying the subtle twitch of her muscles as she reacted to the touch. "You know I did. I always do."

"And I always know." Carly brought her leg up and braced her bare foot on the edge of her desk. Teasing Ray with a tantalizing glimpse of slick, pink flesh. "I love how your eyes feel on me."

"I guess you must." Ray slowly traced a line up the inside of Carly's thigh. She pushed her fingertip beneath the elastic leg of Carly's panties, exhaling as she discovered the silky softness of Carly's labia. "Good thing, too. 'Cause I can't tear my eyes away from you right now."

"That was the idea."

Ray dragged her gaze from the lacy fabric between Carly's legs to the enticing display of her cleavage. "I don't know where to start."

Carly dipped her knee farther to the side, smiling slyly. "I have some suggestions."

Ray leaned in for another hard kiss. Caressing Carly's throat, she whispered, "I think I've made a decision," and pressed Carly backward, laying her down across the desk. "Stay there."

"Yes, ma'am." Carly grinned up at her, slowly running her fingers over the tops of her breasts. "I've been waiting for this all night."

"You should've told me there was going to be an afterparty." Ray dragged Carly's office chair closer, then sat down, pushing Carly's thighs apart so she could roll herself between them. "Something to get me through the small talk."

"You knew you were getting laid tonight. Didn't you?"

Ray grinned, guiding Carly's leg over her shoulder. "Well, I hoped." She lowered her face and took a good, long look at the delicate, silky material that covered Carly's pussy. "Beautiful."

Carly tangled her fingers in Ray's hair, urging her closer. Ray went eagerly. She kissed Carly gently through her panties, moaning at the dampness against her mouth. Poking out her tongue, she sampled Carly's flavor, loving the idea that the layer of fabric between them dampened the pleasure Carly clearly craved. Ray wanted to draw things out as long as she could stand it because Carly always came hardest when Ray built her up slowly.

Carly whimpered at the deliberate motion of Ray's tongue. "No. Not slow." She tightened her hands on Ray's head, arching her hips into the air. "Fast."

Drawing back, Ray grinned at Carly's familiar strategy. "I thought you liked in-control Ray."

"I love in-control Ray. Especially when she makes me come hard and fast."

Ray kissed Carly through her panties again. "I don't believe that." Placing her palms against Carly's inner thighs, she spread Carly's legs as wide as they would go.

Carly inhaled sharply then moaned.

"You like feeling exposed. Vulnerable." Ray hooked a fingertip under the edge of Carly's panties, pulling the material to the side. Just far enough so she could gently lick Carly's labia. "Don't you?"

"Yes."

Ray closed her eyes against the surge of power she felt at Carly's submissive posture. She stroked up Carly's stomach to her soft, lace-covered breast and licked Carly again, then once more, harder. Carly's thighs trembled against Ray's shoulders. Like that, Ray's need to possess Carly shot into overdrive.

"I love these panties," Ray murmured. "And it's time for them to go." She rolled the office chair back so Carly could close her thighs. Carly's triumphant grin didn't go unnoticed. "Don't gloat. I'm still in charge here."

"Sure you are." Carly turned on a seductive smile that made Ray glad she was already sitting down.

Ray curled her fingers under the waistband of Carly's panties, tugged them off, and carefully set them aside. Those were definitely keepers. Ray steeled her expression as she stood and leaned over Carly, drawing so close their mouths nearly touched.

"I *am* in charge." Ray slid her hand along Carly's inner thigh. She could feel Carly's heat inches away from the source, could smell her scent hanging heavily in the air. Knowing that Carly was expecting slow, Ray entered her fully with a single finger, fast but careful. Carly tipped her head back and cried out, an ecstatic shout of surprised pleasure. Ray pulled out before Carly could adjust to the sensation and grazed the slick length of Carly's labia with her fingertip. "Isn't that right?"

Carly made a noise that was somewhere between a laugh and a sob. "When did you get so good at this?"

Ray's confidence soared. They had been working toward this dynamic for months, and she was finally starting to feel at ease with it. Whatever had happened in the past, she was safe when she was with Carly. And she could do anything.

Ray pushed her fingertip far enough inside for Carly to feel it, but not enough to satisfy her need. "We've been practicing. Remember?"

"Oh, I remember." Carly bit her lip and closed her eyes. She lifted her hips, but Ray moved with her. "Please, Ray. I've wanted you all night. You can't torture me like this."

"But I can." Ray rubbed her thumb over Carly's clit, once, twice. Then she removed her hand altogether. "And I will."

Throwing her arm over her eyes, Carly groaned. "Mean."

Ray caught Carly's lower lip between her teeth and bit down until Carly gasped out loud. Instantly she released her, soothing her lip with her tongue.

"Want my mouth on you?" Ray rubbed her mouth over Carly's, felt Carly smile. "Ask for it and you can have it."

"I've been asking."

Ray skimmed her lips over Carly's ear. "Not how I like to be asked."

Carly shivered beneath her and gripped Ray's biceps, squeezing tightly. The sharp bite of her fingernails had Ray so wet, so fast, she knew she wouldn't be able to draw things out much longer. Her only hope was that Carly would hurry up and say the words Ray desperately wanted to hear.

"Please, Ray," Carly breathed against Ray's cheek. "I need my pussy eaten. *So fucking bad.* If you don't fuck me with your tongue *right* now, I'm gonna explode."

Ray shuddered. Carly's incredibly sexy way with words set her on fire like nothing else. Too overcome with the dizzying need to taste Carly to muster a response, Ray kissed down Carly's throat, between her breasts, across her stomach until she reached her destination between Carly's thighs.

Carly clasped the back of Ray's head and forced her closer. Nuzzling Carly's wetness, Ray opened her mouth and had a long, lingering taste. The balance of power had clearly shifted, but Ray couldn't care less. She sucked on Carly's labia, lapping at her with her tongue.

"Oh fuck *yes*." Carly moaned as Ray pulled her leg over her shoulder and dove in deeper. "Just like that. Suck me like that."

Ray reached beneath Carly with one hand, grabbing a handful of her ass and holding her in place. In a moment Carly would be wriggling all over the place—she always did when she was getting eaten out—and Ray didn't want her to get away. Not when she was enjoying Carly so damn much.

For the moment Carly wasn't talking. Instead she moaned loudly, moving her hips in rhythm against Ray's mouth. She could make Carly come as quickly as she wanted, and for all her threatening about taking it slow, the combination of the lingerie and Carly's dirty talk left her with no choice. There was no holding back tonight.

Ray toyed with Carly's opening with the tips of two fingers and Carly's moans escalated from just that little bit of penetration. Ray fought not to just thrust inside and find the sweet spot she knew would send Carly over the edge. But she waited, needing to hear Carly's voice one more time.

Carly seemed to read her mind. "Fuck me with your fingers, baby. I need you inside me *now*."

Circling her tongue around Carly's clit, Ray eased her fingers inside Carly as deep as she could go, curling the tips upward as she thrust in and out. Carly groaned and one hand flew to her own breast, where she tugged at her nipple through the fabric of her bra.

Carly losing control snapped the last of Ray's, and she fucked her faster. She sucked Carly's clit into her mouth, flicking at the swollen flesh with the point of her tongue. Carly cried out, nonsense words, and dug her heel into Ray's back, tightening around Ray's fingers until she came hard.

Within moments, Carly went from clutching Ray close to struggling away. "Stop, baby, I can't take any more."

Ray left Carly with one last, loving lick, then drew back with a satisfied murmur. "Merry Christmas."

"Yes, ma'am." Carly laughed shakily and propped herself up on her elbows.

Ray smiled and reached behind Carly's back, unhooking her bra. She slipped it off Carly's shoulders and tossed it on top of the panties. Carly raised an eyebrow and sat up on the desk.

"You were overdressed," Ray said.

Carly tugged at the hem of Ray's shirt. "You're the overdressed one."

With a self-assuredness she hadn't possessed even eight months ago, Ray slowly eased her shirt over her head. Carly's admiring stare lit a warm glow in the pit of Ray's stomach, making it easy to perform a pseudo striptease while Carly watched with wide eyes.

"Merry Christmas, indeed," Carly said when Ray shed her panties.

Standing naked in front of Carly, Ray was wholly comfortable in her own skin. The first time they'd slept together, the physical and emotional scars of Ray's time in Iraq had made her powerfully self-conscious, but no longer. Carly made her feel like the most gorgeous—and powerful—woman in the world.

Carly stood, took Ray into her arms, and kissed her languorously. She spun them around, still joined at the mouth, and backed Ray onto the desk so she sat on the edge. After a last flick at Ray's mouth she nibbled a path down her throat to a painfully erect nipple.

"Do I get to lick you now?" Carly asked, punctuating the question with a flick of her tongue against the tip of Ray's breast. "Please?"

Ray lay back and spread her legs. "You'd better."

Never one to take things slowly, Carly sat in her office chair, rolled forward, and licked Ray's swollen pussy with the flat of her tongue. Ray cried out and gripped the edge of the desk, amazed by the way her thighs immediately began to quiver. Carly chuckled against her, sending pleasurable vibrations shooting into Ray's abdomen and wrenching a breathy moan from her lips.

Ray closed her eyes and tried her hardest not to come. It was never hard for Carly to bring her off, usually far more quickly than Ray wanted. This was her favorite thing in the world and Ray never wanted it to end. But tonight—with the lingerie and the incredible turn-on of fucking Carly in her office—she was already teetering on the edge of release. Sobbing at the fire pulsing in her pussy, Ray held Carly's face against her and pumped her hips into her mouth. No matter how badly she wanted to make it last, she couldn't help herself. It just felt too good.

Carly's hands crawled up her stomach and settled on her breasts. She seized Ray's nipples in her fingers and pinched, twisting gently. And that was it—Ray couldn't hold off her climax if her life depended on it. She tipped back her head and roared her release, then whimpered loudly when the sensation became too much for her to handle. Well attuned to her nonverbal cues, Carly immediately drew back and let Ray catch her breath.

"No fair," Ray gasped. "Too fast."

Carly kissed the inside of Ray's thigh. "You think you're done for the night?" She peered up at Ray with a devilish smirk. "No way, darling. That was just a warm-up."

Ray struggled to sit up, a Herculean task now that her muscles had turned to jelly. But she did, gripping Carly by the arms and pulling her to her feet. Ray hugged Carly tight, burying her face in the soft skin of her neck. "I love you."

"I love you, too." Carly kissed Ray's hair. "I vote for doing round two at home. In bed."

Ray tipped her head back and gave Carly a hopeful look. "Think you can handle my cock tonight?" One of Ray's greatest discoveries of the previous year had been the wonder of strap-on sex. The very thought of getting Carly on her hands and knees in their bed flooded her with renewed energy.

"Great minds." Carly released Ray and picked up the clothing they had scattered across the floor. "Double-time, soldier."

Carly was so cute when she talked military. Getting dressed quickly—and with a smile on her face—Ray marveled at how Carly made her feel like a lovesick teenager again. Though there was nothing immature about her love for Carly, the feelings she stirred reminded Ray of the all-consuming, world-tilting intensity of adolescence. That was something she had thought she left behind in Iraq, a bone-deep joy she would never feel again. When she'd first come home, fresh from her months being held captive by insurgents, Ray was certain that the part of her life that allowed for love, sex, and happiness was over. That she would never be whole again. Meeting Carly had been a revelation in many ways, but the most shocking part was the realization that she had never actually been whole before now.

"I love you," Ray said again. Now fully dressed, she watched Carly button her shirt, already missing the touch of her bare skin. "I know I just said that, but…I really love you, Carly. And I'll never stop."

Carly gave her a shy smile as she finished securing the last button. "You better not. 'Cause you're stuck with me."

"Good." Ray reached into the pocket of her pants, relieved she hadn't lost the small box inside. "I have a for-real present for you now."

"Oh, sweetheart, trust me. What you did to me just now? Was *definitely* for real."

Ray's chest swelled with pride. She extracted the box she had been carrying around all day and presented it to Carly. "For you."

Carly blinked, and when she looked up there were tears in her eyes. "Thank you."

Ray blushed. "You haven't even seen it yet."

"I don't have to." Carly cradled the box. "I love it already."

"Open it."

Carly unwrapped the small box and cracked it open, lighting up when she saw what was inside. "Oh, Ray. It's beautiful." She pulled out the fourteen-carat gold necklace and the attached veterinary caduceus charm. "It's perfect." Carly turned her back to Ray, handing the necklace over her shoulder. "Would you help me put it on?"

"I'd love to." Ray opened the chain and placed it around Carly's neck, then fastened the clasp. Before Carly could turn around again, Ray pressed a soft kiss to the top of her spine. "Merry Christmas."

"Yes, it is." Carly swiveled and reached past Ray to open a desk drawer. She pulled out a red envelope and presented it to Ray with an excited bounce. "Here's your for-real present. It's not jewelry."

Ray laughed, shaking the envelope lightly. "Yeah, I guessed that. I'm not really the jewelry sort, anyway."

"I know." Carly's smile grew impossibly wider. "I hope you like it."

"I'm sure I will." Ray tore open the envelope, curious what it could be. Inside was a card, and inside the card was… "A photo of a golden retriever puppy?"

Carly's bouncing intensified. "I really hope you're up for it, and if you're not, just tell me. But I spoke to Tanya at the Assistance Dog Institute, and she arranged for you to be a puppy raiser for the new class of service dogs."

Ray's heart started pounding, a sensation she had become very used to over the past three years. But instead of terror or anxiety, it was pure excitement. For as much as she loved dogs, she had never had a puppy before. Knowing that she would be raising one that would one day be to someone else what Jagger was to her was truly phenomenal.

Carly's expression vacillated between elation and concern. "I can't tell—did I just overstep or are you totally geeked?"

"I'm totally geeked." Ray threw her arms around Carly and squeezed hard. "That's amazing, Carly. When do I get him?"

"In three days?" Carly stepped out of their embrace, checking Ray's face again. "I've got puppy supplies hidden in a closet here. So we're all set as far as that goes. You just need to provide the love and discipline."

"For the puppy, too."

"Cute."

Ray waggled her eyebrows and grasped Carly's hand. "Come on, let's get home. All this excitement has me ready for round two. Which, I assure you, will contain plenty of love *and* discipline."

Carly wrapped an arm around Ray's waist and snuggled close. "And to all, a good night."

Radclyffe has published over thirty-five romance and romantic intrigue novels as well as dozens of short stories, has edited numerous romance and erotica anthologies, and, writing as L.L. Raand, has authored a paranormal romance series, The Midnight Hunters.

The characters in this story are featured in the 2010 Prism Award–winning novel *Secrets in the Stone* and the 2007 Lambda Literary finalist *When Dreams Tremble*.

Ice Castles
Radclyffe

Dev Weber hitched the bright yellow, braided nylon tow rope over her shoulder and trudged down the snowy embankment, dragging her loaded skid behind her. The glaring early-December sunlight did little to cut the biting chill of the icy wind that whipped across the frozen lake. Thirty-six miles long and several miles wide in places, Lake George was her laboratory. On days like today the lake felt more like her battlefield, and she was pretty sure she was losing. A quarter of a mile away, the tall, thin outline of her research shack appeared like a matchstick in a snaggle-toothed matchbook, surrounded by other shacks—some no more than four or five feet square—that dotted the frozen surface. Unlike the men and women who sat out the frigid weather inside the tiny shacks, dropping lines through holes in the ice with endless optimism, she wasn't out to catch fish. She was studying them. That was her business, and the work didn't stop just because her laboratory froze. Sun or rain, wind or snow, it didn't matter. The fish still migrated, fed, spawned, and died. And by tracking their movements and lifecycles, analyzing the water that nourished and sometimes poisoned them, she could draw conclusions about the impact of industrial effluent on the health of not only the waterway, but the environment and ultimately, its human inhabitants.

Winter was a dichotomous season. At once barren and lonely, and incredibly beautiful and awe-inspiring. Ice crystals sparkled in the air, fractured by sunlight into millions of tiny prisms. Her breath froze in clouds before her, creating whimsical shapes before drifting away like broken promises. She waved to a few familiar people—locals who populated the waterways in the summer in outboards, trawling fishing lines off their sterns, who couldn't give up the hope of a catch despite the subzero temperatures. Halfway to her shack, she slowed, her attention diverted by the sound of rhythmic pounding. A small 4x4, one of those ATVs that looked like golf carts on steroids, was parked on the ice not far away. Curious, she slogged in that direction.

A dark-haired woman in a T-shirt and jeans knelt on the ice, methodically cutting perfectly square chunks from the frozen surface. She was tall and rangy with muscular shoulders and arms. Just as Dev drew near, the brunette looked up at a blonde in a red and black plaid wool jacket with an expression of such simple joy Dev's heart ached. She missed Leslie most at moments like this, when she was reminded she was alone. She missed that singular connection that let her know she had a place in the world, safe and secure in Leslie's heart.

The two women turned in Dev's direction, and she couldn't help but smile, her loneliness banished for an instant. They were a gorgeous couple, one dark and one light, and by some trick of light they seemed surrounded by a faint glow. As the dark-haired woman rose, Dev's vision shimmered for just a second and she could have sworn the ice ax in the woman's hand was a sword. She shook her head, laughing at her imagination.

"Hi," Dev called.

The brunette casually draped her arm over the blonde's shoulder, nothing proprietary about it, just a natural movement that said this woman was her anchor. Her center.

"You're going to get cold if you stop working," the blonde murmured to the brunette, giving her a look of fond tenderness while plucking at her sweat-soaked T-shirt.

The brunette grinned and rubbed her cheek against the blonde's temple. "But you can keep me warm."

The blonde shook her head, looped her arm around the brunette's waist, and grinned at Dev. "Hi. I'm Adrian. This smart-ass is Rooke."

"I'm Dev. What are you doing?"

"Cutting ice blocks," Rooke said.

Dev nodded. "Yup. That I can see. Why?"

"I don't have any stone."

"Okay. I'm with you so far."

The blonde, Adrian, punched Rooke lightly on the shoulder and said to Dev, "She's a great conversationalist, really. It just takes her a year or so to get warmed up."

Rooke grinned.

The energy that poured from them was like nothing Dev had ever experienced. She'd been around plenty of couples, straight and gay. Friends who she knew without a doubt loved each other. These two, though—these two projected such a sense of timeless unity, she wasn't even certain they were real. Which was ridiculous, because she could see their breath and she wasn't prone to hallucination. "What are you going to build?"

"A castle," Rooke said. "I've always wanted to build her a castle, and now I'm getting the chance."

"Uh-huh," Dev said. *Okay, well, they're a little nuts. Seem harmless, though.*

Adrian laughed. "The Winter Carnival? At the center of town? Rooke is building—"

"Oh!" Dev said. "You're the ice sculptor?"

"Actually, I'm a stone carver, but like I said—"

"Right. No stone." Dev laughed. "So why don't you just buy the ice from one of the commercial pla—" At the sight of the thundercloud rising in Rooke's eyes, Dev reconsidered. "Right. The stone—the ice—that's as much a part of the creation as the final form, right?"

"That's right. The stone—the ice—they are the sculpture."

As Rooke spoke, she stroked Adrian's shoulder, and Dev's fingers ached with the absence of Leslie. She'd seen her at Thanksgiving, two weeks before, but Les had a big case she was trying in DC in another week and had to stay close to the New York office while she prepped. So Les was at her Manhattan apartment and Dev was at the cabin she rented at Leslie's parents' lakeside resort. Most of the time their long-distance relationship didn't bother her. She was often out on the lake for days at a time, camping alone or with a tech on one of the many islands, doing field research. She and Les usually managed to spend more than half the month together, one or the other of them traveling between the lake and the city. But there were plenty of nights Dev slept alone, and too many mornings she awakened with her arms empty and her heart aching.

"I'll have to stop by later and see it when it's done," Dev said.

Adrian rubbed her cheek against Rooke's shoulder. "Do that. You should bring your partner, too."

"I would. She's working this weekend, though."

"We'll be at the castle until sundown," Adrian said with a smile that warmed Dev to the bone.

"Thanks. I'll be by."

Ten minutes later Dev unloaded her gear at her research shack, a plywood structure resembling an outhouse, for want of a better description, and only slightly better constructed. She did have a small propane heater inside, a five-foot-long wood bench attached to the wall to sit on, and some shelves to store her equipment. With a Coleman lantern for light and the heater going, she was comfortable enough. She set up her monitors, dropped her probes through the hole she'd drilled in the ice, and started the data recorders. After unzipping a subzero sleeping bag to use as a cover, she got comfortable on the bench and pulled out a book. When she started to get drowsy, she stretched out on the bench, tucked the sleeping bag around her, and closed her eyes. She awakened to the touch of warm lips moving against her mouth.

"Hey, sleepyhead," Leslie Harris said, kneeling beside the bench where Dev slept. "You know anyone could've walked in here and kissed you?"

"Can't think of anyone else who would want to," Dev said, her heart leaping at the unexpected appearance of her lover. She sat up and made room under the quasi blanket. Leslie scooted in next to her and Dev wrapped an arm around her and kissed her again. Properly this time. Leslie tasted of peppermint and ice. Her skin was still cool from the walk across the lake, but her mouth was hot. Dev had visions of coming in from a raging blizzard to stand by the hearth, the roaring blaze thawing her frozen soul. "God, what are you doing here?"

"I missed you." Leslie unzipped Dev's jacket and slid her hand inside. She nuzzled Dev's neck and nipped at her earlobe. "Do you mind me interrupting your work?"

"Trust me, the fish aren't going anywhere fast."

Leslie stared around the tiny, unadorned shack. "Cozy in here, just the two of us."

"Don't forget the fish," Dev said, kissing Leslie's throat.

"Do you think they can see us?"

"I doubt they're interested." Dev opened Leslie's parka and murmured in approval when she discovered a flannel shirt underneath. She unbuttoned the top three buttons and kissed the warm, soft skin between Leslie's breasts. Leslie's fingers came into her hair and guided her face onto her breast until Dev closed her mouth over Leslie's nipple.

"I've wanted you to do that for the last week," Leslie said, her voice husky and low. "Sometimes I'd be in the middle of a meeting, once even in court, and I'd suddenly remember the feel of your mouth on me, your hands inside me, and I'd feel like I was melting. I couldn't even think for a second." She gripped Dev's hair and pulled her face away from her breast until their eyes met. "I love you so much. Sometimes I think back to when we were kids and I almost let you get away. It scares me to think I could lose you again."

"I'll always be here, Les." Dev made a tent out of the sleeping bag, knelt on the ice in front of Leslie, and opened her shirt the rest of the way. "I love you. I've missed you so damn much."

"I want you," Leslie said, her blue eyes hazy. She fumbled with the waistband of her dark canvas pants, then lifted her hips and pushed them down. Her eyes opened wide. "Oh my God, this bench is cold."

Dev laughed and pulled off her jacket, turning it inside out for Leslie to sit on. "Better?"

"Almost. I need you to warm me up a little bit more, though."

Dev leaned between Leslie's legs, kissing her breasts through her parted shirt and working her way down the center of her stomach. Leslie's belly tightened and her hips lifted.

Leslie sighed. "I've been thinking about this all the way up here. I don't think I can last more than a few seconds."

"Then you don't have to." Dev kissed the hollow inside Leslie's hip bone, then braced her palms on the inside of Leslie's thighs and parted her legs. She ran her tongue lightly between Leslie's lips, savoring the clear sweet taste of her.

Leslie's hips jumped and a small moan escaped her throat. "Oh, baby. Don't tease me today." Leslie tugged at Dev's hair, short fitful movements. Her thighs trembled beneath Dev's fingertips.

"I love how hot and wet you are," Dev murmured.

"Make me come," Leslie whispered.

Dev kissed low on Leslie's belly, then lower, on the base of her clitoris and beneath the hood, light, feathery kisses until Leslie's hands tightened in her hair and signaled she was close. Ever so slowly Dev sucked her into her mouth with the firm steady pressure she knew would take Leslie to the edge. She waited for the sound, for the unconscious whimper that proceeded Leslie's fall into pleasure. When it came, she sucked Leslie harder, driving her over, again and again.

"Enough, enough, baby," Leslie finally gasped, pushing Dev's face away.

Dev laughed and rocked back on her heels. "You sure? Usually when you haven't seen me for a while it's a double feature."

Leslie swatted her shoulder. "I want the second act in bed when my ass isn't freezing."

Dev helped Leslie pull up her pants and then settled on the bench beside her, gathering the sleeping bag around them. "I love making you come."

"Good for me," Leslie said, cuddling against Dev's side, her arm wrapped around Dev's middle underneath her jacket. "You okay?"

"I'll last a while." Dev nuzzled her cheek against Leslie's hair. "You smell like sunshine."

"You smell like woodsmoke. I love that smell."

"How long are you up for this time?" Dev prepared herself for the little bit of disappointment that always followed the pleasure of Leslie's arrival.

"A while." Leslie fished around inside her jacket and pulled out a piece of letter-sized paper. She handed it to Dev. "Got some new office stationery."

"Uh-huh," Dev said absently. She wasn't tracking. Her mind was still a little hazy. Making Leslie come pretty much warped all her synapses for a while. Dutifully, she glanced at the cream-colored embossed paper, noting the name of Leslie's high-profile law firm. Leslie was a partner and had worked damned hard to get there. Dev was incredibly proud of her, even though they sometimes worked opposite sides of an issue. She scanned the names running down the left-hand side, wondering how many new associates they'd added, and then registered the change. Leslie's name wasn't listed under the New York City office any longer. It headed the list under the smaller Albany division. She dropped the stationery onto her lap and cupped Leslie's chin, searching her eyes. "What are you doing?"

"I'm relocating. I'm moving back here."

"I thought you always said you needed to be in New York to handle the big cases."

"I can't stand being away from you. And if the big cases want me, they can come to where I am." Leslie took Dev's face in her hands. "I love you. Time is too short. I'm coming home, so you better start house hunting."

"What, you don't want to live in the cabin at your parents' place?"

"I think I'm too old to live with my mother and father, even if they do adore you."

Dev grinned. "Any place in particular?"

"I only have three requirements—the same three I've had since we were fifteen. I need to wake up in the morning to the scent of pine forest, the sound of waves against the shore, and the feel of your arms around me. I need to be home, where you are. I forgot that once. I won't again."

"I love you, Les." Dev pulled Leslie up by the hand. "Come on, I have a castle to show you."

Laughing, Leslie said, "Okay. A little bigger than I imagined, but why not."

Dev kissed her. "Welcome home, baby."

Julie Cannon is a corporate stiff by day and dreamer by night. She has seven books published by Bold Strokes Books. Her latest, *Descent,* published in July 2010 follows *Power Play*, *Just Business*, *Uncharted Passage*, *Heartland*, *Heart to Heart*, and *Come and Get Me*. Julie has also published four short stories in Bold Strokes anthologies. Recent transplants to Houston, Julie and her partner Laura live on a lake with their two kids, two dogs, and a cat. Visit her at www.juliecannon.com.

The characters in "Come Back to Me" first appeared in *Come and Get Me,* published in 2007.

Come Back to Me
Julie Cannon

Do you remember the first time we met?"

Hey, Lauren, love of my life, I can tell from your deep, rhythmic breathing you're not going to answer. As much as I want you to, that's okay. You need your rest. The last few days have been tough, so as long as you can hear me, that's all that matters.

"We were at that charity thing at the Lincoln Hotel. My life was for shit and even though it was for a good cause, I couldn't wait to get out of there. Then you barged into my life in your little black dress, Charisma perfume, and don't-fuck-with-me attitude. You were the most aggravating woman I'd ever met, and my world hasn't been the same since."

The image of you standing in front of me, your chin high, eyes blazing is as clear today as it was twelve years ago.

"Did I ever tell you that it had probably been years since someone stood up to me like that? Boy, doesn't that ever sound pompous. But then again I was Elliott Foster, investment banker, maker of millions, woman-about-town. Nobody contradicted me or had the guts to say anything out loud. Everybody wanted something from me. Except you. You didn't want anything to do with me. And as shocking as it was, that's when I was hooked.

"I never told you this, but from that minute you were all I ever thought about. It was the weirdest thing. Here I was, thirty-six years old, and it was the first time a woman had totally dominated me. And I had no fucking clue what to do about it. For a smart girl I was pretty stupid.

"I remember when we went to that HRC dinner. You had on that tuxedo vest with nothing underneath. When you took off your jacket, I thought I was going to die. It made me nuts to watch the men slobber all over themselves looking at you. I didn't want anyone imagining doing to you what I wanted to do.

"God, I loved touching you. Your skin was so soft and warm. The way you felt in my arms when we were dancing—it was like nothing I'd ever experienced before. I never wanted to let you go.

"I wanted you so bad. You didn't know, but when you went to the ladies' room I actually scoped out a place where we could be alone. Okay, I admit all I could think about was getting you naked. Or at least getting my hands down your pants. God, if I'd have known it would be weeks before I finally touched you, I would have dragged you away.

"I'll always remember exactly where I was when you threw down the gauntlet. I was wrapped in a towel, fresh from the shower and you were on my answering machine. I can hear your voice now: 'The ball's in your court now, Elliott. I won't approach you again. If you want me, you'll have to come and get me.' I saved that message. I took the tape and put it in my safe at the office. Of course, that was after I chased you until you caught me."

I laugh at my own play on words and you still don't move.

"I wish I could wake you up and show you how much I still want you. I could take you right here, right now, you still have that effect on me. Lesbian bed death is definitely not alive in our house. You were my alarm clock Tuesday morning. No better way to begin the day than by making love with the woman you love."

Neither my voice nor the noises in the hall have woken you. I want you to open your eyes and talk to me. I love it when we reminisce about our life together. I still can't believe you're my girl.

"Remember when we were on that flight to Hong Kong? I don't know what got into you, but I had to bite my lip when you went in me. Thank God it was dark and the blankets were extra large. You were crazy. I remember the shock when I realized your hands were intent on doing more than simply lying quietly on my leg. If I'd have known you'd turn into a sex-crazed maniac I'd have invited you along on one of my business trips earlier.

"Yes, Hong Kong. That was the trip I bought you the Rolex. You were insistent that you didn't need anything so extravagant, but I was not going to be convinced. You deserved the best then and still do every day."

I wonder where it is? Normally if it's not on your wrist it's in your jewelry box next to the Movado, Tag Heuer, and your trusty Timex IronMan. That watch is almost fifteen years old and you still wear it. Was it only a few days ago we joked about how it was one of the last things you had from your single days? That and the dishes in our cabin on Lake Michigan.

"I'm thinking about the cabin. You were insistent we needed a place to reconnect, unwind, and unplug. No cell phones, BlackBerrys, or wi-fi. I remember looking at you as if you had asked me to climb into a rocket and go to the moon. How in the hell was I going to survive without at least my BlackBerry?

"I wanted the best for you, but you had something altogether different in mind. We ended up buying that fixer-upper on the most beautiful five acres I've ever seen. Those first few years we went up there all the time. By the time we were done I didn't want to see another hammer or measuring tape the rest of my life. You almost fell off the roof when we were reshingling. You were so proud of the shed we built for the tractor. You designed the whole thing and it came out great. The dogs love to run and run when we go there. Just thinking about it makes my thumb throb. How many times did I hit it while we were building that addition to the kitchen? I'm surprised it's not as flat as a pancake."

Warmth spreads through my body at the memory of how more than one remodeling project had been interrupted by our never-ending desire for each other. I ended up with sawdust in some very interesting places, but it was nowhere as painful as the case of poison ivy on your butt. In the end the cabin was ours, built practically with our own hands.

"You told all our friends that it was just the way we wanted it, not somebody else's built to their taste. It was the first thing we bought and worked on together. I wasn't sure we could do it. A lot of couples can't work together but we seemed to just know what each other was thinking almost before we did ourselves."

Your hair tickles my face and I gather you closer. We're in a strange bed, but that isn't unusual. We've traveled all over the world together—first class to Paris on our honeymoon, sitting with chickens and goats on a flight in Mozambique. Every place we've been has been paradise because we were together. How did I ever think I didn't need anyone in my life this way? Damn it, those are not tears in my eyes. I'm not going to break down now. Not with you in my arms like this. Deep breath, swallow hard, okay. Back in control.

"Remember Mason and Justin? They scared the holy hell out of me. When you said you wanted us to be foster parents, I thought you were nuts. I knew nothing about children and even less about how to be a parent, especially to kids who needed a foster home. When they showed up on our doorstep that night I was shaking so bad I thought I'd drop Mason when the social worker put him in my arms. He was so tiny. I remember wondering how anyone could beat such a helpless child. You were so good for them. Once they got some good food into their stomach and a few kind words, they really opened up.

"Remember the look on your mother's face when Justin asked her neighbor where her teeth were? I thought she was going to pop a cork. It was her idea to invite the lady in to meet all of us."

I stifle my laugh, but the laughter feels so much better than the tears. Even after eight years I still feel the pain when we had to give the boys back to their parents. They'd been with us for almost three years. God, that was hard. But I'm not going to talk about pain right now. You don't need that reminder.

"All those other kids in and out of our house. All they needed was stability and love. You have a never-ending supply, not just for the frightened children but for the parents that come into your office each day. I'm so proud of you, sweetheart. You care and you help them. You, sweetheart. You make a difference in people's lives every day.

"First the foster kids, then the kids we had together. Grace has your smile and your mannerisms. When she cocks that hip and gives me that look that says I have absolutely no clue, she is all you. Your mother said the same thing the other day. She told me Spence wanted to have a lemonade stand. Our son the entrepreneur. Good Lord, he's only six and already making money. That's my boy."

I can't help but smile at the image of our son waving down cars passing through the neighborhood to land a sale.

"Don't worry about them, honey. My sister's coming down tomorrow to help out. Between Stephanie and your mom, they'll take good care of them. I couldn't have asked for a better mother-in-law."

I feel your heart beat faster when I talk about our children. You had such difficult pregnancies and my heart stopped when you almost lost Spence early on. You were so beautiful when you were carrying our child. You radiated joy and happiness and insisted I feel every move and kick. Even if it was two o'clock in the morning. I was so lucky that you weren't crabby and moody like other women. But my God, you were horny. I think we had more sex while you were pregnant than we did the first few years we were together. Of course, I wasn't complaining.

"I'll never forget the day you went into labor. I was in the middle of negotiations with the union at Strattford. When Teresa came in and handed me a note that simply said *It's time* I completely lost my mind. I ran out of there so fast and down the hall to the elevator. Those thirty floors felt like I was in the tallest building in the world. I still have that piece of paper. It's in that box on the floor of my closet.

"You amaze me, sweetheart. You are always so strong. A minor cut on Spence or Grace sends my heart racing and hands shaking so bad I can barely put on a Mickey Mouse Band-Aid."

I have no idea how you managed to give birth to two children—I can't even conceive of it. But you did, and remember when the doctor put our daughter in your arms the first time? I cried. Me, who never cries. And I didn't care who saw me.

"You taught me how to love, Lauren. How to be a parent, a good parent. You taught me patience, how to slow down and enjoy every second of every day. You trusted me enough to show me love, true love."

I brush my lips over the bandage on your cheek. The doctor says there shouldn't be too much of a scar. But I don't care. You're alive. You will always be beautiful to me. It's finally quiet in the room. The constant beeping of the damn machine finally silenced a few hours ago.

I promised myself I wouldn't beg. Wouldn't do anything to distract you from getting well. But I can't stand it any longer.

"Please, Lauren, wake up."

My throat hurts. I've been talking for hours. Saying anything to penetrate the darkness of the night. The darkness that surrounds me has enclosed you in its grasp and you haven't woken up. I won't leave you until you do.

"We need you, Lauren. Your smile lights up the room, your warmth keeps the harshness of the world away. You are strong when we are weak. You carry us when we can't go any farther. You guide us when we don't know what to do. We love you, sweetheart. No one more than I do."

There's no stopping the tears now. I don't care. I have no pride, no life without you. The nurse is here again to check your vital signs. She's the same nurse I've seen for the last three nights. She looks at me and I see an understanding smile before she leaves as quietly as she always does. The door clicks closed.

I cry without making a sound. Until you and the kids, I'd always wondered if I would ever be able to kill someone. There's no doubt about it now. Without question I could use my bare hands to kill anyone who dared to lay a hand on my family.

I'm glad the nutcase who shot you is dead. Killed by the police when they stormed your office. But I'm pissed I didn't get the chance to kill the son of a bitch myself. I barely remember the detective telling me the details—some guy who'd lost custody of his children when you proved to the judge he was a danger to them. As if the bruises on his kids and his wife's split lip and broken arm weren't enough evidence.

My tears wet your hair. I know you don't mind. Just like the other times we've held each other and cried tears of joy and sorrow. The prayer that repeated over and over again when our children were born fills my mind and I say it again. I have to talk to God, plead for your life.

"Please God, let her wake up. I don't know what I'd do without her. I can't do it without her. I'll do anything if you just let her wake up."

What am I saying? How selfish is that?

"God, don't do it for me. Her children need her. They need their mother. Please let her wake up."

Please.

"Don't cry, baby."

The words are barely a whisper, but they sound like they'd been shouted from the roof top. My heart soars, a wave of relief crashing over me. The first rays of dawn are peeking through the mini blinds. It's Christmas morning and a light snow is falling.

I look into your eyes and I'm home.

About the Editors

Radclyffe has published over thirty-five romance and romantic intrigue novels as well as dozens of short stories, has edited numerous romance and erotica anthologies, and, writing as L.L. Raand, has authored a paranormal romance series, The Midnight Hunters.

She is a seven-time Lambda Literary Award finalist in romance, mystery, and erotica—winning in both romance (*Distant Shores, Silent Thunder*) and erotica (*Erotic Interludes 2: Stolen Moments* edited with Stacia Seaman, and *In Deep Waters 2: Cruising the Strip* written with Karin Kallmaker) and a 2010 Prism award winner for *Secrets in the Stone*. She is a member of the Saints and Sinners Literary Hall of Fame, an Alice B. Readers' award winner, a Benjamin Franklin Award finalist (*The Lonely Hearts Club*), and a ForeWord Review Book of the Year Finalist (*Night Call* in 2009; *Justice for All*, *Secrets in the Stone*, and *Romantic Interludes 2: Secrets* in 2010). Two of her titles (*Returning Tides* and *Secrets in the Stone*) are 2010 Heart Of Excellence Readers' Choice finalists.

Writing as L.L. Raand she released the first Midnight Hunters novel, *The Midnight Hunt*, in March 2010. *Blood Hunt* is due for release March 2011. Her next First Responders novel, *Firestorm*, is due in July 2011.

Visit her websites at www.llraand.com and www.radfic.com.

Stacia Seaman has edited numerous award-winning titles, and with co-editor Radclyffe won a Lambda Literary Award for *Erotic Interludes 2: Stolen Moments*; an Independent Publishers Awards silver medal and a Golden Crown Literary Award for *Erotic Interludes 4: Extreme Passions*; and an Independent Publishers Awards gold medal and a Golden Crown Literary award for *Erotic Interludes 5: Road Games*. Most recently, she has essays in *Visible: A Femmethology* (Homofactus Press, 2009) and *Second Person Queer* (Arsenal Pulp Press, 2009).